Praise for Cars, Cobras, and Concertos

I love the works by Jennifer Johnson. They are just the right size to keep my couch level! If only she would write some "short stories", then my kitchen table wouldn't wobble!!!!
~Saxophonist & Husband of Doris , Jeff Carter

If you could bottle long walks on the beach at sunset and then somehow represent that bottle in writing, her books would be just like only without the rotten seafood undertones.
~Dwight McCormick, stand-up comedian and Presbyterian minister

Finally, a how-to guide that shows you how to fix your car and catch a man! Jennifer Johnson revs the engines in this classic girl-meets-guy-with-a-car tale of romance and wrenches.
~HRH Cheryl Anderson

I'm glad she's getting good use out of that liberal arts degree.
~Jennifer's Mom

Jennifer Johnson is my new favorite author! I LOVE her writing skills. She blends lots of humor, real life issues, plenty of romance and one rockin' cast of characters to create an instantly gripping and engaging novel.
~Reviews by Molly

I really like Jennifer Johnson. She is a wonderful writer and really draws you in.
~Book's Book Picks

A delightful combination of sly wit and sweet romance, Jennifer Johnson's novels are always a treat!
~Margaret Ethridge, rabid fan and semi-stalker

Cars, Cobras, and Concertos

Cars, Cobras, and Concertos

Jennifer Johnson

CARS, COBRAS, AND CONCERTOS
Copyright © 2017, Jennifer Johnson
Trade Paperback ISBN: 978-1-946608-03-1

Editor, Karen Block
Cover Art Design by Calliope-Designs.com

Digital Release, February 2017
Trade Paperback Release, February 2017

Fiction > Romance > Contemporary

Fiction > Romance > Romantic Comedy

CARS, COBRAS, AND CONCERTOS

Mozart and Motor Oil All In One Book.

Libby Miller always considered herself one of the boys and like her brothers, fixes cars in her daddy's garage. But when a tow call for a car with a busted water pump causes her to cross paths with concert violinist, Byron Venable, Libby's life is turned upside down.

Listening to Byron's impromptu concert while she works on his car, Libby discovers an affinity for a type of music that is new to her and a growing attraction to the man whose passion for that music moves her to tears. When it becomes evident to everyone that the attraction is mutual, Skinny Davis, the best friend of Libby's brother, declares his intentions for the girl he's been in love with for years.

Will Libby listen to the enticing music of the beautiful man who's unlike anyone she's ever known or will she open her heart to the man who's been in her backyard all along?

Chapter One

"Libby! Hey, Libby," Vance yelled from the garage office.

"I'm busy. What do you want?" she hollered back. She dropped a bolt from the front wheel bearing of a Honda Accord into a shallow pan and set her wrench on the cement floor.

"Tow. Highway 60 and Wallace."

She straightened and arched her back to release the kinks that'd tied her in knots over the past half hour of laboring over the vehicle. "I am *not* doing a tow."

"You gotta do it. We're the only ones here, and I ain't allowed to drive for two more months."

"Get Mickey."

"He's gone. It's five-thirty."

"Well, what'd you go and answer the phone for? We close at five," Libby grabbed a rag and wiped her wrench before throwing it in her toolbox. Sometimes Vance didn't have enough sense to make change for a dime.

"Habit," her brother called to her.

"Break it. A tow out to 60 and Wallace is going to take me at least an hour." Libby closed her toolbox and cleaned up her work area. "Who is it? Somebody we know?"

"Nope."

Libby heaved a deep sigh and walked through the door separating the garage from the office. Getting information out of Vance was like pulling teeth. "Woman? She alone? I don't have room in the cab for a bunch of kids and a dog."

Her brother Vance sat at their dad's desk and thumbed through a biker woman magazine. "Man. He says he's got an appointment at eight, and he would appreciate anything we could do to aid him in his prediction."

"You mean his predicament?"

"Huh?"

Libby snatched the magazine out of his hands and crumpled it in her fist.

"Hey!"

"Why are you still here? You're doing nothing to help me."

"I ain't got no ride. Skinny's picking me up when he gets off work." He grabbed for the magazine but Libby moved it out of his reach. "I paid seven bucks for that. Have some respect."

"You talk about respect with this magazine?"

Vance shrugged and curled his fingers in a gesture of 'gimme'.

"Did you tell him to call a cab?" He lunged for the magazine, and Libby whapped him on the head with it before dropping it on the desk.

"Nope. I told him the tow truck would be there in twenty minutes. Get going, big sister."

****

Libby spied the Toyota Camry parked on the road at a respectable distance and the man leaning against the passenger side staring into the field beyond. She drove past, then turned to position the truck in front of the car. Checking for traffic first, she jumped out of the cab and walked toward the car.

Out of the corner of her eye, she saw the man approach. Glancing up from the car, her gaze caught. In a tuxedo complete with tails, he strode toward her. His hair slicked back from his face, and his face briefly registered surprise before he smiled making Libby's breath catch.

"Mr. Venable?"

"Yes. Thank you for coming." He held out a hand, and Libby hesitated before she accepted the shake. Who shakes hands anymore? And with a tow truck driver no less?

"What happened?"

"I noticed an acrid scent. I checked the thermostat. It was running hot, so I pulled over and called."

Acrid scent? *Hmmm.*

Libby sniffed. She didn't smell anything. She gingerly touched the hood of the car. "Something burning? Did you notice smoke?"

"Perhaps a vaporous expulsion rather than smoke."

Libby snickered. "Do you kiss your mother with that mouth?"

He grinned in response. "Not recently, no."

Libby's breath hitched at the curve of his lips and the dimples cut on each side of his cheeks. He was so pretty. His honey-colored curly hair rustled as a car flew past them on the highway, and his dark gaze twinkled at her.

Oh, yummy. She'd like that cake served with a side of whipped cream. Shrugging away her pretty picture, she marched toward the passenger side of the truck and gestured him to follow. She opened the door and picked up a clipboard.

"Did you turn the car off, or did it shut off on its own?"

"I turned off the car."

Libby nodded. That was a good sign. "You sure you want it towed?"

"What other choice is there?"

"We can wait for it to cool off, pour some water in it, and drive it to the garage."

"Couldn't you tow it to the garage and get someone to fix it now? I'm in a bit of a hurry."

"What?" She gestured to his clothes. "You getting married?"

"No."

"GQ shoot?"

"That's a joke, right?"

"Yeah. A joke." He was in Eastern Kentucky with a monkey suit on asking if she could fix his car in the next hour and a half, and he thought she was making a joke? She shook her head. "So, do you want me to tow it or not?"

"I want you to tow it, yes."

"Do you have another ride?"

"No." He paused, his pretty eyes clouded. "Can't I ride with you?"

Libby glanced at his clothes—not a smudge anywhere. Seriously? He wanted to ride in the truck? With her? She held out the clipboard for him to sign. "You could, but your car isn't going to be fixed tonight. We closed at five."

He took the clipboard, reached into his jacket with his other hand and retrieved a silver pen. Liberty watched his fingers as he signed the bottom after a brief glance at the document holding him responsible for the bill. He had beautiful fingers, the nails were clipped short and clean. "It's nearly six now."

"Tell me about it."

"The garage is at Carter and Sixteenth, correct?"

"Yes."

"That will do." He presented her with the clipboard with a flourish. "I'm going to the Pendleton Arts Center. According to the GPS, it's only a couple of blocks."

"You're going to walk from the garage to the Arts Center?"

"Sure. Why not?"

Libby studied his shiny black shoes. They didn't look comfortable for walking, but that was his problem. Not hers.

She stretched out her hand toward him, palm up. "I need your car key."

He reached into his pants pocket, the movement showing his ebony cummerbund. His hand withdrew from his pocket, and he deposited his key ring onto her hand.

Three keys on a simple ring. Home. Work. Car.

"Car key only." She bounced the keys once with her palm. "Hate for you to be locked out of your house tonight because your key ring's here with me instead of in your pocket."

When Libby looked up at him, he was watching her, not the keys on her hand. He blinked, his dark chocolate gaze lingering on her. She tamped down the urge to pull her hair out of the elastic band she'd secured it with about seven o'clock this morning and do a fluff and shake, like she'd seen women do on the hair conditioner commercials.

Ugh. Is this what she had reverted to after five minutes with the pretty boy penguin?

Huffing, she tucked the board and paper under her arm, freed the key from its ring then dropped it in the vicinity of his hands. She threw the clipboard on the seat and did her best to ignore GQ as she began to hook up the car. In ten minutes, he sat on the bench seat with only a box of air filters and the clipboard between them. His cologne mingled with the old grease and man sweat of the cab creating an interesting aroma. Libby inhaled and decided she'd like to sniff Mr. GQ Venable in a space where her brothers' stink wouldn't compete with his girly-man smell.

He made no attempt at conversation, which was fine with her. If he opened his mouth and started asking how a girl like her ended up driving a tow truck, it'd kill her pretty fantasy of him. Nothing would be worse than that unless he started talking about the weather. As they passed Giovanni's, Libby wondered if he was a snob. She'd never known a man to be so quiet. Certainly none of the men in her family were. Geez, they yacked all the time.

"I'm Libby," she offered.

"I'm sorry?"

"My name. Libby Miller."

"As in Elizabeth Miller?"

Libby hesitated. Most people didn't know her real name. She'd been Libby for as long as she could remember. "Well, actually my given name is Liberty, but most people call me Libby."

"What's your middle name? Please don't tell me 'Belle'. I might have to report your parents for child abuse."

Liberty chuckled. "Ann."

"Liberty Ann. It has a nice ring to it."

Libby shot him a look to judge whether he'd meant the pun. He stared through the windshield but his mouth quirked up at the corner.

"What's your first name, GQ?"

"Byron. Lots of potential for humor there."

"Man. And I thought my parents gave me a bad name."

"Indeed. Count your blessings, Liberty Ann. There's always someone worse off than you are."

Indeed. Who says 'indeed?' Was he some kind of actor?

"Yeah. I figured that when I had to stop what I was doing to come tow you."

When they arrived at the garage, Libby maneuvered the truck to the front of the double bay doors and cut the engine. She unhooked the car and parked the truck in its spot across the road. As she crossed the street, she noticed Byron leaning into the backseat of his car, the tails of his Tux trailing to his thighs. He stepped back and straightened with a black leather case cradled in his hands.

Some kind of instrument, she'd bet.

He was going over to the Arts Center in his penguin suit after all.

If he was going over there to buy something or to listen at a concert, he wouldn't be dressed that way. What would he look like in ripped-up jeans and a T-shirt? Probably not as yummified as he did standing outside her daddy's garage. Every guy looked good in a tuxedo. That's why men wore them to fancy dances and stuff.

Libby walked past him to the driver's side and opened the front door. Kneeling down she felt for and pulled the hood lever. The lid clicked its release, and she shut the driver's door.

"Pendleton is that way." She pointed behind her as she made her way to the front of the car.

Lifting the hood, she studied the motor.

Vaporous expulsion. Who talked like that? She shook her head and placed her hand near the engine. Warm, but not hot. It had been almost an hour since GQ had called though. She peered at the water filter reservoir and noted there was no water line. Opening the cap, she leaned over and looked inside.

Dry as a bone.

Well, that ruled out the thermostat. Obviously, it was working fine—alerting the dummy owner that since his cooling system was not working properly, the engine was indeed running hot and vaporous expulsions were likely.

Libby retrieved the water hose and filled the reservoir, pouring water on the engine as well for good measure and slammed the lid. Satisfied the engine would survive long enough for her to pull it into one of the bays, she marched to the office, unlocked it, and opened the garage door before pulling the car into it. Vance was gone. Obviously, Vance's pesky friend, Skinny had made it by to pick him up. She opened the hood again and pushed the toolbox cart close to the car. If it was something minor—a loose hose or something—maybe she could get it fixed and send him on his way.

But if it was something major, then what? How was GQ going to get home? The car had Virginia plates. Was he stranded out of state? Should she tell him where the car rental place was?

Not that it was *her* problem.

She doubted people like him ended up on the street just because of a broken-down car. If he was on his way to Pendleton, he obviously knew someone there. They'd help him out with a ride or a place to stay overnight.

I am not going to worry about it. I tow cars. I fix cars. I do not take care of tuxedo-clad men.

Libby shone the flashlight into the engine as she looked for any leaks. What was causing the problem?

She pulled the cart back then walked to the wall where she hit the switch, which lifted the car above her head. When she took her hand off the switch, a sound registered in her ears.

Music.

Violin?

Yes.

What stereo was playing? The garage was surrounded by downtown businesses so after five in the evening things got pretty quiet as a rule. If Vance had left on the radio, she would have noticed before now, although nothing remotely resembling this had ever come out of the speakers in the office.

Libby followed the music to the bay door, and stood dumbstruck.GQ was playing a violin on the pavement outside of the garage. His bow gracefully moved over the instrument while his fingers fretted on the slim neck. Under his hands, a sad melody poured forth filling the air with its melancholy message. A car approached and slowed to a crawl either to view the handsome man or to hear his beautiful music.

Maybe both.

Libby shook her head to focus on her task which was…what? *Oh, right.* Overheated engine. She walked under the hydraulic jack and shone the flashlight above her head into the bottom of the engine of Byron's vehicle.

The melodic notes meandered around her, filling her chest with emotion.

A trickle of water dripped from above her and fell near her face, then another.

Aha. It was the water pump. Just as I….

The pitch of the music became higher and moved into a minor key. Libby turned her face toward the door and listened. She stepped backward and watched him, his upper body swayed as he manipulated the violin. Behind him, a car had paused at the curb with the window rolled down.

His tone softened until she could barely hear the melody, then switched keys and the pace quickened as the volume increased. Liberty sniffed and blinked. She reached up and wiped her cheek.

Was this a tear or water from his leaking pump?

She glanced up at the car and noted she wasn't the target of the water falling in steady drops from the engine.

Well, I'll be damned. Byron Venable's pretty music is making me cry.

Liberty hadn't cried since…when?

Oh, yeah. When Mickey dropped a tire jack on her foot and broke it. That had been three years ago.

She hit the switch to lower the car and stood by the wall as the vehicle came to rest on the floor of the garage. Byron's music stopped, and he approached her. Libby noticed his audience on the street had grown to four cars, and the people inside clapped their appreciation before driving away.

"Nice concert. Did they throw you any coins?" Libby loosened the pump as she spoke.

"I forgot to leave my case open on the ground."

"Too bad. You coulda put it toward your repair bill."

"So it's fixable?"

She removed the alternator so she could reach the pump. "Oh, sure. Everything's fixable. So far, I've found a problem with the water pump which would cause your car to overheat. I'll look it over and make sure there aren't any other problems, but your vehicle's not going to be ready until tomorrow at the earliest."

Byron gazed at her. "Okay." He tucked his violin under his arm and pulled a white handkerchief from his breast pocket. Stepping close to her, he held it close to her face. "May I?"

"May you what?"

"May I wipe your cheek? You have a smudge."

"Oh…kay."

He smiled his thanks as if she were doing him a favor, then caressed her skin below her eye where she'd cried.

Libby froze at the contact.

He touched the other cheek as well. How many tears had she shed? She inhaled and caught his sweet scent. She'd never known a guy to smell so good. Her hands itched to wrap around his waist, but she resisted. He was so out of her league as to be on a different planet. If she touched him, she'd get dirt and grease all over him, and he was on his way to the Arts center.

"You moved me. I usually don't…umm…cry. The music was so pretty."

Byron grinned. "What a nice compliment. Thank you."

Libby walked two steps backward, so she wouldn't embarrass herself by sticking her nose next to his white shirt.

"I've kept you too long already. I'll be on my way. Thank you, Liberty Ann." He cradled his violin and moved toward the bay opening.

Libby sighed in appreciation as she watched him walk away from her.

No, Mr. Byron Venable. Thank you for your pretty face and music.

She smiled and picked up the water pump. Maybe before she left for the night, she'd sit in his car for a few minutes and smell his goodness she was sure lingered in there.

****

The next day Libby drove the truck onto the garage pavement and backed up, arcing to get the towed car in a better position to go into the bay. When she jumped out of the cab Mickey, her older brother, studied her from the tire pile. His twinkling gaze told her he was up to no good. She decided to ignore him and started unhooking the car.

His footsteps approached. The tire he had been holding bounced on the concrete.

"Hey, Hot Stuff."

Hot stuff? Libby glanced up at him before pulling the wench free. She stood to move the truck giving her brother her full attention.

"What did you just call me?"

"Go to the office, Libby. Your payment is waiting on you." He turned on his heel and rolled the tire into bay two.

She moved the truck to its parking space and walked toward the building. Her eyes scanned the lot and found Byron's car missing. Shoot. She'd missed him. Sighing, she opened the door to the office to find out what her idiot brother was messing with her about.

And there it was sitting on top of the customer counter like a beacon of color in the otherwise dingy room—two dozen blood red roses in a cut crystal vase.

Oh, wow.

Gene Miller, her dad, appeared from the other side of the flowers. Vance came in from the garage joined by Mickey.

"What is this about?" she asked.

"Why don't you tell us? We'd like to know how come you're getting roses for towing a guy's truck," Mick said.

"Yeah. Hehehehe. I ain't ever got flowers for a tow," Vance added. "Maybe I shoulda stuck around last night to make sure you kept your pants on."

"Vance," Gene chided. "I don't want to hear that kind of talk."

"We're just a little concerned, Dad, as to what this guy is up to. I mean, who sends red roses for a reservoir replacement?" Mick gestured to the vase.

"A weirdo. What happened last night?" Vance skinched his eyes at her as if to ferret out the truth. "Or don't you want to say?".

"Shut up," Libby snapped. She marched across the room and snatched the florist envelope from the plastic holder amidst the spray. *Oh, my gosh, weren't they lovely?* "If either one of you ever did a lick of work around here, maybe you'd get something more than Dad's foot on your ass."

The envelope was addressed to Liberty Ann Miller and had dirty fingerprints on it.

"And you better not touch my stuff anymore. These flowers have my name on them so keep your dirty grubby hands off."

Vance laughed and slapped Mickey on the back who grinned in return. Liberty's teeth clinched. She looked around for something to beat them with.

Gene finally spoke. "All right, boys. Get back outside to the garage and leave her alone. You've had your fun. Go on now."

Carefully, Liberty picked up the vase and walked into the business office. She set the flowers on the desk and sighed in enjoyment. She turned the envelope over and unsheathed the card.

Music should strike fire from the heart of man, and bring tears from the eyes of woman

—*Ludwig van Beethoven*

Thank you, Byron

She clutched the card to her chest as she gazed at the roses. She'd never gotten roses before. Not even one. The closest she'd come had been daisies from her Grandma on her sixteenth birthday. She leaned forward and touched a velvety petal then pressed her palm on the tops of the flowers. With a last girly sigh, she gathered up the vase and carried it with her to the front office.

"Dad, did you talk to Byron Venable when he came in to get his car?"

"Yep." He peered at her over his readers.

"You didn't let Mick and Vance harass him, did you?"

"They didn't know they had anything to harass him about. The flowers didn't come till later." Gene plucked his glasses from his nose and set them on the paper he'd been reading. "After you wasn't here for him to thank properly."

One rose seemed a little out of place so Libby pulled it out then tucked it in another spot. She smiled and counted them.

"You must have made quite an impression."

"He made one on me."

"And another impression today, I suppose."

"Twenty-four today. Maybe I'll marry him. You think a man who plays a violin would want to marry a grease monkey?"

Gene laughed. "The question is would a woman who fixes cars want to marry a fiddler?"

She sniffed the buds but couldn't detect any scent. "Maybe he's already married. Probably to some heiress with straight teeth and a straight nose."

"Nah. He ain't married."

Liberty stopped her admiration of her roses to look at her dad. "How do you know? Did you ask him?"

He slapped the newspaper he'd been reading on the counter in front of her. "Didn't have to."

The picture on the paper caught her attention—Byron in his tux with his violin tucked under his chin. The caption read, *Byron Venable, Musician in Residence at Marshall, opens the Artist Series at the Pendleton.*

A small box beside his picture gave several facts of Byron including his education, marital status, and his twelve-month stint in Huntington.

"Think he knows any Bluegrass? Seems a shame to bring a boy into Kentucky who can't saw a proper fiddle."

"There's more than one way to saw a fiddle."

"You talk like you heard him. Did you go see him last night at the Pendleton?"

Liberty cupped a bud and rubbed her cheek against it. "He played here last night while I was working on his car."

"That right? That why you didn't charge him for the labor?"

"Hmm," she answered in the affirmative.

"Oh, boy." Concern filled his tone.

Libby She picked up her vase and headed to the garage.

"Where are you taking them flowers?"

"Out here so I can enjoy them while I work."

"That vase is going to get broken," the man predicted.

She opened the door to the garage and yelled, "I'm bringing my flowers out here, and if either one of you knuckleheads gets within five feet of them, I'll bust your lip. Got it?"

"Libby?" Gene called to her from the doorway. "You was kidding about marrying him, right?"

Chapter Two

That evening Libby, freshly showered and in comfy sweats and T-shirt, walked into the living room.

Vance and two of his friends, Skinny and Stevie, congregated around the counter separating the living room from the kitchen. Laughter filled the room.

Great. Now she had to deal with the three stooges. And they were way too close to her flowers.

Skinny spotted her. "Hey Libby,"

Stevie cast her a mischievous grin. "Hey, Libby," he repeated, but the way he'd said the words raised her hackles. He reached over and moved the vase. "So, Vance says you, like, came up with a new payment plan at the garage."

She clenched her fists and fought the urge to thump him. She raised her head and breezed by him on her way to the kitchen. "Vance can't add two and two. He doesn't handle billing."

Stevie knuckled Vance in the ribs. "Oooooo. What a burn, bro."

Vance swatted Stevie's hand away. He looked at Libby and lifted his lip in a sneer. "So, I guess you're *handling* the customers now. Is that just the men, or do you *handle* the women too?"

Stevie guffawed.

"Why do you let him talk to you like that?" Skinny asked.

Libby chose not to answer Skinny. If Stevie would quit laughing, Vance would quit soon enough. Trading barbs with him just prolonged his disgusting jibes.

There was something to be said about living at home with her dad and brother, as well as her older brother and his wife and kids next door. But what was that something?

Sometimes Libby wished she were an orphan.

She could count on Dad going to his room and watching TV till he fell asleep, and lots of times she could count on Vance going out with one of his buddies and not getting home until Libby had gone to bed herself. Payday wasn't until next Friday so, obviously, her brother only had enough funds for a burger and fries. He and his fellow idiots would loiter in the living room the rest of the weekend.

"Can't y'all go to Skinny's place?" She found a glass in the cabinet and held it under the ice dispenser on the freezer door. "Your odor's stinking up the place."

Skinny said something but she couldn't make out what he said over the clunking of ice cubes. With her glass full, she pushed the water button. "What'd you say?"

"I said, so what's the deal with the roses?"

"Yeah, what is the deal, Libby? Your new layaway plan? Hawhawhaw!" So Stevie thought he was a comedian too. Where was a tire iron when you needed one?

"Shut up, Stevie," Skinny snapped.

Libby drank from her glass and stepped over the threshold. Her roses sat on the counter opposite to where Stevie and Vance sat on the raised barstools. Skinny, who'd received his nickname when he was eight had outgrown it about a hundred pounds and six years ago when he'd graduated high school. He stood with folded arms over his massive chest covering up the Howling Angels logo on his shirt. A serpent tat curled around his right bicep, its head raised and mouth open wide ready to strike. The pose reminded Libby of an exclamation mark to Skinny's mood.

"Why'd you get a bunch of flowers from one of the customers?" he asked.

"None ya, and quit scowling at me."

"So you're seeing somebody? Since when?"

"It's none of your business if I am or am not." Libby attempted to step around him to retrieve her roses, but he blocked her. With a huff, she raised her foot and kicked her heel into the side of his calf. He doubled over from pain, and she elbowed him in the back of the neck.

"Oww! Libby, that's not fair. You know I'm not going to hit a girl." Skinny ducked away from her and reached up to rub the injured flesh.

"I'm no girl. I'm a woman." Libby pushed through her brother and Stevie, grabbed her vase, and stalked out of the room.

"Well, why don't you act like one every once in a while, for crying out loud," he called after her.

The taunt stung, and hours later Libby sat on her bed and stared at the roses. What'd Skinny mean she didn't act like a woman? She acted like she acted. Not that she'd had much of a role model. Her own mom had died when she was five. She only had snatches of memory of her at all.

Libby crawled across her bed and opened up her nightstand drawer and lifted out a box of dryer sheets. Freeing one from the box, she held it to her nose. The scent brought the image of Mom standing at the dryer, so tall next to Libby's childhood frame.

"Hey Mom, how come you put the paper in the dryer with the clothes?"

"Those are dryer sheets, sweetheart. They make the clothes soft and smell nice." The woman grasped one in her hand and reached down rubbing Libby's cheek with it and holding it close to her nose.

"Ooo. That does smell nice."

The smile her mom gave her with the scent of dryer sheet in her nostrils was the clearest memory Libby had, the only time she recalled her voice or words.

It sucked not having her around.

Libby's sister-in-law Josey was the only other woman in the family, and most of her time was spent taking care of the three terrors that were Mick's sons. Libby loved the little snots, but geez, they were like tornadoes when they tore through a room. They had destruction down to an art form.

Libby sighed and looked at the clock. Close to midnight. Maybe the boys had broken up the home party by now, and she could watch something on the big TV. Opening her door, she padded down the hall to the living room and hit the light switch. The television was off, and she scanned the room for the remote.

Was it too much to ask that Vance could put it next to the recliner where it belonged?

Libby sat on the couch and felt between the cushions. Heavy footsteps approached, and Skinny appeared.

He scowled at her.

"Hey, what did you boneheads do with the remote?" she asked.

He stalked over to where she sat with her hand swallowed by the couch. The serpent was poised.

"Well?" she asked.

Reaching down, he grasped her shoulders, hauled her to her feet, and kissed her hard on the mouth.

It was over quick, and Skinny was gone.

Just turned around and walked right out the door.

Libby touched her lips and stared at the door.

What the heck was that about?

****

Libby lay on a rolling mat under a 2001 Explorer. The music she'd been playing on the radio stopped abruptly.

"Turn it back on, Vance," she yelled without missing the rhythm of her wrench loosening a bolt. She'd started listening to classical music while she worked, and Vance hated it.

"Vance isn't out here."

Skinny.

She hadn't seen him since he pulled that stunt the other night.

Libby shifted and raised her head enough to see his shoes. "What do you want, Skinny?"

With the toe of his boot he nudged her ankle sticking out from the car. "To talk to you."

"I'm all ears." *You jerk.*

"To see you while I talk to you."

"I'm busy, as if you didn't know. I've three more cars

after this one to get done by five." She freed the bolt and hooked her fingers through the clamp.

"Arms and head down," he announced before grabbing her foot and pulling.

When her head cleared the car, she didn't even bother to sit up. Just glared. "So talk."

"I can't talk to you when you're on the ground. Why ain't you using the lift so you don't have to lay down to work?"

"Because my neck hurts when I have to look up into the engine half the day. Now what do you want?"

"Ouchie, my neck hurts when I work on the big engines," Vance crooned.

"Vance, get over there and find the hole in that tire and fix it before I smack you one," she said, as she rolled on her side and got to her feet.

Skinny glanced over at Vance before turning his attention to her.

Libby went to her radio and turned it back on though she turned down the volume. "You going to tell me what the heck that little stunt was about the other night?"

Skinny followed her and stood there with his hands clenched at his sides.

"Just spit it out, Skinny."

"I...I...do you want to go out?"

She lifted her hands in exasperation. "Go out where? I'm working here."

"No. Later. Like a...you know...." He stepped closer to her and his voice dropped. "Sort of a date maybe. With me."

Sort of a date maybe with me.

Libby blinked at him, his meaning sinking in slowly.

Unbelievable.

"Are you serious?"

His mouth thinned, and he nodded once.

"With me?"

Another nod.

"Hey! Hey, Skinny, did you come to get Libby to work

on your cycle? 'Cause it'll cost you at least two dozen roses in addition to the bill. She's got princess wages now." Vance's voice rang out across the garage from where he stood next to the spinner.

Libby stalked over to him. Grabbing his thumb, she twisted his arm up and behind his back making him double over.

"Owww! Owww! Dad, Libby's hurting me!"

"What'd you do to her?" Gene hollered through the door from his office.

Libby let go and shoved Vance giving him a dope slap as he stumbled forward before catching his balance. Libby wiped her hands on the front of her coveralls.

"Hello."

All of Libby's nerves stood at attention at the sound of his voice.

Byron.

He stood just a few feet outside of the bay wearing charcoal pants and a wide-striped, blue, button down shirt under a caramel colored jacket. His hair was slicked back from his face except for a thatch which hung over his forehead.

Oh, no. No!

Had he seen her beat on her brother?

"Umm….Hi." Libby took a step toward him.

He looked so crisp and beautiful, like he'd just stepped out of a clothing catalog.

He shifted, and Libby caught a glimpse of something white in between his jacket and shirt.

He was wearing a white scarf.

Libby blinked.

Oh, great day in the morning. He accessorizes.

Libby shook off her awe and searched his face for any clue he'd seen her get violent with Vance.

He smiled at her, and Libby's heart stopped for a few seconds.

"Car running okay?" It was the first thing that popped into her head.

"Well...yes."

Uh-oh. There was definitely a hesitation there.

Had she messed up his car?

Libby took another few steps toward him. "Is it running hot again?" She searched the lot for his car and spotted it on the curb.

"No. It's not running hot, but it's...." Byron's gaze roamed over her face, dropped briefly, then met her eyes.

What color were his eyes? Dark chocolate—warm. Oh, he had nice skin. Like coffee with a lot of creamer in it. But as fair as his hair was she'd have thought his skin would be paler. "What?"

"It's making a funny noise."

Right. The car. Funny noise. Libby put her hands on her hips. "Pull it up here in front of bay one."

"Don't you have enough cars to work on?" Skinny asked from behind her.

Byron strolled over to his car. He had a natural grace in his movement.

Bet he's a good dancer.

Bet he doesn't dance to the same music I do.

Libby walked close to the curb and waited as he got in his car and started it. She cocked her head to listen.

"Didn't you say you've got three more cars—" Skinny began.

"Shhh." Libby held a silencing hand to him and listened to Byron's engine. It sounded okay so far. She stepped back and pointed to where she wanted Byron to park the car then approached the driver's door when he opened it. "Leave it running and pop the hood."

At the front of the vehicle, Libby waited for the telltale pop of the release. She lifted the hood and propped it open.

Mick appeared by her side. "Making a noise, huh?" He grinned at her. "You missing any tools?"

Libby shook her head. She cocked her head over the engine. Nothing out of the ordinary, but then again, this was only the second time she'd seen this car. Byron drove it every day. He'd know if there was an odd sound. She straightened and looked for him. He stood aside, on the pavement—like a spring flower growing through a break in the sidewalk.

"When do you hear the noise? she asked. "All the time?"

Byron walked toward her and stopped next to the car. He placed both hands on the right quarter panel and turned towards her. "Mainly when I accelerate."

"What's it sound like?"

He parted his lips and executed a perfect tongue trill mimicking a cat purring.

Libby's stomach fluttered, and her skin at the back of her neck tingled as if he'd touched her there with that trilling trick. She stared at him unable to speak.

Mick slid in between Liberty and Byron. "And it's only when you press down on the gas?" He tested a few nuts and clamps to be sure they were tight and reached for the oil stick and pulled it. "When's the last time you gassed it up?"

"Not since before it ran hot and Liberty towed it in."

Her knees went weak at the mention of her name. He didn't just say it. He caressed it.

Mick fished a cloth out of his pocket, wiped the stick, and placed it in the reservoir before removing it again and studying the oil level.

"Why don't you ride with him up to 29th Street and back and see if you can hear it?" Mick counseled her. He wiped his hands on the rag and stuffed it in his pocket. His eyes twinkled. "Stay in the front seat, though, and hurry back. Mrs. Barker's not going to be happy with you, if she don't get her Cherokee back today."

Byron cast an apologetic glance at her. "This is inconvenient. I can make an appointment and come back another day."

"No. That's okay. It'll just take a few minutes."

"Yeah?" Vance called as he rolled a tire by. "Is that how long it takes the princess? Must be—"

"Vance!" Gene yelled at him from the doorway. "Get

over here, boy, and get this tire on the car. Customer's waiting."

Libby shot a grateful glance at her dad over her shoulder and lowered the hood. She tried to sniff to see if she smelled bad.

Grease and rubber, probably. If only he'd come by earlier in the day before the belt job on the Honda.

Sighing, she opened the door of the passenger side and slid in. Soft breezy music flowed from the speakers. It was a lot prettier than the music she'd found on the public radio station out of West Virginia. The door opened, and Byron sat down next to her fastening his seat belt.

He smiled at her. "So, to 29th Street?"

"Yeah. You'll have to go down a block. That's a one-way street."

Why did I say that? The sign was as plain as day.

He adjusted the music to a lower volume, shifted gears, and made a sharp U-turn to get on the road. He crossed the next road and turned left at the following intersection. Libby listened for any purring, but only heard regular engine noise.

"If you hear it, let me know," she said.

He didn't reply, and Libby assumed he was listening for the wayward sound. So many questions played in her head as he drove to 29th. Why was he in Ashland? The newspaper article said he was working in Huntington. What did a musician in residence do anyway? Teach violin lessons? Play for whoever wanted to hear a song? Did he take requests?

Did he know "The Devil Went Down to Georgia?"

Libby fought the smile that threatened to break out on her face.

"It's so odd. I'm not hearing it now."

Not uncommon. If she had a nickel for every time someone brought in a car with an odd noise and she'd practically tear the thing apart and still be unable to pinpoint the origin, she'd be rich. Reproducing the exact conditions when the noise occurred wasn't easy. Had the motor been cold? Had the car been on a hill, or accelerating rapidly....

"Were you going really fast when you heard it?"

He shrugged. "Not overly so."

Not overly so.

She loved how he talked.

"Where were you? In a neighborhood, or on the interstate, maybe?"

"At one point I was on Highway 23, but I also heard it driving around downtown."

Libby rolled down the window and leaned forward.

The traffic light at 29th loomed in front of them. It changed from yellow to red. Libby faced him, studying his perfect profile. He watched the light through the windshield. "I really did hear something."

"I'm sure you did. It could just be a vibration of a part I knocked when I was working on the engine. If you want, we'll check it out. Make sure nothing's loose.

He turned left, went down two blocks, and turned left again. That would bring them back to the garage.

"What did the guy mean about staying in the front seat? Is it possible you might hear differently from the back?"

"Oh." Libby gave a self-deprecating snicker and waved her hand. "That's my brother Mick. Don't pay any attention to him. He's just being a smart aleck."

Three blocks to go, darn it. Why couldn't he have taken a wrong turn?

Libby searched her brain for something clever to say, some question which would give her more information about him without seeming too personal. "What you doing over here, anyway? I thought you were over in Huntington?"

"I had some business at the Paramount." The Paramount was the theater downtown. It often hosted plays and musical acts.

"Are you playing there?"

"Perhaps."

"Is it a secret?"

"No. It's just talk now. There's really nothing to keep secret or report."

Libby digested that bit of information.

"It's always appropriate to make contact with local theaters and concert halls to make contacts and lend help, if needed. It's a good practice."

"Sounds like you're politicking."

His lips parted, and he graced her with a beautiful smile. "I suppose that's one way of putting it, yes. What have you seen at the Paramount?"

Libby didn't want to answer that question. She'd seen shows there as a kid on field trips, but otherwise she hadn't been back. When was the last time she visited? Sixth grade?

She shrugged. *Bummer.* She had nothing in common with this man, except the search for an engine noise.

"You don't remember?"

"Not really. It could have been a reprisal of School House Rock."

"Ahh."

The garage came into view, but the red light caught them. Libby inhaled deeply hoping to catch a whiff of his sweet masculine scent. She had to figure out what that cologne was.

"I guess you go to a lot of stuff like that."

"Sometimes. I try to support my fellow artists."

"I saw Roy Clark a while back. But that was in Charleston. I guess he doesn't count though."

Byron laughed. "Of course, it counts, my dear."

My dear.

In all her twenty-five years, no one had ever called her 'my dear'.

Affectionate Appalachian terms tended to be more like 'baby' or 'sweetie pie', even 'hillbilly,' if said with the right tone. Not 'my dear.' The last person she'd heard say that was Rhett Butler, and it had started with 'Frankly.'

"Are you for real? Who talks like that?"

His smile fell, but the humor remained in his eyes. The traffic light turned green, and he moved forward, and steered into the garage lot. Putting the car in park, he left the engine idling. Turning to Libby, he spoke. "'Put off that mask of burning gold With emerald eyes.'"

Libby blinked at him. "What?"

"It's a poem by William Butler Yates. Do you like poetry?"

• "My brothers can recite some pretty good limericks. They usually start with a guy from Nantucket, so probably not anything you'd want to hear."

His lips parted again showing white teeth. "Liberty Ann, thank you for your time." He reached over and took her hand in his. "'O no, my dear, let all that be; What matter, so there is but fire In you, in me?'" Raising her hands to his lips, he kissed her knuckles "I like you," he whispered against her skin.

Placing her hand back on her coverall covered leg, he exited the vehicle, came around to her door, opened it, and escorted her out.

Without another word, he drove away leaving Libby standing on the pavement staring after him.

What was that all about?

He was so pretty—seemed so nice, but she was too dumb to know what the heck he was talking about.

She rubbed her face with the knuckles he had kissed.

Not in my league.

Sighing, she walked to the building. Entering the office door, she spotted Vance behind the counter. He shot her a big goofy grin.

She held out her hand. "Give me your cell phone."

"What for?"

"'Cause I need it for a minute, that's why."

He took it out of his pocket and handed it to her. Scrolling through his contacts, she found Skinny's name and dialed his number.

He picked up on the first ring.

"Hey, this is Libby. Did you want to go out tonight or some other night?"

Chapter Three

Libby parked her car and walked into the restaurant she and Skinny had agreed on. She'd stipulated nothing in Ashland. There was no way she wanted to run into anybody they knew, so they crossed the state line and decided on a place in Huntington. And she'd told Skinny she'd meet him there. No sense in starting out the night with Vance sniveling because he wasn't invited to go.

When she opened the door and walked in, Skinny stood up from the bench he'd been sitting on. His eyes roved over her.

"Is that what you're going to wear?" he asked.

Libby looked down at her torn jeans and black pullover sweater. Well, it wasn't exactly prom threads, but then again this wasn't the prom.

She met Skinny's gaze. He was wearing jeans, too, and for once, a shirt which didn't look like he'd run over it a few times with his motorcycle.

"What?"

"I kind of thought you'd wear a dress or something."

Libby laughed. "I don't even own a dress." She cuffed him on the arm. "Geez, you didn't tell me this date had a dress code."

He rubbed his arm and glared at her. "No hitting on the first date, okay?"

"Does that include hitting on me? Because I can tell you, Skinny, the night's not looking promising at this point."

The waitress stepped up to them with menus in hand. Libby noticed her gaze lingered on Skinny. "Are you ready to be seated?" she asked him.

He nodded and walked behind her through the

restaurant, and Libby followed them both. Skinny claimed the chair on the far side of the table so Libby sat on the chair across from him. The waitress lingered as she placed a menu just so in front of Skinny and took their drink orders.

He was clueless about the poor girl.

Guess she was into tats and T-shirts stretched tight over big muscles.

Skinny immediately began looking at the menu not giving her to the time of day, and she plopped Libby's menu down on the table and left.

"Why don't you give that woman some attention? She's practically drooling over you and you ignored her."

Skinny raised his eyes to hers. His glance strayed briefly to where the woman had gone. "I don't check out other women when I'm on a date." He flipped the page and followed his finger down the margin.

"You wait till the next day, huh?"

"Yeah." His finger stopped, and he scowled at her. "No. Would you stop it? Any other woman would be pissed at some chick checking out her man. And you think it's a joke."

Libby blinked.

Her man?

Did Skinny think they belonged to each other now?

"This is me. I give you a hard time every other time I see you, why do you think I'd treat you differently tonight?"

He pursed his lips as if thinking about it. Finally, he shrugged. "What are you getting?"

"How much money you got? I'm leaning toward the steak, but if you're broke, I'll just get a burger."

He glared at her. "I guess it was too much to hope that you could be nice for once in your life."

Libby laughed. "Would you lighten up? Obviously, you like the abuse or else you wouldn't have laid that kiss on me the other night."

He shut his menu and slapped it on edge of the table. Sitting back, he folded his arms over his chest and stared out across the restaurant.

Who knew? Skinny has feelings, and I've hurt them.

"All right," *you big baby*, "I'll try to play nice. What're we going to do after we eat?"

"I dunno. Movie?"

"A movie? We can't get to know each other at movie. We sit in a dark room and stare at a screen." *Or sit in the back row with the fourteen year olds and make out.* And no way in heck, was Libby going to do *that*.

Not with Skinny Davis anyway.

"We've known each other since we were kids, Libby. I think we know each other already."

"I know you as my little brother's annoying friend. We've never been together without Vance irritating the stew out of me."

"Yes, we have. Last year we went to the baseball game together."

Libby searched her memory. *Oh, yeah*. The Legends had been playing in Lexington, and Vance got sick at the last minute. She'd gone in his place. "There were five other people on that trip. It wasn't a date."

"It was. We sat next to each other, and I bought your beer."

"It was dollar night, you doofus, and I didn't have more than two."

"Three."

"It wasn't a date."

"You kissed me."

"I did not!"

"Bottom of the ninth, and the bases were loaded. Evans hit a homer."

Libby's heart melted a little bit. *Oh, yes*. That had been a beautiful play, and it had put the Legends in the playoffs. She probably had kissed Skinny, she had been so excited. She probably would have kissed Hitler if he had been sitting next to her that day.

A gal gets carried away sometimes.

"I don't consider that a date since you're just now telling me it was one. If there's no knowledge beforehand, or even during, until a year after the fact, it is not a date," Libby said firmly.

"Y'all ready to order?" a sweet voice crooned.

She was back. The drooler.

Libby held up the menu to her. "I'll have the steak. Burn it."

Later that night Libby gave Skinny a breezy good night and drove home alone. She pulled her truck into the yard of the dark house and was nearly to the porch when a headlight blinded her. A familiar motorcycle pulled in the driveway, and Skinny dismounted and walked toward her.

Hmmm. What was this about? Was he here to see Vance or her?

"Hi."

"Hey, what's up?" She recovered her keys from her bag and extended the house key toward the door lock. His hand covered hers. She jumped and the key ring fell to the porch floor.

"Are you ready to say good night?" he purred.

Her skin prickled at his tone. Never had she heard Skinny talk that way.

This evening hadn't been unpleasant. They'd had a good dinner and gone on to see a slasher flick over a shared bucket of popcorn. But that didn't necessarily mean she intended to thank him with anything more than a handshake.

Libby looked up at him. The porch light illuminated the snake well enough. Funny how the tat seemed a little playful at the moment. "How do you say goodnight, Skinny?"

His inhalation filled the silence of the night. He tugged on her hand pulling her closer to him.

Uh-oh. "I don't think—" she began.

And Skinny pounced. He was all over her, tongue in her mouth, all gross and large and...wet. *And—ouch!—he just squeezed my boob.*

Libby shoved him away and wiped all of his spit off her mouth. "Don't do that. Geez!"

"What?"

"Get all on me like that. Is this how you end all your dates?"

"I thought we had a good time," he said defensively.

"We did until you followed me home and tried to choke me with your tongue and grabbed me. Man!" She punched him on the arm. *Take that, you stupid snake.*

She picked up her keys from the porch floor and unlocked the front door. Opening it, she headed inside.

"Wait."

"I'm done with you for the night, Skinny." She pushed the door shut, but it didn't close. Skinny was already on the threshold. *Geez, take a hint already.*

She walked into the living room with him stomping behind. Vance was on the couch. The images on the big TV turned Libby's stomach.

Libby stalked over to the TV and hit the power button. "What did Dad tell you about watching porn in here? You're disgusting!"

Throwing the remote in the vicinity of his head, she went to her bedroom and slammed the door.

Men. She hated them all.

****

Libby came back from lunch and walked into the garage ready to finish a brake job on the Toyota Sienna for that preacher chick. Dad was always so particular about any work they did on the van. Libby couldn't figure out whether he was scared of her or trying to earn his way into eternity by providing good service for one of God's workers.

Taking a long sip of tea from her to-go cup, she set it on the shelf over her workspace and studied the empty spot on the concrete. Libby scanned the immediate area. Where was her tool cart? She always put her cart next to the wall when she left the garage for any length of time.

Dad had put a password on all adult content channels until further notice. On top of that, Skinny had told Vance about their date. Her brother hadn't spoken to her since, and that had been two days ago. Vance and Mick knew better than to mess with her stuff. If Vance had done something to her tools in retaliation, she'd do more to him than twist his thumb.

Libby picked up her tea and walked into the office. Dad was at his usual spot behind the counter. "Where's Vance?"

"I sent him to the parts store. Why?"

"I think the little snot hid my cart."

Gene's eyes crinkled over his cheaters as his mouth turned up in a grin.

"Go ahead and laugh. I've got the lady preacher's van halfway done. Do you want your immortal soul in peril because Vance is acting like a ten-year-old?"

His smiled disappeared. "He'll be back in a few minutes. In the meantime, look around."

Libby walked past the desk to go in the back office. "If there's one scratch, one tiny dent on any of my stuff, I'll hurt him so bad he'll wish he hadn't been born."

"Now, come on. It's a harmless prank. If you wouldn't react like you do, maybe he wouldn't pull stunts like this."

Typical. Vance acts like a little brat, and it was her fault.

The office wasn't big enough to hide much. Libby stood at the door and gave it a cursory glance. She grasped the bathroom keys hanging from the nail on the doorframe and exited through the front door to check the bathrooms.

Nope and nope. Where'd he put it? It's not like it was a lug wrench he could put in a drawer. Her cart was waist high. She stepped over the cracked sidewalk and circled behind the building.

Libby hadn't heard from Skinny either. Was that good or bad? It hadn't been a horrible date, well, not until he'd kissed her at the end. Revulsion scuttled up her spine at the memory of it. *Yuck.* He'd come onto her like a freight train. Do some gals really go for that?

Turning the corner, she glanced at a couple of cars parked on the east side of the building. Left there by customers who didn't have the money to pay for the work they'd done. Dad called these cars his layaway lot. After so many months, he'd call Silas Winthrop, a local lawyer who usually got them the title to the car so they could sell it to recoup some of the money they'd put into it for parts. What it meant was they always had a couple of extra cars available to drive.

She wouldn't put it past Vance to hide her cart in one of the cars. If it wasn't in any of the storage rooms, she'd check the trunks. Rounding the corner, she took her keys out of her pocket and unlocked the door to the tire shed. Turning on the light in the windowless room, she perused the space. Tires were haphazardly piled everywhere. Obviously, Dad hadn't been in here in a while. He'd have a fit if he saw all the clutter. Vance took care of most of the tire work and oil changes, leaving the more difficult jobs to her and Mick.

Libby smiled. Vance's day just got a little harder. He wouldn't be allowed to go home until he got this room back in order. Dad would make sure of it.

But no tool cart.

She shut the door and locked it then entered the far bay where Mick did most of his work. He had a vintage van resting there with the hood up. The van should have been retired years ago, but the owner was stubbornly determined to make it to three hundred thousand miles. Mick had replaced so many parts on it, they'd dubbed it Frankenvan. He swore the last six months' worth of work had paid for his vacation to Dollywood. Well, and he'd made a side trip to a massive junkyard in Tennessee hoping to find some replacement parts for the old thing.

Crossing the middle bay where Vance worked most of the time, Libby resisted the urge to pick up some of his tools and hide them in a drawer in the office.

The tow truck pulled up, and Mick stepped out of the driver's side. Vance slunk away and headed to the office.

He was so busted, and he knew it. Libby decided to wait him out not giving him the satisfaction of knowing he'd ticked her off. But he better not have messed up her cart or he'd be sorrier than he'd ever been.

Mick walked into the building. "Hey," he called.

No mirth in his tone. Obviously he wasn't in on the stupidity. This time.

Heading over to his space, he picked up a ratchet and got to work. Libby hoisted her cup and took a long drink. She turned on the radio, and soft guitars filled the area. The cavernous area echoed the strains of the music. It had a Latin flavor to it, like she'd heard a time or two when a Mariachi band had played at a Mexican restaurant in Huntington. Would Byron Venable like it or did he only enjoy the classic kind he'd played last week as she worked on his car?

She sighed.

Worlds apart. Why think about him anymore? She'd probably never see him again, unless his phantom noise came back.

And even if it did come back and he brought the car to show her, then what? Nothing. She didn't belong with a boy like him. Even with his horrible kiss, Skinny was more her type. They liked baseball and beer. Libby was willing to bet the only thing Byron drank from a bottle was expensive wine.

Mick turned on the Tommy lift drowning out Libby's introspection soundtrack.

Movement out of the corner of her eye caught her attention. Vance had exited the office and stood with his hands in his back pockets staring at her. She returned his look and waited.

"What's your problem?" he snapped.

"I'm waiting on my tool cart."

"Well...what makes you think I have it?" Defiance sparked his eyes. *The jerk.*

"Did I say you had it?" She knew Dad hadn't said anything. He lived by the 'only get involved when it got violent' theory of parenting.

"No."

"If you've seen it, I'd like to know. I want to get these brakes done."

Vance huffed. He stalked up to her and spit near her boots. Libby's fist clenched automatically, but she straightened out her fingers.

I won't let him get to me.

"What the hell is the deal with you and Skinny?"

"What do you mean?"

"Are you screwing him?"

Libby shook her head in amazement. "We went out one time. What do you think?"

"How long have you been after him? How long has this been going on?"

"Nothing is going on. He asked me out, I said okay, and we went out. It isn't that big a deal, and nothing much happened."

"What's nothing much?"

"Vance, look. I don't really owe you any details about my dates. I don't ask you about what you do with your girlfriends, so how about giving me the same consideration."

"I don't date your friends."

"Well, if you did, I certainly wouldn't want to hear about it."

"You need to stay away from Skinny."

"Why? Who are you trying to protect? Me or him? Don't you think I'm good enough for your BFF?"

His nostrils flared, and he took a step toward her. What was this about really?

Vance didn't answer her—just stared her down. Libby refused to look away. This standoff was making her want to call Skinny and and go out with him again, if for no other reason than she wanted to show Vance he couldn't tell her what to do.

A door slammed, and Libby heard metallic rattling moving across the concrete floor. She refused to be the first one to look away. And she didn't have to. Vance's eyes slid in the direction of the far side of the garage, and Libby followed suit. Mick was pushing her cart toward her.

"You know how this got in the back of the

Frankenvan?" Mick asked.

She walked toward him and took it. "Nope. Thanks for finding it though."

Mick turned to his baby brother with an eyebrow raised. Vance dropped his eyes and left the garage without a word.

"What's that about?"

"He's jealous because Skinny and I went out and didn't invite him."

Now both of his eyebrows rose. "What about the fiddler?"

"He's a client. I've only seen him to work on his car."

Mick sniggered. "Josey started out as a client too." He followed Libby to the car and watched as she opened the top of the cart and inspected its contents.

"Seems like you never did find out what was wrong with her car."

Josey'd driven up in a '69 Camaro with the trademark twin stripes on the hood and trunk one day, and Mick's tongue had been so far out of his mouth, Libby was surprised he hadn't stepped on it. At first, she had thought it was the car that had Mick so worked up, until she saw her brother with Josey. They'd gotten married six months later.

"I sure did. It needed me to marry Josey, so I could be co-owner."

Libby snorted. Josey may have agreed until death do them part, but she'd refused to have his name on the title. They'd had a huge fight about it and the wedding almost hadn't happened because of it.

Mick gave Libby a self-deprecating smile. "She said if the next one's a girl, she'd give me the car outright."

Libby shook her head. *What an idiot.* "And you believed her?"

Mick blinked. "What?"

"She's only let you drive it a few times, Mick. I think she was lying, you know, because she's crazy." Libby rolled her eyes. "Geez. I hope you guys stop at four, no matter if this one's a girl or not."

****

A letter with Liberty Ann Miller in a neat scrawl across the envelope lay on the top of the counter when she came into work one morning. Her dad was on the telephone so he didn't speak to her as he pushed it toward her.

Weird.

She never got mail at the shop.

And certainly not to…Liberty Ann.

Her breath caught.

Could it be from Byron?

She tore open the letter and looked inside. She tapped the envelope and two tickets to a concert in Huntington for Friday night fell onto her palm. A folded paper of card stock fit snug inside the envelope, and she actually had to pull it out.

Please bring a friend and be my guest. Byron.

Bring a friend and be his guest? Who the heck could she take? She carefully placed the tickets back in the envelope as she studied his note. Such beautiful handwriting. The way he wrote his B was *so nice.*

The concert was two days from now. Was Byron actually performing, or did he just have some extra tickets he wanted to share? Propping the envelope open, she flipped the tickets to read the front. Park Night Music. What did that mean? Did Park Night mean the kind of music he played? Did she want to go? Yes, especially if he was performing. But who would go with her. Skinny? Yeah right. Even if she could drag him along, taking one guy so she could drool over another one wasn't a good idea. Even if the drooling was done from the audience.

Dad hung up the phone. "Whatcha got there?"

"Byron sent me tickets to a concert. Wonder if he's playing in it?"

"Call and see."

"Call who?"

"What's the ticket say?" He held his hand out, and she placed one of the tickets on his open palm.

"Marshall. Park Night Music," he read the words aloud.

"Well, if he invited you, he at least has to be there. Right?"

"I don't have anybody to go with."

"Go by yourself."

"By myself? That has pathetic written all over it."

"Libby, I didn't raise you to be a wimp. Go and enjoy it. Don't be like them girls who can't even go the toilet unless they got a bunch of women holding hands together."

"This isn't the toilet. This is a ticketed performance. What will it look like if I'm sitting there with an empty seat next to me?"

"You'll have a place to put your pocketbook."

"I don't carry a pocketbook."

"Dog."

"No dog, either."

"Just go. Take Josey with you."

"Who'll keep the boys?"

"Their daddy."

Libby stared at her dad, and they both burst into fits of laughter.

"Good one, Dad. You kept a straight face for almost two seconds."

"I know. It wasn't easy." He reached a finger under his glasses and wiped a tear from his eye. "Those boys would have the house burnt down by the time you and Josey got back, and Mick would be clueless as to where they got the matches. That boy really needs to be a more attentive father."

"Like you?"

"Yep."

Chapter Four

That night Libby and Josey stood in front of Josey's open closet. She pulled out a flowing turquoise dress and held it up. "I can't wait until I'm back down to my pre-pregnancy size again. All of these cute clothes, and I haven't been able to wear them in years."

"That's because you haven't not been pregnant in years."

"We like having the kids close together." Josey's wide-eyed gaze met hers.

"Why?" She raised her hands in emphasis. "They just gang up on you that way."

"Here. Try this on." She held the dress for Libby to take.

But Libby shook her head. "It's all glittery. I don't do glittery."

"Why not? What's wrong with glittery?"

Libby sighed. "I'm not a dress kind of person. Can't I just get a pair of slacks or something?"

"No. This is a concert. You've got great legs, but no one ever sees them, Libby. You're never going to get a man when you're wearing coveralls every day of your life."

"This is a mistake. If he doesn't like me in coveralls, then he isn't going to like me period."

"I'd kill for legs like yours." She reached into the closet and produced a short ivory dress on a hanger. "Here. There's no glitter or bows or lace. It's a simple cut, and ivory is classy. It's lined so you don't have to worry about a slip. With boots the whole look will be elegant."

"I don't do elegant."

"In this dress you don't have to. It'll do it for you."

"Can I wear my work boots with it?"

"Nope, but I've got some other boots that will have Byron Venable panting for you." She reached up on a shelf and extracted a large box. Throwing off the top, she held up a black knee high boot. "Panting. For. You."

"I'm not sure I can walk in those things."

"Oh, pshaw. The heel's only two inches. My granny could walk in these. Take off your clothes. Let's try this on."

Libby shook her head. "I'm not taking off my clothes in front of you."

"Why not? We've got all the same parts, sweetie."

Libby stood there wondering how she got talked into playing dress-up with her sister-in-law. *Ugh.* She'd never done anything so girlie in her whole life.

Josey motioned her to hurry up. Next she'd start counting like Libby had seen her do with the boys. It amazed Libby that counting one and two worked. What did they think would happen if their mom got to the dreaded three?

Uh-huh. I am not taking off my clothes in front of anybody.

Josey sighed in defeat. "Fine. I swear I don't know why you are so modest. Mickey would walk naked through the house all weekend if I'd let him." She draped the dress on the bed. "I'll run downstairs and check on things. Put this on, then come out and let me see." Walking to the door, she walked through it and shut it softly behind her.

As soon as Josey was gone, Libby locked the door. Grabbing the hem of her sweatshirt, she stripped it off. Unbuttoning her jeans, she pushed them down and stepped out of them.

Catching a glimpse of herself in the full-length mirror on the closet door, she ran a hand over her hip hooking her thumb under her blue satin and tea lace panties. The matching push-up bra had promised plump breasts increased by a full cup size. She struck a pose in the mirror and studied her curves.

Skinny had said she needed to act like a girl every once in a while. If he had any idea how much of a girl she was under her Craftsman twill coveralls, he would have tried to jump her long ago. She knew how guys acted when a woman presented herself in all the trappings.

Which was why nobody knew of Libby's secret love for pretty underwear.

Not even Josey, and she was the one who first turned Libby on to the idea when she'd bought her two matching panty and bra sets two years ago with the unapologetic comment, "Every woman wants to feel pretty. This way you can feel pretty even when you are in Testosterone Central at the garage."

She'd set aside the gift with an eye roll, but Josey's gesture had touched her. In the privacy of her room later that day, she'd tried on the garments and had been in the closet with Victoria's Secret ever since.

Libby had seen enough of the laundry at the house to know Josey loved lingerie. The large collection of pretty scraps of material and lace was probably why she'd spent more time pregnant than not in their six-year marriage.

Josey had some kind of power over Mick that went far beyond sex. He worshipped her, but he also shut away a part of himself from her without any guilt or remorse. She never saw the meticulous way he worked an engine or placed a bet on the horse with the craziest name at the Derby or got all sappy and knocked the price off some work because an old lady gave him a sob story.

Libby didn't want that kind of relationship with a guy. She wanted full disclosure—to share the work stories and hang out together because they liked to do the same things. She should like Skinny, if only some other woman would teach him how to kiss first.

Maybe she'd suggest it to him.

She walked to the bed and sat on its edge. Picking up the boots, she slid them on and closed the zipper. Standing, she watched herself in the mirror.

Admiration for her image battled with shame. It was okay to think she looked like a hottie, wasn't it?

Too bad she was too embarrassed to call Josey in here

to get her opinion.

What would Byron do if he saw her dressed like this? Would he act like Skinny had acted the other night?

Under that GQ persona, was Byron Venable, musician in residence, like every other guy she'd ever known?

****

Libby followed the usher down toward the stage hoping she didn't trip and tumble down the stairs and bust her butt. Shouldn't they have a rail or something? She glanced behind her to be sure her dad was still with her. After a lot of handwringing on her part about having no one to go with, he'd offered to accompany her and was presently wearing his standard church outfit—khakis and a blue button down shirt.

The usher kept going. Where were their seats anyway? Why hadn't she looked on the ticket?

She tugged at the skirt of the dress. With the boots and the hem, she had her knee and a few inches above showing. When she'd asked Josey about borrowing some leggings to wear underneath, Josey had refused.

"Give him that sliver of bare skin, Libby. Oh, it will drive him wild!" She'd grinned like the cat who ate the canary. Dumbfounded, Libby had studied that expression.

I am no good at this.

"And quit walking like a...a bull stomping in the Pamplona Encierro."

Libby's eyes narrowed. "A bull stomping in what?"

"Walk like a woman. Don't stomp around. Think of a pony prancing. The enthusiasm. The grace. The beauty." Josey placed her hands on Libby's hips. "Loosen them up. Fluid."

Libby stepped away from Josey's groping and held up a hand. "That's it. I am no Eliza Doolittle, so can it, Professor Higgins."

Josey shook her head. "What am I going to do with you?"

"Mama!" John John ran up to her and fisted their mother's shirt followed closely by Tony wielding a plastic sword. He whacked his brother on the back.

"Boys! Boys! Cut it out."

Libby used her nephews' distraction to stomp quickly away from her well-meaning sister-in-law.

Shaking away the memory from earlier tonight, Libby spotted Byron standing in front of the stage talking to someone. Her breath caught in her throat. Dressed in a yellow sweater vest with a dark blue striped shirt underneath, he looked like a clothing model. He nodded at what the guy next to him said and smiled. Then his gaze traveled from his companion upward, meandered over her, and away.

In a second, his attention was back on her and—*yes!*— he laid his hand to his heart as he watched her come down the aisle stairs.

Prancing pony. Loosen them up. Fluid. Oh, please don't let him think about a stomping bull.

His lips moved, and she read his words from the span of space between them.

Excuse me, please.

He walked toward the aisle and waited. The usher walked by him, and Byron lifted his hand and took hers. Bending slightly forward, he kissed the knuckles of her hand.

"Liberty Ann, so kind of you to come tonight."

In the next moment, his hand and lips were gone, and he greeted her dad with a handshake. "Hello, Mr. Miller. We're on the front row right here."

We're on the front row?

"You aren't playing in the concert?" Libby asked as they walked to their seats. Not quite in the middle, but close enough.

His gaze caressed her, and Libby was so glad she'd borrowed the dress and boots, had foregone the leggings, and left her hair down.

"No. I'm in the audience with you. Shall we?" He gestured to the chairs.

Libby grasped the armrest and lowered herself onto the

cushioned seat, glad she hadn't tripped once in Byron's presence.

Her dad settled next to her with a sigh. He bounced on the chair a couple of times. "Nice place to park our carcasses. Hope I don't fall asleep."

Libby grinned at him. "Me too, Dad. They'll be able to see us from the stage." She paused. "Thanks for coming with me."

"Meh." He shrugged. "Been a long time since we did anything father-daughter related. I figured we was overdue, if you didn't want to take no one else."

"I'm glad you suggested it." Her bare legs caught her attention and she tried to pull down the hem of her dress. Not much luck. The dress was riding up showing way too much thigh and right here on the front row. Why hadn't she brought a jacket to cover up with?

She peeked at Byron to see if he was looking at her legs. His face was raised to the stage watching people who appeared to be students of the college take their places on chairs arranged in a semi-circular pattern.

Should I be disappointed or relieved?

She shimmied in her chair and tugged at the edge of her skirt again to cover more skin. Why hadn't she tried sitting in the dress before she agreed to wear it tonight? With the bulletin the usher had given her earlier, she covered some of her leg.

"What's wrong?" her dad asked. "You sitting on a pinecone or something?"

"No," she whispered to him. "I'm not comfortable in a dress."

"Then why'd you wear it?"

"Josey told me to."

Gene pursed his lips and raised his eyebrows in a *what were you thinking* expression.

The lights dimmed, and a woman stepped onto the raised platform at the center of the chairs. A clear tone sounded from what Libby thought was an oboe. Then all of the other instruments joined in with the same note.

Cool.

Tap. Tap. Tap. The conductor raised her stick a moment, then the music began.

The concert lasted perhaps an hour with a ten-minute intermission. When the concert ended, Libby sighed in appreciation.

Really nice.

She'd never sat front row at a concert before. Who was she kidding? She'd never been to a concert before where an orchestra played.

The beauty of the music had relaxed her, given her a sense of well-being.

She glanced over at Dad. He sat with his mouth open, and his eyes closed. She nudged him with her elbow.

He startled awake. "What?"

She leaned over to him. "Naptime's over."

"Okay."

The lights came up, and Libby turned to Byron. "Thank you. I enjoyed that."

Gene stood, and she and Byron followed suit. Her dad looked at him. "How's the car running? Still got that noise?"

"It's intermittent." He shot an apologetic glance at Libby.

"Why don't you take Libby home? Maybe the noise will show up, and she can figure it out."

Embarrassment heated her face. Did her dad really just unload her on the guy? She shook her head. "I'm sure you've got better things to do than drive me all the way back to Ashland. Bring it by tomorrow. I can look at it."

Byron's mouth parted in a smile. "It would be my pleasure to take you home."

"That would add an hour to your night," Libby argued.

"It would be his pleasure." Gene gave his daughter a look like she was being unreasonable for refusing. "I'll see you later. Good night, all." He nodded to them both and walked to the stairs without looking back.

Reluctantly, Libby turned to Byron. "I'm sorry. He's

usually asleep by this time. He hasn't stayed up past eight in a long time. I'll just go catch—"

"No, really. I'll be happy to take you home, Liberty Ann."

Liberty Ann. She loved how he said her name, as if he liked the taste of it.

****

With his violin in the backseat, Byron drove them east toward Kentucky. He was taking the back roads, the long way to Ashland.

"Crossing the bridge into Ohio would have been quicker," Libby commented.

"Really?" His tone told her he knew this already. Libby smiled in the dark, but a sound caught her attention. She crooked her head to listen.

A low vibration.

"Take your foot of the gas."

The car slowed, and the noise disappeared.

"Do you want me to pull over to the side of the road?"

"No. Go ahead and accelerate again." She rolled down the window, pricking her ear.

Was it a belt? No, a belt wouldn't purr like that. It would screech. Libby thought back to the job she'd done on the water pump. If he hadn't noticed the sound before she'd worked on the car, then it could have been something she'd done. Or maybe the overheating had stressed something else. What?

"Would you like to stop somewhere to get something to eat?"

"Uh-huh. I want to nail down this noise. Go to the garage."

They continued on for a few miles. After a while the noise stopped.

"Have you noticed it happens when you first start it up, but disappears later?"

"No."

"Are you sure it wasn't happening before I worked on your car?"

"I didn't notice it before you worked on the car. That's not to say it wasn't occurring."

"Do you usually listen to the radio when you drive?"

"Often I do, yes."

So, if he did listen to the radio, then the sound could have been going on for months, and he wouldn't have noticed.

Cooling fan? That would be intermittent, especially in city traffic. She'd check it first. When they arrived at the garage, Libby directed him to pull up to the closed bay door and exited the vehicle. Luckily, she had finished the exhaust issue in Maybelle Paxton's car, Libby's last job of the day. Her workspace was clear.

She unlocked and went through the office turning on the lights then opened the garage door signaling for Byron to pull his car forward. He did so, and she walked to the driver's side.

"Pop the hood."

"You don't have to do this. I can bring it by tomorrow."

Oh.

Libby snapped out of mechanic mode. She focused on Byron instead of his car for the first time since the noise had distracted her. She'd blown it. She'd forgotten that this could have been a date. He'd asked her out to eat, and instead she'd told him to go to the garage. He'd taken the long way back, and she'd listened for engine noises instead of listening to him.

This is why I have no boyfriend.

She shook her head in self-derision and stalked over to her tool cart, her boot heels clicking on the cement.

I'm with a guy who could pass for a GQ model, who sends me red roses, and what do I do? Grill him about his car problems. He wants to take me to a restaurant, and I demand he take me the garage so I can get all dirty with his car.

I'm an idiot.

She reached under the hood and freed the clasp, lifting it and grabbing the stand to prop it. Stepping to her cart, she opened the hinged lid and sorted through its contents. Byron was out of the car now and standing aside silently.

Maybe he had had another date anyway, and he'd had to get out of it because of the stunt her dad pulled. He'd excused himself for a few minutes to get his violin. That's probably when he'd explained the situation to the woman.

Sorry. I just got saddled with my mechanic. I sent her tickets to the concert, and, well, you know what they say about no good deed goes unpunished.

He'd probably given her one of those smiles that make a woman's knees all gooey.

Libby picked up her flashlight and looked under the hood. Shining the beam on the cooling fan, she looked for bent or chipped blades. The area around it didn't show any shiny places which may have been skimmed by a bent blade. She bent over and grabbed a blade and ran her hand over it, then the others. Her fingers skittered over the edges. Hanging the light from the hood and aiming it to the engine, she reached forward and took hold of the harmonic balancer testing its tightness. It shifted.

Aha.

A harmonic tone echoed in the room.

Byron's gotten his violin out.

He began to play a slow melody, different from the one he'd played before. Libby paused for a moment.

The other piece he'd played the night she'd met him had been sad. This one…was….what? A little playful, but more than that.

Sort of…seductive.

From under the hood, Libby realized her dress was likely riding up. She hoped she wasn't mooning the poor guy. With her free hand, she reached back and felt the hem. *Darn it.* Nearly to her butt. She pulled, but doubted it helped. Straightening, she glanced back at Byron who continued to play, but his fiery gaze stupefied her, his eyes the color of liquid onyx. His lips curved in a smile, and he dipped his head in acknowledgment.

Of what though?

Of having an eyeful of her panties? What panties did she have on?

Oh, no. The emerald green with the black lace.

She wrenched the dress down for good measure and moved to the other side of the car. At least when she bent over the next time, she wouldn't flash him.

She judged the size of the bolt she'd need to torque and opened a drawer and pulled out the wrench. It was too small, so she got the next size up and reached over to tighten it. *Shoot.* She couldn't reach that far. She'd have to move back over to the other side.

The music continued, the notes falling down around her, blanketing her in their beauty. Her body tingled as if Byron had touched her, as if he were....

She walked to the corner of the car and peered at him around the open hood. His hand held the bow as he moved it back and forth across the face of the instrument, as if he were caressing her somehow through the violin, by the strokes of the bow over the strings.

His eyes were closed now, but his lips parted as she watched, and his tongue licked his lower lip.

Is he doing this on purpose? Does he know what he's doing to me?

If she hurried, she could get the balancer tightened and let him take her home. He'd put the violin away, and she could keep her panties on and covered.

Just do it.

Fix the car.

She walked around the car again and leaned over. Reaching the bolt with her wrench, she gave it two good turns and straightened. Going to the front, she lowered the hood then leaned on it with arms crossed enjoying her own personal concert.

His eyes, open now, watched her. For a moment she lost herself in their dark depth.

Byron continued to play, his fingers moving up and down the neck of the violin then further up, sawing the bow hard across the strings fast and high until the final note rang out around them. He lifted the bow up and with dropped his other hand holding the violin so that it rested at his waist.

The buzz of the lights seemed so loud in the sudden quiet as the last note of Byron's music died away.

Libby didn't know what to say. Her heart pounded with emotion and desire. She resisted the urge to jump him.

She had to have been misreading his 'come to me, baby' look. Guys like him didn't go for women who had grease under their fingernails instead of pretty polish on them.

Right?

Pushing off the car, she walked to the shelf along the wall, and took a cloth out of a box of orange solution she used to clean grease off her hands. She wiped her skin, taking extra care to get the smudges in between her fingers. Placing the cloth aside, she picked up a towel beside the box and dried her hands. Looking down at the dress, she checked for any smudges on the cream-colored material. If she got Josey's dress dirty, her sister-in-law would not be happy. By some miracle, it was clean.

Finally she found her voice. "Byron, what a beautiful piece of music. Did you make it up?"

He shook his head, his eyes still so warm. "That was Tchaikovsky."

A girly sigh escaped her mouth.

That Tchaikovsky. He sure knew how to make love with a violin.

"Are you ready to go home, Liberty Ann?" Byron's voice caressed her ears as his violin had moments before.

"Can we take the long way?" The question slipped out, so she hurriedly added, "I'm interested to know if I found your problem."

His lips parted in a grin. "The long way it is."

The trip back to her house was only a couple of miles, but Byron headed in the other direction. Crossing the bridge, he followed the river on the Ohio side, skimmed West Virginia, then took the highway back into Kentucky.

And the engine made no purring noises whatsoever.

Libby considered it a victory of sorts. Maybe she couldn't have GQ, but she sure as heck could touch his engine parts while he played sexy music for her ears alone.

She directed him to the Miller household, and he steered the car into the driveway, and cut the engine.

Libby's heart thundered in her ears. She'd ask him in for coffee, and if he accepted, that meant he liked her, that the hot looks he was shooting her way wasn't just because she was willing to fix his car pro bono.

"Thank you for fixing my car," he said.

"Sure."

He left the car, and in a moment he had opened her door, and helped her out. His fingers held hers as they walked together to the door.

On the front porch he squeezed her hand and let go.

"Would you like to come in for a while for…coffee?"

"I better not. Perhaps a rain check?" He softened the rejection with his perfect smile.

Disappointment rocketed through her. "Sure."

"May I have your telephone number?"

"Umm…okay."

Byron reached into his pocket and retrieved his cell phone, and touched the digits on the screen as she recited it to him. A hundred desperate questions poured through her mind. *When are you going to call me? Do you like me? Why would you play that music which makes me want to jump you then refuse to come inside for coffee?*

He returned the phone to his pocket, and stepped backward. "Until next time, then." Pivoting on his heel, he strode to his car as if he were late for an appointment.

Libby walked into the dark entrance foyer with a mixture of emotions churning in her heart. Would he call her?

A lone lamp lit the living room. Libby started toward it to turn it off

"Hey," Skinny said from the corner of the couch.

Libby stopped. Skinny's gaze meandered over her. "Hey yourself. What are you doing here, and where's

Vance?"

He placed his arm along the back of the couch as if he were settling in. "He went to bed." Tossing his head back, he finally settled on her face. "He said you went out on a date."

Libby shrugged.

"How did it go?"

His tone was casual, but Libby went on the defensive. Crossing her arms over her chest, she spoke. "Skinny, you and I went out once. That doesn't mean we're exclusive."

"It could mean that."

Libby sat down on the other side of the couch. "I like you, but I don't like how you came onto me like a freight train."

He was silent for a moment. He flicked his hand toward her. "You wore a dress for him."

"It was a concert. You're supposed to dress up for those things. This isn't mine. It belongs to Josey."

"You look pretty in it."

"Thanks." Libby turned to him, propping one booted foot on the couch. His eyes dropped to her legs. *Oops. Bad move.* She touched both feet to the floor.

Skinny leaned forward, resting his elbows on his thighs. "Are you going out with him again?"

"If he asks me, I will."

"Will you go out with *me* again?"

"I don't know. Are you going to ram your tongue down my throat?"

"That's how people kiss," Skinny said in an offended tone.

"No, they don't. A kiss should be...." The sensuous music from the garage flowed through her mind. "It should be slow and tentative, like you're testing the waters. You stick your toe in first to see if the temperature is okay. You don't just dive in."

Skinny shook his head in disagreement. "I dive in or I do a cannonball. Nothing like the shock of cold water on a hot day."

Libby laughed. "I believe that about you. But when you kiss a woman, you should be gentle, like you have all night to just kiss her."

"I can try to kiss you like I have all night." He bit his lip. Straightening, he pivoted to face her. "I like you, Libby. I've liked you for a long time."

"I don't think I'm the girl for you."

"You could be the girl for me." He slid across the cushion. Closer. "I'm loving these boots. They're really revving my engine." His lecherous grin irked her.

"You see? That's what I'm talking about. Is that supposed to turn me on? You talking about your revving engine?"

"You're a mechanic. I'm trying to talk in your vernacular."

"Well, don't," she snapped then took a deep breath. *He's trying, and I need to be nicer.* "Pretend like I'm a woman who wants pretty words and soft touches."

His brow furrowed. "Your boots really...make your legs look hot. How's that?"

Libby's insides warmed. "Better."

He stood, his large frame filling her visual field. "Maybe you can wear them more often."

Libby tilted her face and looked up at Skinny. She lifted her hand and he took it pulling her to her feet. "You can be charming when you try. I would like to kiss you, but promise me just a lip kiss, between two friends like we are. Can you do it?"

He grinned. "I don't know. The boots are hard to resist."

"Then quit looking at my legs." Libby reached her arms around him and lifting her head, she touched her lips to his. His mouth was warm and pliant beneath hers. Drawing back, she watched him. "Was that nice?"

He nodded. "Nice. But a little tame."

This time she kissed him on his cheek. "Good night, Skinny." She felt pressure on her backside. "And get your hand off my butt unless you want me to show you what these boots are really for."

Chapter Five

Libby stood behind the counter at the garage waiting for Catherine Euclid to tell how she'd popped this tire in a manner which was entirely someone else's fault. The woman ran up on so many curbs that her tire replacements on top of their regular order got them a discount with the supplier.

"And there I was with a chicken wrap with ranch dressing in one hand and trying to hold Princess Taffy back with the other, and the steering wheel veered to the right, and the next thing I know, I hear thump, thump, thump."

"More like a whump, whump, whump, I'd say," Mickey amended while he hooked the truck key on the nail next to the garage entrance.

Catherine batted her false eyelashes at him. "Yes, more like whump, whump, whump. Thank you for coming to get me. Is your daddy going to be back soon?"

Catherine seemed to have a thing for Gene Miller though he most definitely did not return the sentiment, especially when it came to Catherine's furry appendage known as Princess Taffy.

The dog's beady eyes blinked at Libby from underneath tightly styled fur tied in a pink bow at the top of her obnoxious little head. Libby felt a little sorry for Mick having to ride in the cab with the animal. She probably yapped nonstop all the way from Highway 1667. But too bad. Mickey had lost the coin toss.

"Dad had an appointment in Ironton," Libby said. She didn't say it was at the wings place after the call had come in for Catherine's tow. He liked to make himself scarce when Ms. Euclid was on her way to the garage. "We'll get the tire fixed in about twenty minutes, if you don't mind waiting. You and Princess Taffy."

"That would be wonderful. I'm supposed to be in Huntington by four-thirty for a River Arts lecture and violin demonstration."

Mick and Libby looked at each other.

Nah. Couldn't be. He wasn't the only violinist in the Tri-State Area. She opened her mouth to ask but clamped it shut again.

Byron had had her number for nearly a week now, and he hadn't used it.

"Who's doing the lecture, Miss Euclid?" Mickey asked.

"Call me Catherine, please. Brian Something. He's a musician in residence. That means Marshall pays him to come here to play and teach music. Isn't that divine? A musician in residence. Don't ever say West Virginia doesn't have class."

"Do you mean Byron Venable?" Libby asked.

"Yes. I do believe that is his name."

Princess Taffy yapped in agreement.

"Can anybody go to the lecture?" Mickey asked.

"What's it matter, Mick?" Libby glared at him.

His eyes widened innocently. "In case I might want to go, Lib."

"Yeah, right." She held up her arms wide apart. "You're here. Culture is over there."

"Then maybe I need to go. Where is it, Miss Euclid?"

"Uh-uh-uh, my precious boy. It's Catherine."

"Miss Catherine."

"Just Catherine."

Mick opened his mouth to echo the woman's words, but Libby shot him a dirty look.

He conceded. "Catherine."

"It's at the public library. They have an auditorium. Such a nice facility."

"It sure is," Mickey said.

"You went to a library? On purpose?" Libby asked.

"Yep. The Big Foot hunters were there. I took the boys. You know they've had several sasquatch spottings in

Ohio."

"Oh, dear me," Catherine replied. She clutched Princess Taffy to her chest.

• Libby looked at the fur ball. Doubtful that the sasuatch would waste its time on that hairy little nibblet.

At four-thirty Libby walked through the auditorium doors dressed, once again, in borrowed clothes from Josey—a soft sweater dress the color of dark chocolate with perfectly coordinated leggings and boots.

Libby felt like a stupid Barbie. Even her feet were in the same ridiculous arch as the doll. She stumbled into the room, thankful that she regained her balance instead of being sprawled on the floor.

Mickey had milked Catherine of all pertinent information, then called Josey in to bully Libby into going.

"You've got to go," Libby said.

"He's not interested. If he were, he would have called me by now."

"He invited you last week, and instead of going parking with him in some romantic hideaway, you demand he take you to the garage so you could play with his car."

Properly chastised, Libby had given in.

She found a chair near the back though with only about twenty-five people there it was hard to blend. Byron wore a charcoal suit with a silvery tie. Someone handed him a headset microphone, and he put it on and adjusted it. His violin sat in its open case on a high table near him. A woman introduced Byron, and he shook her hand then walked around the podium to stand in front of it. He launched into a brief history of the violin and spoke of several of his favorite composers. Then he picked up his violin and began to play.

This was the third time she'd heard him play, but the first that she wasn't at work. The music he played today wasn't what she'd heard before. There was not the sadness from the first night or the sensuous nature from last week. Though both pieces were beautiful, they seemed impersonal. Showy even.

When he finished, he put his violin away, and the audience clapped. He nodded his head in gratitude, and his eyes met hers. One corner of mouth turned up.

Great. He spotted me. I've graduated to groupie status now.

Still. Her toes curled in Josey's boots.

People stood, some going to the front to meet Byron. Others congregated together, and a few walked toward the exit.

What should she do? Go up and talk to him, but what would she say? He'd think she was stalking him.

Josey had forbidden her from talking about his car, so that shut that topic out. They hadn't really talked about anything else.

This is stupid. Why did I let her talk me into coming?

Libby headed to the door. Outside of the room, someone touched her elbow. She turned and looked into Byron's face.

"Hi," he said.

"Hi."

"Thanks for coming today. I didn't know you were involved in River Arts."

"Oh. A lady at the…someone told me you were—"

"Yoo-hoo, Libby!" Catherine hurried toward them with a big smile on her face. "Darling, I hardly recognized you with a clean face."

And I hardly recognized you without Princess Yappy.

She touched Byron's forearm. "Byron, this is Libby Miller, my mechanic. Who knew she liked high art music?"

Libby's head hurt from not rolling her eyes.

Byron nodded politely to the woman. "Liberty Ann and I are acquainted. And you are?"

"Catherine Euclid of the Compton County Euclids?"

Byron blinked. "Of course."

Seriously?

"So, you two know each other? Really?"

"I—"

"We've been out a few times, haven't we, my dear?" Byron turned to her for confirmation.

Libby nodded since her tongue refused to move.

Catherine's jaw dropped. "Really?"

"Liberty Ann, you look lovely." He shot an apologetic glance to the other woman. "Would you excuse us, please?"

"Oh, yes. Of course." She hurried back into the auditorium.

"I'd love to spend some time with you, but I've got another obligation in a few minutes."

"That's okay."

"What did you think?" He lifted his violin, which was cradled in his arm.

Libby studied the instrument.

"Uh-oh. You didn't like it."

Her gaze met his. "You play very well, and I'm no expert, but what you played today. It seemed...."

"Yes?"

"Kind of...fluffy."

"Fluffy?"

"You know, like you didn't want to work too hard to play it, and they wouldn't have to work too hard to listen."

A gleam lightened his eyes, and he laughed. "You have very perceptive ears. But I should know that by now."

"Why would you do that? This ladies' club is to promote the arts."

He leaned close to her, his lips brushing her ear. "Most of their conversation with me was about the hors d'oeuvres and the color scheme. They want a program from me that compliments the pâté. Nothing too complicated or obscure, and they wanted to have it here instead of at the concert hall at the university, so no piano or music students handy. So I keep it simple, give them what they want, and everyone's happy."

Tingles ran up and down Libby's spine at his soft words spoken in her ear and the way his breath teased her hair. She breathed in the sweet tang of cologne, tempted to rub her face against his neck like a cat rubbing its mouth along a piece of furniture.

He stepped away, and Libby swayed a bit.

"See you soon?" he asked.

"Sure," she replied, not believing it.

She took the stairs down to the ground floor. Skinny sat on a chair in the lobby, his eyes downcast, and a frown across his face.

"Skinny? What are you doing here?"

He stood, his expression changing when he saw her. "Hey. Are you alone?" He wore black denim and a black T-shirt that looked new. Ebony boots with silver-topped toes completed the ensemble.

Wow.

"Yeah."

His blue eyes studied her warily. "Wanna go get something to eat?"

"I guess so." Libby returned his stare. "What are you doing here?"

He began to walk to the entrance, and she fell into step beside him. He walked through the door and held it until she caught hold of it. Outside, he turned on the sidewalk to her. "Angelou's is two blocks up. Want to walk it?"

Angelou's was a bar and grill. Their wings were the best in Huntington.

Libby nodded, and they turned west to the restaurant.

He wasn't going to answer her question, but it was obvious. Him being in the lobby wasn't a coincidence.

"Who told you?"

"Vance."

"Huh. You know, he told me to stay away from you. Seems odd he'd tell you where I was."

"He didn't exactly tell me with the intention of me coming over here."

"Then why did he tell you?"

"I think his reason was to let me know you and...what's his name...had hooked up, so I might as well *give* up."

And yet, here Skinny was...*not* giving up.

Libby tripped. She skittered forward, and Skinny's arms were around her before she landed.

"Whoa there, Grace." He righted her, and his hands were gone.

"Thanks." She watched the sidewalk as they continued. These boots were definitely not for walking in. Her feet hurt from her toenails to her ankles. "Maybe two blocks was too far after all."

"We're almost there. Want me to carry you?"

Libby shot him a glance, and he winked at her.

"Over your shoulder, on your back, or in your arms?"

He quirked an eyebrow at her legs. "Over the shoulder, I think. Better view, that way."

She snickered. "I'm going to be more careful."

In a few minutes they sat at a booth with two mugs of beer on the table between them. They fell into an easy banter and shared a plate of cheese fries and a double order of wings. Skinny excused himself to go to the restroom, and when he returned to the table, he had a speculative gleam in his eye.

"Libby," he said reaching for a fry. "You came over here to see that guy, right? The violin player? Did you get to see him?"

"Yeah."

"Do you...*like* him?"

Libby watched Skinny. His mouth held a hint of a smile, as if he had a secret. What was his deal?

"I don't like playing games. Spill it."

"I think he's here, and I think he's...with his boyfriend."

"What?"

"That guy who was at the garage the other day is in the bar with another guy, and I'm telling you that other guy is as queer as a three-dollar bill."

Libby bristled at Skinny's words. She sat back and glared at him.

He held up his hands in a gesture of surrender. "Don't shoot the messenger. I'm saying that my chances of coming out the winner on this deal just improved about a thousand percent."

"Is this deal you're talking about winning me?"

Skinny's face fell. "If he's a...." He stopped at her glare. "If he's gay, Libby, you really don't have a chance."

"How can you look at a person and know if they're gay or not?"

"The guy he's with was a walking advertisement for the rainbow connection."

"What does that even mean? And anyway, just because Byron is with somebody who might be gay, it doesn't mean he is."

"There's a good chance that he is. I wouldn't be caught dead with a f—"

"Don't say it."

Skinny ran his hand through his short hair. "I guess you'd know...since you've been out with him. If he's hit on you, then you know he's not." He shook his head and glared at some spot across the restaurant. "*I* wouldn't go out for a beer with one."

"One probably wouldn't go out for a beer with you either." Libby stared morosely at the table. The half-empty platters of food didn't seem so appetizing any more.

Was it true? Was Byron gay? Was that why he hadn't come into the house with her the other night? Was that why he hadn't even touched her on the porch?

Skinny reached for a wing and began to eat it.

Libby tugged a napkin from the dispenser and wiped her hands. "Are you going to be done soon? I'm ready to go."

****

Libby had chosen pants this time, but they were girlie pants—all low on her hips and tight. She'd have to pull them off by peeling them down her legs. Thankfully, Josey had laid out a sweater that hit Libby at mid-thigh since sitting down in these pants would give anyone sitting behind her a view of parts of her she didn't want to expose—not what she was going for tonight. Honestly, who designed the popular styles these days? Obviously, someone who had a butt crack fetish. Libby reached up and scratched her shoulder.

And this sweater, while it covered the problem of the pants, was itchy. It looked like cotton candy—the color as well as the texture, all fluffy and weird.

Libby didn't even like pink. Not even on cotton candy. Especially not on anything she put on her body.

When the doorbell rang, she cast one last disparaging look at herself in Josey's mirror and headed downstairs.

There stood Byron in the living room with Marcus hanging on his khaki pants' leg. But it was Byron's button down shirt which captured her attention.

Cotton candy pink.

Josey laughed when she caught sight of Libby. "Oh, my gosh. You guys match! Isn't that cute?"

Libby pivoted on the stairs to find something else to put on, but Josey ran to her and stopped her. She leaned close. "Oh, don't be like that. It's providential. A matched set. See?"

"Don't read too much in it," Libby whispered, then spoke aloud as she allowed Josey to pull her down into the room. "It just means you and Byron should be shopping buddies."

Byron smiled and bounced on his heels. "It means we both have excellent taste."

"Yes," Josey agreed.

"I'm not into pink," Libby complained.

"Maybe you will be before the night is over," Josey murmured in her ear. "So, try to act like a girl, okay? He looks positively yummy, and you might get lucky."

A few minutes later she sat next to Byron in his car. "So where we going?"

"I thought we'd head over to Mead's Crossing. There's an excellent restaurant there which serves soul food."

"Soul food?"

"Hmm-mmm. Ever had it?"

Libby shook her head. "No, but I'm game. Somehow you didn't strike me as the type."

"The type?" His tense tone alerted her that she'd hit a

nerve.

"You know, that likes that kind of food. Forgive me for saying so, but you seem to be the kind of person who likes food that they call cuisine and charge an arm and a leg for."

"What? You think I'm a snob?"

"You kind of dress like one."

He tapped his fingers on the steering wheel. "I'm a chameleon. If I change my skin, then I can blend in really well." He glanced at her.

"So, what you're saying is the people at the university dress like snobs, and since you're a musician in residence, you feel that you have to dress like one too."

"Something like that."

"And this soul food place isn't really a dive that serves good food. It's a trendy restaurant where the rich kids go."

"We shall see."

"Have you been there?"

"Yes."

"And so will pink fit in well?"

"I think any color is welcome. That's why I like it."

He drove through Ceredo and Huntington until they were on the other side of the city. Pulling the car into a parking lot for a storefront building with blacked-out windows, Byron cut the engine, jumped out, and was at her door opening it before Libby had even grasped the door handle. She figured he was making up for the fact that in times past she'd gotten out of the car before he had a chance to help her.

He held out his hand to her and she stared at him in confusion. "Shall we?" He bowed slightly.

"Shall we what?"

He grinned and reached for her hand, gently tugging it. She followed his motion and swung her legs onto the pavement, then stood. He didn't drop her hand as he pushed the door shut, and they walked to the building. Large script painted on the door declared the restaurant 'Soul-Full.'

Inside the restaurant was a lot cozier than she would

have guessed. Warmer—decorated in dark maroon and purple swags on the walls, with black and white Formica tables and chairs. An African-American man stepped forward in greeting.

"Byron! Good to see you, man."

Byron dropped her hand to shake his. "Zeb, I'd like you to meet Liberty Miller. Liberty Ann, this is Zeb Rogers. He and his wife, Jackie, own the Soul-Full."

Libby also shook his hand. "Nice to meet you."

"And you, too, Liberty. Let me get y'all a place to sit." He procured two menus from a stack on the counter next to him and motioned for them to follow him. He wound through a room full of tables, most of which were occupied. *Wow.* If the crowd was any indication, the food must be pretty good.

At the back of the room, Zeb stopped in front of a wall of a curtains. He reached forward and pulled a cord, and a small section opened revealing a table booth in front of a plate glass window overlooking the river.

Oh, wow.

"Nice, huh?"

"Yes."

"Curtain open or closed?"

"Open, I think. And if you and Jackie have a few minutes, come sit with us."

Zeb's teeth shown bright against his dark-hued skin. "We'd like that." He extracted a small notebook from his pocket and took their drink orders and informed them what the specials were, then promised to be back in later with his wife.

A young Latino woman brought their drinks and an appetizer of biscuits with a side of melted butter mixed with corn syrup. "Jackie said if you don't want something sweet first, she'll send out the corn pone chips with collard and garlic dip."

Libby's brows raised in appreciation. She wasn't sure what pone was, but it all sounded great.

"You like biscuits?" Byron asked her.

She shook her head in amazement. "You just don't seem like a biscuit kind of guy."

"Remember, I'm a chameleon." He reached for a biscuit and one of the small glass bowls of butter mixed with syrup.

Libby, too, reached for a biscuit. When she bit into it, it practically melted in her mouth. "Wow. The biscuit alone is worth coming here."

"Try the syrup with it."

She did so and groaned in appreciation. When the biscuit and most of the syrup was gone from her little dish, she wondered if she could get away with licking it clean.

Yes, it was that good.

A white woman with ruby colored hair approached their table. She wore a waist apron over her ebony velvet dress. "Hi ya. I'm Jackie. She grinned down at both of them. I hear we've been invited to join you."

"If you have time," Byron said. "Do you?"

"I think we can spare a few minutes."

Byron pushed his plate toward Libby then stood and moved to sit next to her. Jackie sat on the bench he'd just vacated.

Libby smiled at Jackie, liking her immediately. "I'm Libby."

"Where you from, Libby?"

"I live in Ashland."

"Aha." Jackie nodded. "Across the state line. How'd you two meet?"

"She rescued me."

"Really?"

"Not exactly. His car overheated, and I drove the tow truck. I towed his car to the garage."

"And she was able to deliver me in time for a concert at which I was performing."

Zeb appeared and slid onto the bench next to his wife. He leaned over and kissed her on the cheek. "How's this, babe? We actually get to sit down at a table together at dinner time."

"And yet, there's no food in front of us to eat." Jackie noted in mock sadness.

The woman who had brought their drinks came forward with a platter laden with four plates. She set one plate in front of each person at the table.

A surprised expression settled on Jackie's face. She turned to her husband.

"You were saying?" he asked.

The sun, already low on the horizon, set across the river providing a beautiful setting to their dinner. Libby enjoyed the conversation with Byron's friends. They were so down to earth, not at all who she thought he'd hang out with.

So, maybe I'm the snob.

When they'd finished eating and the plates had been cleared away, the conversation turned to Jackie's musical talent. "You know, she hasn't played in weeks, By," Zeb said.

"We've been short of help," Jackie added. "I don't feel right playing if there's work to be done in the kitchen."

Zeb shrugged at Byron from across the table. "See what I mean?"

"Giving your patrons nice music to listen to seems like good help to me," Byron commented.

"Yeah. Me too. Hey, man, tell me you brought your violin. Maybe you can coax her to play something with you."

"I always have my violin," Byron informed his friend.

"Zeb." She leaned into her husband. "We've not done anything for half the night here."

"So? The dishes will wait on us. Come on."

Byron stood up and walked toward the exit, and Zeb slid off the bench seat so Jackie could go retrieve her guitar.

"The food was delicious," Libby said. "I'm glad Byron brought me here."

"Thanks. We're glad he did, too. He's a good guy."

"Yes. Do she and Byron play together a lot?"

He smiled. "She took lessons out at the college, and her teacher brought Byron out here one night. They convinced her to get out her guitar, and the three of them played. It was great."

"Who is her teacher?"

"Paul Lee. Do you know him?"

Libby shook her head. The name meant nothing to her. Was he the same man Skinny had seen in the restaurant? "Is he....?" Libby searched for a diplomatic way to ask if he were gay.

"Asian? Yes. Well, descent anyway. He's been a citizen for about ten years."

The waitress came to the table with a large piece of red cake on a white plate. "Jackie said to bring this out here," she said setting it in front of Libby along with a folded napkin and a fork.

"Thanks, Mara," Zeb said.

"Yes, thanks." Libby stared at the cake. It was blood red with white icing.

"Dig in. It's red velvet cake. I made it myself."

Libby picked up the fork, but hesitated. "Red velvet?"

"Because of the appearance, of course. That's not just food coloring either. I use beetroot juice."

Libby's gaze met his. "You want me to eat this, right?"

He smiled. "Try it. If you don't like it, I'll bring you out the banana pudding."

"I'm not a fan of beets."

"You've never had beets here. I can make anything taste good."

"That fried chicken was the best I've ever eaten. I don't know about beet cake though."

"Red velvet. The beetroot is just for the coloring."

Libby pushed the prongs of the fork through the corner of the cake, lifted the small piece to her mouth, and was immediately in love. An involuntary *mmmm* came from her mouth as she chewed.

"See?" Zeb sat back, his eyes sparkling merrily. "Can't I bake as well as cook?"

"You *can* bake as well as cook." Libby ate a much larger piece and dipped the fork in her mouth a second time to get all of the icing.

Byron and Jackie had come back with their instruments. Jackie sat on a stool with her guitar on her lap, and Byron stood next to her. They were speaking to each other, but Libby wasn't close enough to know what they said. Byron nodded and brought his violin to his chin. With his bow hovering, he watched Jackie who began to play. Immediately he joined her. The music was slow and soothing.

Byron's body swayed in tempo with the movement of the bow. Libby had never known anyone who obviously loved music as much as he did. She'd never been out with a man who was as pretty as he was. His curly hair wasn't blond so much as it was gold. He looked good in pink, but really, he looked good in everything she'd seen him in.

Most of the men she knew had no concept of style. Was it because he was gay, or did some straight guys like clothes too? Who could she ask? If she talked to Josey about it, she'd say something to Mickey. They'd probably make jokes about Byron.

She didn't want that. Not any of it.

The music invaded her thoughts, comforted her, and the problem of crushes and cruelty faded. She finished off the cake and gathered the leftover icing from the plate on her finger and brought it to her lips. She sucked off the last bit of cream cheese icing with regret and appreciation.

Byron's gaze caught hers and held. He smiled, and Libby wondered if he could read the ecstasy of red velvet on her face. Hopefully, without any vestiges around her mouth. She licked her lips to be sure.

A napkin appeared in front of her. She glanced at Zeb.

"Just in case you're checking for icing and not trying to distract By."

Libby snickered. "I hate to waste any of it on a napkin." She wiped her mouth anyway.

"I'll cut you a piece to go."

The music meandered around them overtaking Libby once again. She watched Byron. He and Jackie reached the end of the piece.

The room had quieted when they began to play, and everyone applauded in appreciation.

"Canon in D?" Byron said to Jackie, and she nodded. Moving her fingers up the neck of the guitar, she played several chords before Byron accompanied her with long tones stretching the length of the bow before taking the lead in the melody. The piece was short, and when it was over, Jackie and Byron both smiled in acknowledgement of the clapping around the room. When they began to put away their instruments, someone called out, "More!"

"That's all we've practiced," Jackie replied to the patron, which elicited laughter.

They came back to the table, and Zeb stood. He leaned down and kissed his wife. "Beautiful."

"Thanks." Jackie's face glowed. "I better get back to work. Liberty, it was so nice to meet you." She strode across the room with her guitar.

Zeb shook Byron's hand. "Want a piece of Red Velvet, By?"

He shook his head. "Don't tempt me. Just the check."

"Nope. You earned your meal tonight."

"We played less than ten minutes. Hardly enough as payment for two delicious meals."

"Jackie enjoyed doing that. You've made her happy. That's worth it." He glanced at his watch. "Stay as long as you want. I'll bring out some cake in a take home box for you, Liberty."

Zeb excused himself. Byron placed his violin in its case on the other bench and sat down next to her.

"What do you want to do now?" he asked.

Make out. Was that an option?

Surely if Byron were gay, he wouldn't have chosen to sit next to her. He wouldn't have held her hand as they'd walked into the restaurant. His leg wouldn't be brushing against hers right now.

Libby resisted the urge to touch his hair. "I don't know. Got any ideas?"

With only the candle flickering on their table and the shade of the curtain, his brown eyes appeared black in the low light.

It would be so easy to lean forward and kiss him. Would he want that? Would he return the kiss just to be nice?

"What did you think of Zeb and Jackie?"

"Very nice. I think they must do a great business. The food is wonderful, and they both seem very hospitable."

"She runs the business end of it, and he's a fantastic cook. When they met, he was about to close the restaurant because his bookkeeping skills were killing him. A friend recommended her, and she came in, got the books straightened out, and they fell in love."

He leaned back against the seat and watched her as if he were waiting for her to say something.

When she didn't, he went on. "Her parents disowned her when they found out."

Libby made a sound of derision. "That's stupid. He's salt of the earth."

"He's black."

Libby cast him a disparaging look. "What's your point?"

He studied her for a moment.

"You don't have a problem with it, do you?" Libby said. "I mean if he treats her right, and he's a good person, that's the important thing. Right?"

"I suppose so."

Disillusionment niggled at Libby. If Byron was uncomfortable with Zeb and Jackie's bi-racial relationship, why had he brought her here for dinner? Had he hoped to be able to play with Jackie? No. That had been Zeb's idea.

"I think they make a nice couple."

When they left the restaurant and he drove her back home, he initiated no more contact between them. Their conversation turned to lighter issues, though his comments at the restaurant bothered her. Had her racial comments dissuaded him? Was he a closet gay racist?

In silence they walked to the front of the house.

Butterflies fluttered in her stomach, but she didn't know whether it was from anticipation of a goodnight kiss or disappointment that Byron wasn't as perfect as she thought.

He took her hand and leaned forward, depositing a peck on her cheek. Squeezing her hand as he smiled down at her, he bid her goodnight and turned to go.

Libby watched Byron walk back to his car lit by the streetlight. Opening the front door, she walked into the dark house and to her room. Stripping off Josey's clothes, she lay on her bed and replayed the evening in her mind. It was like they had been on a double date with Zeb and Jackie. Is that how Byron had planned it? Had he purposely picked a place where they didn't have to be alone? Some place where he wouldn't run into any college buddies?

She hadn't invited him in the house this time. But maybe she should have. Would he have accepted her invitation to come in? Could they be making out on the couch right now? Or was she just fooling herself?

Was Skinny right?

Was Byron not interested in the female sex at all?

Chapter Six

Libby stood in the kitchen and looked up.

There was pee on the ceiling.

These kids are going to kill me.

Marcus crawled into the kitchen. He still had his diaper on, but that was all. He obviously wasn't the culprit.

A crash from the other room, and John John screamed. Not a 'my brother is killing me' kind of scream. More like 'my brother just took something from me, and I'm going to kill him' kind of scream.

"Tony! John John! Get in here right now," she yelled.

The screaming continued. Libby left the disgusting mess and followed the noise.

"Which one of you peed all over the kitchen?"

"It ain't pee, Aunt Libby. It's Marcus' bottle milk," Tony said.

"Gimme! Ahhhh!" John John jumped on Tony who held an action figure of some kind, and the two boys collapsed in a writhing ball of boy dirt and skin.

Libby glanced at the clock. Josey and Mick had only been gone twenty minutes. Libby thought of calling her dad, but wondered how much help he'd be. Josey didn't trust him, since the last time he'd babysat he'd put Tony and John John in the dog kennel. The boys had begged to go in there, according to Gene. And they'd settled down and gone to sleep on the dog pillow inside. Josey had been livid when she arrived home. Not only had Gene locked them in there, but he'd refused to show any remorse for the deed.

"They loved it," he said. "They even let me give them a bath with the flea shampoo."

The flea shampoo had cinched it. Grandpaw hadn't

been allowed to babysit since then. Libby thought Josey was crazy. The boys had never been seriously hurt while Dad had watching them, and the flea shampoo incident was the only time that Libby ever knew of that the boys had willingly submitted to having their hair washed.

Libby reached down and tried to separate them. Somebody kicked her in the shin. "You boys want to go in the dog kennel?"

She got Tony by the scuff of the neck and John John by the arm.

"We ain't allowed in there no more," Tony declared.

John John screamed. "Want my Ranchu Man!"

"Give it back to him."

"This is my Tarantula Man." Tony blinked up at Libby. "He flushed his down the toilet."

"No! Mine!"

"When did he flush it down the toilet?" Libby hoped it wasn't in the last twenty minutes.

Tony threw the action figure, and it hit the other little boy in the face. John John screamed again and clutched his nose.

"Tony." Libby sighed. "Go to your room." She turned him toward the stairs and pointed. "Now."

"Don't have to. You're not my ma."

Thank goodness.

The doorbell rang. Libby sprinted to the front of the house. *Please let it be Josey.* Maybe she decided she couldn't be without her boys for an entire evening or maybe she forgot her key....

The figure Libby glimpsed through the window was definitely not her sister-in-law.

Libby opened the door. Skinny held two pizza boxes. "How about some pizza?"

"I'm not sure you want to be here. The little terrors are in full throttle."

Skinny shrugged. "They're little kids. You can't handle them?"

Libby laughed. Obviously, Skinny hadn't spent much

time with Mickey's kids. She gestured to the boxes. "What are you doing? Working a second job?"

"No. Thought you might like some company."

Marcus crawled by Libby and she reached down to grab him on his way out the door. She picked up the baby and settled him on her hip. "You better come in before somebody escapes." She stepped back, and Skinny stepped inside closing the door behind him. Marcus screeched and struggled to get loose. When Libby refused to put him down, he flailed his arm. Libby blocked his little fist as he attempted to whap her on the chin.

She glared at him. "Stop."

Another scream.

Geez. How did Josey stand it?

Libby locked the door before releasing the baby. He immediately crawled to the door and beat on it.

Skinny looked at the boy. "What did you do, feed them sugar or what?"

Tony ran by and knocked the pizza boxes from Skinny's hands. He tried to grab them, but they tumbled to the floor. The lids stayed on, but the boxes were upside down now.

"Hey, you little shit," Skinny shouted.

"Skinny! Don't call him that."

Tony jumped up and down in glee. "Little shit! Little shit!"

John John joined him. "Shit! Shit!"

"Are you happy now? You taught them a new word." Libby crouched down to pick up the boxes. She carefully turned the boxes over and walked to the dining room table.

"Jesus Christ, Libby, they're out of control."

"Jesus Christ! Jesus Christ!" the boys echoed.

Lovely. We've added blasphemy to the list.

"Shut up, you little...kids," Skinny commanded.

"Shut up! Shut up!"

Libby peeked under the pizza lid and sighed at the gooey mess. "Boys! Enough! Tony, I told you to go to your room."

"Jesus Christ. Shut up, you little shit!" Tony yelled.

John John chortled.

Skinny charged at them, but Libby intersected grabbing him by the arm. "Don't. I'll handle it, but don't do or say anything else."

"Well, handle it then."

"You should go, Skinny. It's not going to get better. They're little kids."

"They're not kids. They...owww!" He jumped.

Libby looked down. Marcus sat back on his haunches and grinned a toothy smile. Drool trailed from his mouth to Skinny's pants leg.

The man shook his head and marched to the door. "I pity Mickey. I pity all of you." He pulled at the knob, and nothing happened. Shaking it briefly, he shot a panicked look at the baby who crawled rapidly toward him. Releasing the lock, he opened the door and slammed it shut behind him.

"Jesus Christ, where is that little shit going?" Tony asked.

"Tony, I'm going to get a bar of soap and stick it in your mouth, if you repeat any more words you heard Skinny say."

"What's it taste like?" Tony opened his mouth and stuck out his tongue as if he were waiting for a doctor to examine his throat.

"Horrible." She took his hands and led him upstairs. "You're going to your room for a few minutes to cool off."

"Noooo. Noooo, Aunt Libby."

"Nooo, Anlibby," John John repeated tugging her from behind.

"You're going." She grabbed the toddler before he tumbled down the stairs.

"I'm not!" Tony started to cry.

Libby rolled her eyes. It wasn't like his room was a dungeon. As punishments went, going to your room seemed rather lame. All of his toys were in there. It was a great place to be. Of course, she wasn't going to inform him of that.

"If you put me in my room, I'll hate you forever!"

"Really?"

They reached the landing, and she ushered him to his room, nudged him inside and shut the door. He opened it immediately screaming at the top of his lungs. Libby expected him to run out, but he didn't. He collapsed on the floor and kicked his legs.

John John ran into the room and Tony kicked him. John John fell on the floor and began to cry.

From her pocket, her phone vibrated. If it was Josey, Libby was going to tell her the deal was off and to get home now. She took her phone out and looked at the screen.

Byron.

She scooped up John John and headed for the stairs. Answering the phone, she placed it to her ear. "Not a good time, Byron. I'm in a warzone."

Over the loud screaming, she thought she detected Byron say, "What?"

"I'm babysitting my nephews. Can I call you later?"

She hung up the phone without waiting for his answer. Marcus was halfway up the stairs, and Libby reached down to pick him up before he fell.

Things didn't improve with Tony's time out. To get Libby's attention, he began to throw his toys out of his room. Some of them hit the wall and tumbled down the stairs. When that didn't work, he repeatedly slammed his door.

With the baby gate secured at the bottom of the steps, Libby hollered to the second floor. "The longer you keep that up, the longer you're staying in there."

A hardback copy of some kid's book flew down the stairs.

"And when you come out of your room, you're cleaning up your mess too, or you won't get any pizza."

"Hate you forever, Aunt Libby!" Slam! Slam! Slam!

"Don't slam that door again, Tony, or you'll be sorry."

Slam!

Shoot. Now how am I going to make him sorry?

Libby folded her arms trying to figure out how to get a five-year-old to feel remorse. Marcus sat on the floor near the banister. He gave her a puzzled look and made a garbled sound. Libby stopped and peered at him. "Marcus?"

Realizing he was choking, she held him up and stuck her finger in his mouth.

"What have you done, Marcus?"

Turning him upside down, she pressed his stomach to her thigh and thumped his back. A Lego flew out of his mouth. For a second he was silent, then he wailed. Righting him, she clutched him to her. "Oh, buddy. I'm sorry. Sorry. Sorry."

She looked around for a safe place to put him and spotted the highchair.

"I'm staying in here forever," Tony yelled, and a shoe sailed down the stairs.

"It looks that way," Libby muttered. She tried to slide the baby into the highchair, but he was too big. Glancing underneath the tray, she tried to figure out how it detached. A large blue button was on the side, and she depressed the button nudging it up with her arm. After a few unsuccessful attempts, she had Marcus situated in the chair much to his displeasure.

Big tears rolled down his red face.

Libby ran in the kitchen and got some rice cookie things Marcus liked to chew on. She emptied several on his tray but he ignored them.

Another shoe hit the wall on its way down to the first floor.

Libby realized she hadn't seen nor heard John John lately.

A really bad sign.

"John John?" she called.

"I'm calling my mom!" Tony yelled.

"Want me to get you the phone?" Libby yelled back.

A kid's boot was his reply.

"John John, where are you?" The front door was still closed. She checked the den and the back door. In the kitchen she looked into the laundry room and pantry. No John John, but the bathroom door was shut. She attempted to twist the knob.

Locked!

"Are you in there, John John?"

The toilet flushed.

Geez! Can these kids at least tag team instead of throwing all their crises at me at once?

Libby knocked on the door. "Let me in, buddy."

Another flush. Marcus was still crying in his high chair.

Libby looked at the knob. She ought to be able to pop the lock if she had a small enough screwdriver.

"John John? Say something so I'll know you're all right.

"Shut up."

Libby sighed. She walked to the kitchen cabinet and opened the top drawer. Silverware. Next drawer down had towels. But the bottom drawer—*Aha*. Tools. She rummaged through several screwdrivers, none small enough for what she needed it for. Another flush that didn't sound quite right.

Libby paused and turned to the door. A puddle appeared under the door and grew. Libby pulled the drawer out and dumped it on the floor scattering its contents. She chose a skewer and charged across the room. Forcing it in the hole, she heard the satisfying click and threw open the door. John John stood next to the overflowing commode and stared up at her innocently.

He pointed to the toilet. "Shit."

The water looked clear. "You're not fooling anyone. I know you flushed something down the commode, but I'm pretty sure it's not what you're telling me."

He reached his hand into the water, and she held his arm. "No. Dirty water. Yucky." She shook her head with a grimace. "Don't play in it."

She opened the cabinet looking for the plunger and

when she heard splashing, she saw John John hadn't followed her advice.

"John John, no! Get your hand out of there." She rushed to him, but he screamed and ran out of the bathroom. Deciding to let him go for the moment, she went back to the cabinet and retrieved the plunger to work on the toilet.

It was a good thing Josey and Mick weren't paying her for this babysitting gig because they didn't have enough money in the bank for what these little monsters were putting her through.

Ding dong.

With the plunger still in her hand, she walked by Marcus. With his red drooling face, he looked a pitiful sight, as he continued to cry. Sighing, she dropped the tool and released him from his prison, holding him to her.

"Shh. Shh." She bounced him as she had seen Josey do. "It's all right. All right, buddy." Making her way to the front door as a pillow fell down the top two stairs, Libby saw John John was already at the door trying to open it. "I'll get it," she told the toddler.

"No! Me!"

"Aunt Libby! Can I come out now? Now!"

Libby opened the door, and there stood Byron Venable with violin case in hand. Tonight he wore smoky gray pants with a maroon and white shirt, all the creases in all the right places.

"Hey!" John John said. "Shut up, Jesus Christ!"

Byron studied the child and bent down on one knee. "Hello," he said holding out his right hand for a shake. "How do you do?"

The boy stared at the man ignoring his outstretched hand. "What that?" He pointed to the black case sitting on the concrete next to Byron.

"This? This is my magic. Would you like to see?"

John John's eyes grew wide. His head wobbled in reply.

"Take my hand then, and help me up."

John John grabbed his hand and leaned backward. With

a groan, Byron straightened into a standing position holding his case with his other hand. He let the little boy lead him into the house. Libby patted Marcus' back attempting to quell his wailing. He took a shuddering breath and wiped his face on Libby's shoulder his cries muffled by her shirt.

He stopped in front of Libby. "Oh, my goodness, what is wrong, little one?" His kind face registered concern. His calm demeanor radiated outward. Libby realized her teeth were clenched, and she loosened her jaw.

"He choked on a Lego and I fastened him in the highchair while I tried to get that one out of the locked bathroom." She indicated the little toilet clogger with a nod of her head.

"C'mon." John John tugged on Byron's hand. "I wanna see magic."

Byron reached behind him with their joined hands. "Let's shut the door first." John John would have slammed it, but Byron stopped him. "Gently," he cautioned the child.

"Why?"

Together they nudged the door to its frame then Byron took the child's hand once again, and they walked into the living room. "When we are quiet, we make room to listen to things that we couldn't hear otherwise." They sat down on the couch, and Byron placed his case on the coffee table.

Libby walked to the couch and watched. John John had his hand on Byron's shoulder. The little boy's attention was riveted on the black case.

"Hey! Who's here? Aunt Libby!" Tony yelled.

John John stood up on the couch and hollered, "Shut up, you little shit! We're s'posed to be quiet for magic!"

"Aww, come on! I wanna come down! It's not fair!"

The little boy jumped off the couch and ran to the banister. "Tony, shut up! Shut up!" He slapped the rail a few times and shook it for emphasis.

"You shut up, John John! I'm going to clobber you

when I get out of this room. Aunt Libby!" His clock radio hit the floor and tumbled down the stairs.

Marcus who had quieted somewhat, opened his mouth and let out a pitiful wail.

Three quick notes emanated from Byron's violin, each one higher than the next. Then he launched into a dramatic piece on his instrument.

All three boys fell silent. The two downstairs turned their heads to look at Byron who had stood to play. His eyes were closed, as if he were alone and not in the midst of little kids who could easily have torn his violin in pieces if they got their hands on it. It was on the tip of Libby's tongue to tell Byron to put it away before something bad happened, but for the first time since Mickey and Josey left, the kids were attentive to something other than destruction.

The peace she'd had a taste of earlier returned with the waves of music filling the house.

Byron opened his eyes and walked toward her. "Who's responsible for the disarray on the stairs?"

"Tony. I told him he had to clean up, when he's allowed to come out of his room."

"When is he allowed?" He continued to play as he spoke, the melody perfect.

Libby shrugged and leaned her face against the top of Marcus' head. "I guess when he quits throwing stuff down the stairs."

"Ah."

Admiration tugged at Libby. Byron was incredible.

"I wonder if you would remove this small gate from the stairs."

Libby shifted Marcus to her side, reached down, and pressed the bar to release the baby gate. Lifting it, she leaned it against the back of the couch. "Do you think it's a good idea to have your violin out around them?"

Byron met her gaze. "This is Johann Sebastian Bach. This partita works well as a distraction from mourning, crying, and accompaniment for cleaning."

As if that justified putting the violin in danger.

He bent toward the little boy who stood slack-jawed in front of him. "What is your name?"

"John John Frasier Miller."

"John John Frasier Miller, would you clear a path for me so I may walk up the stairs. I must speak with Tony."

Immediately, the child began shoving toys and shoes to one side.

"Gently," Byron counseled him. "So we can hear all of the music."

"Hurry, John John," Tony called.

With his hand still clutching the bow, Byron paused and tapped John John. The child turned and gave Byron his attention. "Take your time," Byron countered softly. "This is Tony's clutter. Let's not make it yours. All right, sir?"

"Okay."

"Very good. Let us continue." He began to play again.

In a few minutes, one side of the staircase was clear, and Byron ascended while the notes of Bach poured from his strings. The music stopped, and Byron spoke. Tony replied. Their words weren't loud enough for Libby to understand. More discussion followed, then the music resumed, and Tony appeared. He gathered all of the things he'd thrown out of his room. Libby watched him with her mouth open.

In a few minutes, Marcus whimpered. Since he hadn't fallen asleep, Libby decided he had calmed down enough to eat. Going to the table, she opened the pizza box and tore off a small piece of cheese pizza for the little guy. He held out his hand and took it from her bringing it to his mouth. He hummed in appreciation, and Libby noticed he was mimicking the music coming from upstairs.

Incredible.

Later the boys came downstairs, and Byron put the violin away. Libby put pizza on paper plates for them, and directed them to the living room. She reached for the remote control.

"Won't they eat at the table?" Byron asked.

"I figure the TV's the easiest. They can watch while

they eat."

"Let's try the table." He held out his hand. "May I choose the channel?"

She placed the remote on his palm. He peered at it, then hit the 'guide' button. Surfing through the channels, he chose one of the classical music stations.

Of course.

They gathered at the table and ate. It was the first time Libby had ever seen Tony and John John sit still.

"Where'd you get that violin?" Tony asked.

"My parents bought it for me."

"For your birthday?"

"For Christmas actually."

"I didn't see magic," John John commented.

"I did," Libby said.

"Where?"

"You and your brothers. Your mom and dad are going to be very proud of you guys picking up all your toys and cleaning up your room."

"That wasn't magic." John John scoffed.

"Magic is when something unexpected happens. I think you young gentlemen have impressed your auntie," Byron quipped.

"Yes. The auntie is very impressed."

With only a few outbursts and a minor tantrum, the rest of the evening went well. Libby retrieved two toys from the toilet and disinfected the bathroom and kitchen floor while Byron, the boys flocked all around him played games on the computer with them. After the children settled into their beds, Byron played Brahm's Lullaby and a piece by Beethoven which Libby forgot the name of.

Later Byron and Libby sat on the couch. She leaned her head back and rolled her neck to look at him. "Man, you're good with kids."

"I've worked with kids a lot. School programs and workshops. I've gotten to play at a few Shriners' hospitals in the cancer wards. Children respond really well. Studies have shown high art music encourages calm behavior and promotes healing."

"Maybe Josey needs to have it piped into the house all the time." She turned towards him and touched his arm. "Thanks for helping tonight. I never asked you what you called for."

He shook his head. "I can't remember now. It was probably something about how lovely your eyes are."

Libby snorted. "My lovely eyes. You, Byron Venable, are too charming for your own good. I've never seen my nephews under someone's spell before."

"You know what they say." He reached over and took her hand in his. "Music soothes the savage beast."

His touch warmed her hand, the rough skin of his fingertips rubbed over her knuckles as if he were fretting a chord.

"Which note is that?" she whispered.

He grinned as he moved closer. "C."

"Your life is all about music."

"'We are the music makers, and we are the dreamers of dreams.'" Nearer still, his face was close to hers, his ebony eyes mesmerized her.

"'Wandering by lone sea-breakers and sitting by desolate streams,'" Libby continued the poem.

Surprise registered in his gaze.

"Don't be too impressed. *Charlie and the Chocolate Factory's* one of my favorite movies. The old one. Are you going to kiss me?"

"I was considering it, yes. I've never kissed a mechanic before."

"I find that more comforting than you know." Libby shifted, her body humming in anticipation. "For the record, I've never kissed a mechanic *or* a violin player."

Byron lips curved in a smile a second before his mouth touched hers. "Have I told you I like you?" he said, his words spilling into her mouth.

"Yes." She inhaled through her nose taking in the heady aroma of whatever cologne he wore. She attempted to deepen the kiss, but he withdrew, his mouth moving to her cheek, then neck.

"We'll only have one first kiss." He murmured next to her skin making her shudder. "I want to savor it."

Libby closed her eyes to savor the sensation of his teeth nibbling her neck, the warmth of his body next to hers, the sweet tanginess of how good he smelled, the stiff cotton of his starched shirt under her hands. He trailed kisses to her jaw, building a desire in her for a closer connection with him.

Oh, my gosh, the anticipation.

Libby fastened her mouth onto his, exploring and tasting. Liking the slight raspiness of his face against hers, enjoying the long-anticipated joining of tongues, wanting more. He leaned away when she began to unbutton his shirt and covered her hand with his effectively stopping her.

"Don't tell me you're not that kind of boy. Please," she panted. All of the uncertainty blossomed from Skinny's comments, and Libby searched Byron's eyes for reassurance.

"We're babysitting in your brother's house. I'd prefer us not be caught in a state of undress by anyone. It feels rather like a teenage episode here to make out on a borrowed couch." He punctuated his statement by giving her the sweetest, slowest kiss she'd ever received, and she forgot to breathe. He stroked her back, ran his fingers up and down her spine as if he were playing his violin. He brushed her lips once more before sitting up, and Libby realized they were already horizontal.

Wow.

He reached forward and picked up the remote control. "How compatible are we, do you think?" He grinned at her. "Three guesses on what I like to watch on television."

Libby sat up and swung her legs to rest her feet on the coffee table. "No brainer. BBC."

"Nope."

"Public television."

Byron laid a heart on his chest and shot her a mocking

dark expression. "Have you judged me, dear lady?"

She snickered. "Cinemax?"

He pressed a button and Animal Planet appeared onscreen. He leaned back and put his stockinged feet closer to hers. "May I put my arm around you and snuggle while we watch *River Monsters?*"

"Might I enjoy a copious handful of your butt during commercials?" She leaned into him and settled into his side.

Hugging her to him, he kissed the top of her head. "Are you making fun of me?"

"Yes. Is that okay?"

"Sure, my darling. Just don't pinch me too hard while gratuitously groping. Hmm?"

Chapter Seven

Josey and Mick walked in the kitchen door, and Libby looked over the back of the couch at them. "Hi."

"How did it go?" Josey asked.

"Great." No need going into the overflowing toilet, the new vocabulary, or the Lego incident. "How was the parent-teacher conference and PTO meeting?"

"Tony is a good boy at school, but he's having some problems with listening."

"Byron, Libby." Mick nodded to them both as if there was nothing unusual about Libby being in the arms of a man on his couch. "Baby." He leaned down and kissed Josey. "I'm headed upstairs. I'll check on the boys."

Byron straightened, and Libby sighed in resignation. *I guess the snuggling was over.* She watched him put his socked feet into his leather loafers. Libby stood up and shoved her own feet in her sneakers. She watched his bowed head and tucked her hands in her pockets so she wouldn't be tempted to run her hands through his beautiful curls.

She should have messed with that hair when she had the chance.

Josey gave her a thumbs up when Byron wasn't looking. "I really appreciate you babysitting tonight. They really didn't give you any trouble?"

Libby arched her eyebrow at her sister-in-law. "You just better be glad that Byron showed up. He pulled some kind of Pied Piper trick with them and actually got them to behave for once."

Josey shifted her attention to Byron who had stood.

He shot her one of his GQ-smooth smiles. "It was a good time."

Josey's mouth fell open in shock. "It was a good time?"

"The boys were a captive audience."

"What'd you do, tie them up?"

****

Libby's cell dinged alerting her that she had a text. She wiped her hands and fished her phone out of her coveralls. *Hello.*

She smiled at the text Byron just sent her.

She texted him back. *Hiya.*

I'm texting my boyfriend. I have a boyfriend. Do I have a boyfriend? After those smoking hot kisses on the couch, Libby figured they were an item. But they hadn't talked about it—not made any promises or commitments to each other. He'd kissed her one more time outside of the house, and they'd parted ways.

On Sunday he'd asked her to go with him to Charleston, but she'd declined. She'd promised her dad she and Vance would clean out the gutters on the house, and she knew if she backed out, Vance sure as heck wouldn't do it without her.

Want to take you out for lunch. Are you free?

Libby's heart sped up at the message, but looked down at herself. She was filthy.

Not dressed for lunch date.

Please.

Libby huffed. She dialed his number and heard a phone ring. Puzzled, she turned around and spotted him standing in the door between the office and the garage. Today he wore a black turtleneck and sleek black pants. Her mouth began to salivate.

"Have I told you how beautiful you are?" His voice reached her across the garage then purred the same message in her ear through her cell.

Ignoring the fluttering of her stomach, she shook her head in derision and closed her phone. She really didn't want him to see her like this. Especially when he looked like that.

She walked over to him. "What are you doing here?"

"Trying to convince you go get something to eat." He

stepped toward her with an outstretched arm, but she moved back.

"Don't. I'm gross. I stink. Don't get near me."

"Oh, is this your plan? Play hard to get?"

"Look at me." She gestured to herself. "You know you don't want to be seen with me."

He growled softly in his throat, and cupping her hip, he nudged her to him. "I know I desire to be seen with you while we sit down at a table together eating lunch."

For a second, Libby forgot how to breathe. She glanced around to see if they had an audience. Vance and Mick stood side-by-side at the tire pile watching. Byron crooked his head. "What is that? Sounds like Ciccione."

Libby ignored her brothers. "That's the radio."

"Huh." He smiled down at her, and Libby marveled. A hot guy wanted her in her coveralls to have lunch with him.

He must like me.

"You should eat. With me. Soon. Don't you think so?" He patted her back.

"I'm going to get you dirty."

His chocolate brown eyes twinkled. "If I'm lucky."

****

Friday night Byron was busy so Libby was at the house when Vance, Skinny, and Steve came into the house with plans to watch a movie. Skinny cornered Libby in the kitchen. He'd called and asked her out a few times, but she'd turned him down. She figured they were overdue for a heart-to-heart in person.

"How ya doing, Skinny?" Libby looked at him from where she sat at the kitchen reading an article about smart cars in Popular Mechanics. His snake tat stared menacing at her, its mouth open and ready. She pushed a chair out from the table with her foot. "Wanna sit down?"

"Okay." he turned the chair around and straddled it. "It's Friday night. We ought to go grab a bite."

She laid the magazine on the table and focused on his face. "Not going out with you. I tried it, and it didn't work out."

"You only tried it one time. You should give me another chance."

"I like you, Skinny, as a friend." Libby reached over and patted his arm. "It's not happening between us. All right? You like a girl who you can do the Nestea plunge with. That's not me."

"What's that mean, the Nestea plunge?"

"It's a metaphor."

"A what?"

Libby ran her fingers through her hair and sat back. Case in point. "You like my brother, Vance, right? Y'all like to do the same things. You like to hang out."

Skinny's eyes narrowed.

"Well, I don't like him. If I weren't related to him, I wouldn't even want to be around him. But he's one of your best friends. You get what I'm saying?"

"He's a guy, Libby. I do guy things with him like gaming and hunting."

Libby spread her hands out on the table. "What do you consider things to do with a woman?"

A grin spread on his face.

Libby tutted in annoyance. "Other than that."

He shrugged. "I don't know. Going out to eat. Watching a movie."

"What else?"

"Why the third degree, man?"

"Because I don't like how you've put me in a box here. Just because I work on cars doesn't mean that I don't like to go to the opera or go to a museum, you know?"

"Hey, I asked you to start dressing nicer, didn't I? That's your doing that you'd rather clomp around in army boots. You dress like that, people make assumptions."

"That's another thing, I ought to be able wear whatever the heck I want to, and if you were any kind of man, you'd be fine with it."

"A guy likes his woman to look like a woman. Not one of the guys."

Libby ignored the fact that he was referring to a woman

as belonging to a guy. The only thing stopping her from jumping down his throat about it was assuming he was not referring to her. "A real man likes his woman to look like how she wants to look, Skinny."

"Don't you let your pansy-assed boyfriend set the standard for the rest of us. A real man, if he's not a closet fag, doesn't out dress the girl he's with."

Fury rose up inside of her. She jumped out of the chair with fists clenched. "I've finally met a real man who makes me feel like a real woman. And you don't even compare."

She stomped out of the room, found her keys, and left the house. In the car, she drove until she'd calmed down. By then she was in Chilicothe across the bridge from Huntington. She parked in a drug store parking lot and texted Byron.

Miss u

It bordered on the pathetic, but Byron probably wouldn't mind. He was wonderful. He'd never given her any hint that what she wore or what she did wasn't good enough for him.

Busy but would like to see you

When?

Anytime. Will begin a concert in few minutes in downtown Huntington. Corner of 2nd and Riverside.

Libby sighed.

Not dressed for concert

No dress code. All are welcome. Join me.

I don't want to be the only one in jeans.

You won't be. Trust me.

Libby stared at the screen. Closing her phone, she tucked it into her pocket and started the car. She drove across the bridge into Huntington and headed toward downtown. 2nd Street was a one-way street, so she had to go down two blocks to get to the corner. She didn't see an auditorium or theater. Where was the concert? A group of people congregated outside of a parking garage next to a homeless mission shelter. Music reached her ears, and she searched for a violin among the people in the band.

Everyone was dressed in casual clothes—ratty clothes even. Three people had violins tucked under their chins, but Libby had passed them in her car and nearly hit another car because she was looking at the curb instead of traffic. She concentrated on driving and found a parking space two blocks up. Easing the car in the space, she jumped out and jogged back to where she'd seen the musicians.

The music grew louder as Libby approached.

Where was Byron?

Nearly to the edge of the crowd, Libby's breath caught when she recognized him. A red ball cap he wore backwards covered his hair. Other than his violin tucked next to a sports jersey, Byron blended in with the rest of the people standing on the corner. His fellow musicians were dressed similarly—like everyone else including, Libby suspected, the people staying in the shelter. Byron's faded jeans were so frayed she wondered how they hadn't fallen completely apart.

"Hey," a man approached her with a Styrofoam cup in his hand. "They have coffee. Can I bring you a cuppa?" His warm smile welcomed her.

"Sure. Thanks."

"Cream and sugar?"

"You know it."

He nodded and disappeared. In a moment, he returned and handed her the cup. "The shelter's filled up, but they still got coffee to keep you warm at night."

Libby sipped from the cup. "You don't have a place to stay tonight?"

He smiled, his teeth glinting in the near dark. "There's always a place to stay. Whether you're looking at a ceiling, the rafters under a bridge, or the stars. Only thing that changes is the scenery." He held out his hand. "Name's Beau. It means good-looking in French."

She shook his hand. "Name's Liberty. It means freedom in English."

Beau laughed. "Yeah. Liberty. Hell, yeah. I like that name." He looked around. "Who you here with?"

Libby nodded toward Byron. "The fiddler in the red hat."

"Really?" Beau's tone alerted her that he was privy to some insider information. He gave her a once-over.

"What?" Libby frowned. "You think he can do better?"

"No, ma'am. Haha! You could though, like with me."

"I'll keep that in mind, Beau. Can I pay you for the coffee?"

"I got it for free."

Libby found two twenties in her wallet. "Here. It's supposed to get down to freezing tonight. Maybe this will help with the scenery."

He looked at the bills and shot her a look of appreciation. "Liberty. That means freedom. Thank you." He stuffed the bills in his pants' pocket. "Come with me. I'll get you closer to the band."

Beau tapped on a man in front of him. "Make way for freedom, man."

Libby followed him through the throng of people until they were at the front of the crowd. Two women played violins along with Byron. One man sat down in front of a keyboard, his hands moving across the keys. Two other people played cellos and one woman played a double bass.

Libby didn't recognize the music they were playing, but it was pretty. The street corner concert lasted about thirty more minutes, and they finished their last note to an eruption of applause. Byron met her gaze and wove through his playmates to her.

"Hello." He gestured around him with his bow. "What do you think?"

"Amazing. I thought you were working tonight."

"I am. I was guest lecturing with some music majors, and we decided to put on an impromptu concert. How many people would you say are here tonight?"

Libby looked around. "Maybe sixty?"

"They didn't think five would stay and listen."

"It's kind of cheating, isn't it? Setting up next to the homeless shelter? I mean, what else do they have to do?"

Byron's gaze glittered. "The shelter opens at seven. They could be inside where it's warm, but they've chosen to be out here because they appreciate the music."

"Why didn't you have the concert in there?"

"We didn't think about it. We chose this spot because there was plenty of room to set up and for a crowd, if one gathered." His mouth turned up on one side. "There's always potential for audience so a good musician plans for that." He gestured with his chin over his shoulder to the people casing their instruments. "They were lamenting how this type of music is considered antiquated and largely unappreciated by the masses, how it won't exist except digitally in a hundred years, so I said part of the issue is making it available to people on the street, and we took a field trip."

"You're a very good musician-in-residence."

A woman in a long trench coat approached them. "Hey, that was beautiful." She held out a grubby hand to Byron.

Instead of shaking it, he grasped her fingers, bent forward, and kissed her knuckles. Gazing into her face, he gave her one of his killer smiles. "It was my pleasure, Madame."

She blinked at him, and a tear escaped from the corner of her eye. "No one's touched me except to hit me in years."

"What is your name?" Byron asked her.

"Lucy."

"May I have your permission to give you a hug, Lucy? You certainly deserve one."

"Okay."

Byron turned to Libby. He held his violin and bow to her. "Do you mind?"

Libby took the instrument from him. His offer shocked Libby because even from where she stood she could smell the woman's body odor. Obviously, it didn't bother Byron.

He opened his arms, and the woman stepped into his embrace. He wrapped his arms around her and squeezed for a moment before releasing her.

"Are you somebody famous?" she asked.

He shook his head.

"You oughta be."

"Why, thank you."

Later the people in the ensemble gathered at a house near the university. Libby sat on the couch while people milled around the living room. Byron had excused himself when they arrived. In a few minutes he came back and sat down next to her placing his hand on her leg, patting her affectionately. He reached over and took her hand twining their fingers together.

Libby watched their hands resting on her blue-jeaned thigh. The toffee skin on his hand contrasted with her lighter skin, his thumb rubbed hers.

"Don't worry," he whispered. "I washed my hands."

Libby smiled at him. "What'd you do? Use the bathroom?"

"No. I hugged a homeless woman. But I washed my hands with soap."

"Did you wash your lips too?"

"I tried, but, well, if I'm going to get sick, I'm probably already infected."

"Why did you kiss her hand?"

"She looked like she needed someone to cherish her and kissing her hand was the most efficient way to do it in that moment." His eyes searched hers. "Do you ever feel as if you need to be cherished?"

"I feel cherished right now."

"I'd like to kiss you, but I've got hand sanitizer all over my mouth."

Libby chuckled. "Lay one on me. I need my lips sanitized." She leaned into him and lifted her face to his.

He placed his mouth on hers briefly before withdrawing. "Do you like to sing?"

"In the shower, I do pretty well. Why?"

"Because they're getting the karaoke machine out. Everybody has to sing. House rules, and I must confess,

I'm a horrible singer."

Rochelle, the double bass player Libby had met earlier called to Byron from across the room. "You're going first, By, so we can get it over with."

"Yeah, and exorcise your horrible caterwauling from our ears with the rest of the singing," Jean added.

"Your cruelty only serves to motivate Liberty Ann to be kinder to me, so go ahead with your taunts."

"Get up here, but no Michael Bolton or Abba this time. I had nightmares for a week," Noah, the cellist said.

Byron sighed in mock resignation. "I hope you'll respect me in the morning." He stood and strode to the microphone. Peering down he continuously pushed a button next to the screen beside him. Libby assumed he was searching for a song to sing. A grin spread across his face, and he pointed to Noah. "You're going to be so sorry." He grinned and pushed a button on the screen.

A tune began to play from the speakers. It wasn't one Libby recognized, but by the time Byron got to the chorus of being the 'Happiest Girl in the Whole USA', Libby had tears running down her cheeks from laughing. She wasn't so sure if the humor was because Byron was chortling more than he was warbling or from him singing 'zippidy doo dah.'

Nicholas, the keyboard player went next. His mannerisms were so effeminate that it struck Libby he might be the guy Skinny had seen Byron with. When he belted out an amazing version of a classic by Eartha Kitt, Libby was convinced but she reserved judgment.

Was it any of her business whether Nicholas was or was not anyway?

Libby set aside the thought, caught up in the antics of the karaoke. When Jean called her name, Libby stepped forward. She scrolled through the menu.

"I don't really know any of these songs," she confessed.

Jean stood next to her. She touched the menu bar. "You ever go to camp as a kid?"

"Yes."

The woman's eyes glimmered merrily. "Great." She pushed a button, and a list of camp songs appeared on the screen. "You ever sing any of these?"

Libby read through the titles. She nodded, and pointed. "That one."

Jean handed her the microphone, and a polka beat started. Libby raised the microphone to her lips and began.

"The cutest boy I ever saw was sipping cider through a straw...."

When the party broke up later, Byron and Libby walked to her car. He had ridden with someone else downtown so Libby offered to take him home. After they settled in the vehicle, he directed her toward campus.

"I'm surprised no one was drinking tonight," Libby commented.

"Can you imagine how out of hand the karaoke would get if we were drunk?" He shook his head. "We'd actually consider ourselves decent singers and want to do it in public. It would be really embarrassing then."

"It's odd. All of them are college students, right?"

"Graduate level. They've sown their wild oats for the most part, except for Nicholas who still likes to kick up his heels from time to time. But someone in the group is a recovering alcoholic, and out of deference to her, we don't drink."

Libby digested that bit of information for a few minutes. "Is Nicholas gay?"

"Why do you ask?"

"He's got that graceful girlie way about him and he sang Eartha Kitt."

"Does it bother you?"

"Not really. I don't agree with it." Byron didn't say anything, so Libby added, "He sang Eartha Kitt very well."

"Turn left at the next light," Byron directed. He didn't challenge her opinion which struck her as rather interesting. She figured he'd want to debate her. Libby plunged on.

"Do you and Nicholas hang out much?"

"He's also a musician-in-residence, along with Rochelle.

We started here at the same time three months ago, so we've gotten to be rather close friends." He pointed at the windshield. "Here's the campus. You can pull into that parking lot."

Libby did as he directed and found an empty spot. "Has Nicholas...I mean...do you..."

Byron leaned against the door and turned to her. Though it was dark, she saw his relaxed expression. "What is it you want to ask me, Liberty Ann?"

"Most guys I know...they wouldn't be comfortable being friends with a... person like Nicholas."

"Why is that, do you think? Is it because they have a moral objection to a person like Nicholas, or it is because they are afraid his sexuality is contagious?"

"Maybe some of both. But there are...men and women who feel pressured to...try to blend in... you know, like you were talking about earlier being a chameleon."

"Ahh." Byron breathed out the sound. "This isn't about Nicholas. This is about someone else."

Libby watched him and waited.

"You would like reassurance that I'm a heterosexual, am I correct? Can't you tell?"

"I used to think so, but the very fact that you're not offended makes me wonder. And earlier tonight you sang about being a girl. It was funny, but maybe you didn't mean it to be."

"What? You think the thought of waking up next to you wouldn't make me want to sing 'zippity doo dah'?"

"I believe the words are 'Thank you, Lord, for making *him* for me' and 'I'm the happiest girl', and I think you even talked about shoes."

"Well, I guess I could have changed the words to fit the gender, but it gets confusing if I do that."

"You're making a joke, but I'm serious. It's your business if you are. I don't have to agree with how you live, but if you're just being nice to me or...if I'm misreading your signals, then I'd like to know."

He didn't speak for a while, and as the pause

lengthened, Libby's discomfort elevated. Finally, Byron spoke. "To be comfortable with who we are, to be able to be with someone who makes us thankful to be alive, to have the freedom to love another person because we're better together—all of these are gifts."

"You're dancing around the issue."

He shook his head. "I don't want to argue about it. I don't feel the need to convince the world I'm right about my opinions."

"Okay. You don't need to convince the world. But maybe I'd like to know where you stand."

"I consider sexuality more of a continuum than an either-or. Being around Nic doesn't bother me. Someone who is more rigid than I am will likely have a problem with him. But he's a nice guy. He's one of the most gifted musicians I've ever met. I'm proud to say he's my friend, and I value that friendship. That's who I am."

"And who you are is not gay...right?"

Byron smiled. He shifted and leaned toward her. "I like women, especially this one," he whispered before kissing her.

Relieved, Libby returned his kiss. When she banged her knee on the gearshift, she yelped.

"Are you all right?" Byron sat back and rubbed her knee. "Do you want to come inside? That tall building there is where I live."

"That's a dormitory."

"Yes."

"You live in a dormitory?"

Byron crooked his head in acknowledgment. "We live in the dorm with the music majors. We are literally musicians-in-residence."

Libby pulled the keys out of the ignition. "Can you have company?"

"I have a bed, a kitchenette, and a desk in my room. There's not much comfort for entertaining guests, I'm afraid."

"How big's the bed?" Libby asked.

"Rather small." He gave her a smoky grin that curled her toes. "Would you like to see?"

They walked hand in hand inside the building and rode in the elevator to the fourth floor. "These are all graduate and post-graduate students, so it's really quiet except for the practice rooms which are across the courtyard."

"People don't practice at night, do they?"

"All hours of day and night. The rooms are insulated rather well, but if they open the windows, then there's constant noise."

"Noise, or music?"

"Depends on how much practice the student has had." Byron stopped at a door, which was identical to every other door on the hall. He produced a key and unlocked it, then gestured for her to precede him. She did and found a stark room with the furniture he'd described, plus a large bookshelf. He placed his violin case on the only empty shelf there, and walked to the kitchenette. "Would you like something to drink? I have bottled water and tap water."

Libby shook her head and walked to his bookshelf to read the titles on their spines.

"Does it bother you that people would assume you were gay because you hang around with Nicholas?"

Byron walked to stand next to the bookcase and crossed his arms over his chest. "Why would it bother me? Is it someone who has the right to judge me? Or a woman who thinks I'm not interested?" His eyes lit with an amber fire. "I am. I've attempted to woo her accordingly."

Libby straightened, giving him her full attention. "I like your woo."

"I like your woo, too."

Libby allowed Byron's gaze to draw her in. Her feet moved her forward, as if he were a magnet and she the metal. Stepping in front of him, she reached her hand around and found the hole and a particularly frayed area just south of a belt loop she'd spied when he'd walked toward the karaoke machine earlier in the night. "I really like your woo in these jeans."

His arms gathered her close, and he inhaled deeply, bending his face toward hers, his lips rested on hers and opened, inviting her to taste him, explore his mouth, and she did so willingly. Eagerly. Desire lit inside of her, and she examined the contours of his backside through the rough texture of denim and the hint of skin through soft frays. Byron's hand inched her shirt aside, and his fingers— so sure and yet tentative spanned her back caressing the muscles as if learning their breadth and width. Without breaking contact, he moved to the chair and pulled her along with him.

"The bed," she suggested.

"Not yet," he replied moving away from her mouth and kissing her neck. His hand grasped her thigh and guided her leg away from his lap.

Libby stood and kicked her leg over his legs to straddle him. "How's this?"

"This is good."

"But not the bed?" Libby panted. She wanted him.

"No." He nibbled her lips, and his hand slid under her bra clasp and upward to her shoulder blades then down again.

Libby leaned away to look at him. "How come?"

"I have to...take care of a few things first." His hand continued to knead her back, and Libby resisted the urge to stretch like a cat having its fur rubbed.

He didn't elaborate, and disappointment nipped at the yearning which had consumed her only seconds ago. "Okay."

Maybe he thought they were going to have sex, and he didn't have protection.

"Tomorrow there's a banquet I have to attend. It's for the Eastern District of Musicians. People will be there who have a lot of clout in the industry."

"Are you one of the people with clout?"

His hands settled on her hips, and he nudged her closer to his body. "Look around, Liberty Ann. Does this look like the room of a man with clout?" He grinned as he said it, but the amusement didn't reach his eyes.

"So you have to suck up to the clout people."

"Something like that."

"And afterwards you can woo me on the bed?"

"It's not very impressive, that bed." Byron tucked his face into her shirt, his breath warm against her breasts.

"No, not very." She wound her arms around his head and tugged on a curl. "That's okay though." She kissed his hair. She wove her hands into it and watched the gold strands curve around her fingers. "Where'd you get this gorgeous hair?" She rubbed her face against it. "It reminds me of that story Rumplestilskin. I imagine this is what the straw spun into gold was like."

"The color is from my dad. The kinky curls come from my mom's side."

"Do you have brothers and sisters?" Libby pressed her fingertips into his scalp.

"Two sisters. That feels really good."

Libby massaged the skin near the base of his neck. "Do they have hair like this?"

"Yes. They hate it."

"Are they older or younger?"

"One older; one younger." His fingers began to move across her skin, his thumbs moved in unison under her shoulder blades all the way down her back and crossed at her waist lowering into the back of her pants over her panties. His fingers slid over the satin there.

"Aha. We're both middle children. Flexible. Adaptable." She edged closer to him and, feeling the heat between them, she ground her pelvis against his.

"Very adaptable." His gaze studied her face. "You should go home. That bed's looking more and more impressive."

Chapter Eight

Though the garage was only open a half day on Saturday, Libby stayed on and worked on into the afternoon. Working with her hands left her mind free to think about Byron and their evening together. When the phone rang, she answered it and accepted a tow job.

What did he have to take care of that would prevent him from getting more involved with Libby? Admiration for his scruples filled her. She hadn't pegged him as poor. It hadn't even crossed her mind until his comment about the bed last night. The first day she'd met him he'd been wearing a tuxedo. The second day she'd met him he'd sent her two dozen roses. The flowers had probably cost him over a hundred dollars.

Why would he send her expensive flowers, if he didn't have much expendable income?

Libby cleaned her hands and wiped them on a towel, then shut the hood of the car she'd been working on. Going into the office, she turned on the computer and opened the billing file for Byron. He'd paid with a credit card. It had gone through without any problems. Of course, she'd also knocked off some of the labor because of the mini concert he'd played while she worked on his car. And the second time she'd worked on it, she hadn't charged him anything. That wasn't exactly charity, because it was possible the loose balancer had been her fault.

He dressed in such beautiful clothes, and yet he lived in student housing. Is it because most of his money went for his wardrobe and wooing women?

The next day, Libby sat in the sunroom at Mickey and Josey's house. Tony and John John were wrestling on the floor, and Marcus was cuddled in between the two women.

Gene walked into the room with a newspaper tucked under his arm.

"You see Byron last night?"

"No."

Her dad arched his eyebrow at her. "Y'all still seeing each other?"

"I guess so. Why?"

"Seems like if y'all's an item, he'd take you out to a fancy party." He held out the folded paper to Libby, and she took it.

Straightening out the newsprint, she saw he'd handed her the Lifestyles section. On the front page in color was Byron in his tux smiling for the photograph. Draped on his arm was a woman in a red sequined low cut dress. Her long dark hair fell in perfect waves over her shoulders.

"Who is that?"Josey asked.

"I think," Libby said as she examined the picture. "It is a woman with clout."

****

Byron called her the next day. She didn't pick up, and later listened to the voice mail he left.

"Liberty Ann, I missed you yesterday. Would you call me when you get this message?"

She played the message two more times trying to decide whether to call him back or not. The caption of the photo named the woman as Katrina Bromwell. She had a narrow straight nose and perfect teeth.

Of course. Libby hated her.

He called a second time and left another message. On Friday, he called again.

"Liberty...Libby, I'm going to assume you saw Sunday's paper since you aren't returning my phone calls. I know we haven't known each other that long, but I'm sure you are a reasonable person who wouldn't jump to conclusions based on a photograph in a newspaper!" By the time he reached the end of the message, he was yelling into the phone.

Libby bit her lip. It was the first time she'd seen a hint of his temper.

Interesting.

Well? Was she a reasonable person, or was she the kind of person who would jump to conclusions based on Katrina Bromwell with her sequined-covered boobs right next to Byron Venable's arm.

She called him, but he didn't pick up.

I guess I deserve that. She listened to his voice, and warmth spread through her as if she'd downed a glass of wine.

"This is...Liberty Ann. Since we haven't known each other that long, you should know I'm not a reasonable person. I get jealous when I see you with Katrina Bitchwell hanging her boobs all over you with her perfect smile and beautiful nose." Libby clenched her eyes shut and gave herself a dope slap. *Why did I say that?* "I'm sorry. I know her name isn't Bitchwell. I'm sure she's a very nice person, but I hate her anyway."

Libby closed her phone and pocketed it.

There. Saw the paper. Jumped to conclusions. Returned your phone call. Ball is now in your court.

Thirty minutes before they closed up shop on Friday, Gene came into the garage.

"Libby, tow across the bridge on Highway 7."

"Dad, I can't do a tow in half an hour."

"I already said we'd be there."

Libby slapped her hands against her thighs. "Why did you do that? It's too late to be done by the time we're closed."

"Because we're not closed yet, so hurry up."

Grumbling, Libby took the key and the clipboard and marched out the door. It took nearly an hour and a half to get back to the garage with the car and truck secured. By then she was ravenous. Someone coughed, and when she looked up Skinny stood there.

"What do you want, Skinny? Vance isn't here."

"Are you hungry? We can go grab a bite to eat."

Though it was fifty degrees, Skinny had on a short-sleeved T-shirt with a sleeveless leather vest. The snake's mouth was open as if it, too, were hungry. But she didn't feel like holding onto the snake and the rest of Skinny on the back of his motorcycle. "Sure. I'll drive, okay?"

Skinny smiled, his eyes crinkling in the corners.

Libby drove them out Route 60 to a dive she knew was a favorite of Skinny's. He loved the meatloaf, and Libby loved the pie.

They sat at a table, and the waiter set down menus in front of them. "How 'bout it, Randolph," he said using Skinny's given name.

"Hey, Ben. How's it going?"

"How's your daddy 'nem? I hadn't seen 'em in a coon's age."

"They're good. How's Miss Lily?"

"She's cooking in the back. I'll tell her you asked about her."

The man walked away. Though Libby had seen him here plenty of times, she didn't know him. Obviously, Skinny did.

"So, *Randolph*, how often do you eat here?"

His lips parted in a grin, and he slid his hand back and forth across the table's surface. "Ben is my dad's cousin, and Miss Lily, his wife, is the queen of meatloaf. But she won't tell anyone how she makes it, so I have to come out here if I want some."

Ben brought back two large glasses of iced tea. Libby watched him place a glass in front of her. She'd asked for water, but decided not to say anything. After he left with their meal orders, Skinny leaned back in the chair regarding Libby from across the table. "How was work today?"

She shrugged. "Same old. Same old."

"You were there late."

"Dad put me on a tow almost to quitting time. He stayed till I got back, but not much longer." Libby's phone rang. She took it out of her pocket and looked at the screen.

Byron.

Her heart sped up, but she hit ignore so the call would go to voicemail, then she texted him.

Sorry. @ dinner. Call u later. K?

She glanced at Skinny, and his dark expression snagged her attention. "Sorry," she replied putting her phone back in her pocket.

"Who was it?"

"Byron."

"Did you tell him you're out with me?"

"What's it matter? This isn't a date."

He scowled at her. "Why not?"

"Because we're not dating, and I'm paying for my food."

Skinny's chair scraped across the floor as he moved away from the table. The rest of the meal was shot as far as the company, but the food was still good. Libby made a half-hearted attempt to make nice, but Skinny chose to pout so she ate a second piece of rhubarb pie and drove him to the garage.

Back at the house, Vance and Stevie were hunched over the computer playing a game. Libby snagged a bottle of water from the fridge and headed back to her room. She turned on the television and pulled off her boots and coveralls then put on her robe to go into the hall bathroom to take a shower. With all of the grime from work washed off, she wrapped her hair in a towel and donned her robe once again before heading to her room. In the hallway, she stopped short.

Skinny stood in her doorway. His eyes roved over her figure, and he bowed his head. "I acted like a jerk. I'm sorry."

"Apology accepted." Libby clasped the front of her robe together just in case she was showing more flesh than she wanted to. Having any conversation with Skinny while she wore no panties was a no go.

Skinny didn't move. He folded his arms as if he didn't have anything better to do than to block her from getting on drawers.

"You smell nice."

Libby rolled her eyes. "It's called clean. That's what I

smell like when I don't stink of grease, engine parts, and sweat. Can I get in my room now?"

Skinny stepped away from the threshold. Libby strode into her room and shut the door behind her—or would have if his boot hadn't stopped it.

"Need some privacy here." Her towel started to slip so she held one hand to her head and kept the other at the lapels of her robe.

"I said I was sorry."

"And I said *apology accepted.* Now I'd like to get some clothes on. Go out there and play with your friends."

His eyes dropped to her chest.

Libby sighed in exasperation and pushed him into the hallway slamming the door before he could stick his big boot in the way again. She stood for a moment until she heard his heavy shoes on the hall and down the stairs.

Good.

Throwing on a T-shirt and some sweatpants, she rewrapped her hair in the towel and called Byron.

He didn't pick up again. Was this his way of getting her back for giving him the cold shoulder this week? Give her a taste of her own medicine?

"How immature," she muttered laying her phone on her bedside table and switching off the lamp. She picked up the remote and surfed the channels. A commercial played advertising the local community college. They were enrolling for the next semester.

Hmm. Wonder if they have any music appreciation classes?

Maybe she wouldn't feel like such a dumb-dumb with Byron if she knew a little more about his world. She finally settled on a Sirius channel playing classical music.

She must have fallen asleep because the next thing she knew Vance was shaking her shoulder. "Hey, Princess, there's some idiot outside of my bedroom playing a fiddle."

Libby struggled to sit up, but her hair was twisted in the towel, which had wedged itself in between the mattress and headboard. She flailed like a bug on its back.

Vance laughed. "If he could see you now...."

"What?" She freed her hair and raised up on one elbow to get a look at the clock. It was just past ten at night.

"Idiot outside my window. I'm about to open the window and drop a brick on him."

"Who? Skinny?"

Vance snorted. "No. The flake who thinks he's Mozart."

Libby jumped out of the bed and ran past her brother. Flying down the stairs, she threw open the door and a haunting melody met her. Stepping into the brisk night, she saw Byron on the front lawn playing his violin.

"Byron, what are you doing?"

"Disturbing the peace," Vance called from his window. "I think I'll call the police."

Libby glared up at the second story window. "I'll handle this, so shut up and close your window."

The music stopped, and Byron knelt down to the grass and placed his violin and bow in the open case. Libby sucked in every detail of him—his dark gray suit with the lavender shirt and the purple paisley tie, his black wingtips with black cloth laces threaded through their holes and tied neatly at the top of the shoe. Picking his case, he straightened in a graceful move and meandered to her, his expression somber.

Libby hugged herself as he approached. No man had any business looking as good as Byron Venable did walking onto her bricked walkway. He stood in front of her and waited. Desire shot through Libby like lightning, and she trembled.

He touched her hair moving a damp strand away from her neck. "I'm sorry for bringing you out here. You should go back inside."

He'd noticed her shivering and misinterpreted it.

"Come with me," she whispered.

He nodded and stood aside for her to go ahead of him. Libby walked to the door and walked inside. Footsteps on the stairs alerted her that someone was coming down to the first floor. Gene Miller in a flannel robe and slippers stopped at the bottom stair.

"What in the world is going on here?" he asked.

"Umm," Libby began.

"It's my fault, sir. I didn't mean to bother anyone."

Gene studied Byron. "For future reference, Byron, her bedroom is at the back of the house." He shot a dark look at his daughter. "You can take him up to your room, but nothing better happen in there that would make me pull out my shotgun. Understood?"

Libby returned his look. She wasn't making any promises.

He didn't wait for any affirmation—simply turned around and stomped back to his room. Libby shut the door and headed for the stairs. "Come on," she said grasping the railing.

"Maybe we ought to stay down here," Byron countered.

Libby turned and arched an eyebrow at him. "It's an empty threat. He doesn't even own a shotgun." She started up to her room.

"He might borrow one." Nevertheless, Byron followed.

Once in her room, Libby closed and locked the door. He laid his violin case on top of her dresser and shoved his hands in the pockets of his slacks. Bending a bit, he studied the pictures on the dresser top and the décor of her room ending with her queen-sized bed.

"Now that is an impressive bed."

Libby sat down on the edge and patted the mattress beside her.

He didn't move. "What do you think your father considers shotgun-worthy?"

"A positive pregnancy test."

"Oh." He picked up her hairbrush from the dresser and sat down. After a moment he turned to her. "I'd like the chance to explain about Katrina."

Libby leaned back on her elbows, and Byron shifted to maintain eye contact. He grasped the brush and ran a finger along the handle.

"I can play the violin really well, but that's all I can do.

That violin is all I have going for me."

Libby opened her mouth to contradict him, but he held up the brush. "May I brush your hair?"

Of all the things Byron could have said to her, an offer to groom her wasn't anywhere in the possibilities.

"What?"

"Do you like to have your hair brushed?"

"Nobody's ever brushed it but me."

He scooted back on the bed and tapped his thigh. "Would you sit in front of me, and let me do it?"

"Why?" This was weird. She stood up and studied the space on her bed he'd made between his spread legs. Her stomach fluttered. She turned and sat down, and her eyes met his in the mirror.

He settled back further on the bed, and grasping her hips, he set her back next to him. The unexpected move caused her to tense, but he ignored it. Instead, he gathered her hair from over her shoulders and smoothed it across her back. He was looking at her hair now, and she watched him take the brush and pull it gently through the damp locks. Soon, her body relaxed at his ministrations.

"I've put everything into my music, but everything also means I have to be nice to all the right people. Talent only goes so far. Can you understand that?" The brush paused. Byron glanced into the mirror and met her gaze.

Libby nodded.

"Unless you know people and you get really lucky, it's impossible to make a living at music. Most of my contemporaries play as a hobby. There aren't a lot of fulltime positions, so I do a lot of bartering, and I make a lot of friends." He began to brush her hair again.

"Bartering?"

"Yes." He encountered a tangle, and gripped a lock of Libby's hair with one hand and with tender short strokes, Byron brushed it out. "I play in exchange for favors, goods, and services. I've played over five hundred weddings. This suit was a trade for violin lessons to a ten-year-old. Some of my meals out are about the cost of an evening's worth of music, and my opportunity as a musician-in-residence for the EDM was in part because of a very generous woman who has a tender spot for young men."

"Katrina Bitchwell?"

"Bromwell."

"So, she's older than you?"

"By fifteen years, yes."

Libby's jaw dropped. How young was he? "How old are you?"

"Twenty-five."

Relief rushed through her. They were the same age.

"You're a...gigolo?"

"Define gigolo."

Libby covered her face with her hands. "I can't believe it. You're her boy toy." She peeked through her fingers at his reflection.

A pained expression crossed his face. "It really wasn't like that. Her husband was from Europe. He was a structural engineer who made a lot of money for a car manufacturer and moved to the States after he retired. He was a great supporter of the arts, and Katrina has continued the work he began by sponsoring musicians and artists. She has been very good to me, and she didn't ask for anything in return. But, you know, gratitude engenders loyalty."

Libby turned to face him. "What does that mean, Byron?" He was so close to her, inches away.

He set the brush down on the bed and tucked his hand under the weight of her hair on her neck. Instead of making eye contact, his gaze seemed to linger on his fingers peeking through the curtain of her hair. "It means that I owe her a lot, and I wouldn't do anything to hurt her."

"Were you two..." Libby searched for a diplomatic word. "involved?"

"Yes. Before I came to West Virginia. Saturday was the first time we'd seen each other in about six months. We parted on good terms, and even though I thought she'd moved on, I needed to make sure before you and I got too serious."

Wow. Byron was a gigolo, and he liked her.

"Did you brush her hair?"

A small smile lifted his lips, and he shook his head. "Katrina would have laughed in my face if I asked."

"She *is* a bitchwell."

"No." Byron rested his hand on her shoulder and gazed into her face. "She wouldn't laugh at me for asking. She'd laugh because it would seem silly to her. She has a personal hair dresser who comes to her house, so why would she need me to brush her hair?"

"Because it feels nice."

Byron's gaze dropped to Libby's lips.

Yes!

The urge to close the couple inches between them ballooned in her, her heart aching in her chest from its palpitations. She shifted a bit more, turning more fully toward him. Byron's hand nudged her forward closer to him. He tucked his face into the crook of her neck, his tongue touching the hollow at her shoulder and his fingers massaging into her skin. Libby dropped her head back giving him better access. She snaked her hands under his jacket and around to his back feeling his muscles through the crisp material of his shirt. Nibbling his way up her neck, Byron trailed a line of kisses across her jaw.

He whispered against her, "Liberty Ann, your skin is so sweet."

Libby loved it when he said her given name, as if it were a secret code that no one else knew—a key unlocking the door to all the special thoughts and feelings she'd kept hidden away waiting for someone like him to discover the room and marvel over its treasures.

His lips brushed against hers, once, twice, and Libby opened her mouth to him letting him in.

She pushed against the confines of his jacket against his back.

"Can we lose this, please? There's an empty hanger in the closet."

Byron drew back, a teasing glint in his eye. "You want

me to hang up my jacket?"

Libby fingered his tie, enjoying its silky texture. She pulled at the knot to loosen it. "Wouldn't want you to wrinkle it."

He shrugged out of his suit coat and, grasping it in one hand, laid it across the foot of the bed. Libby shifted with his movements working to undo the tie.

"How the heck do you untie this thing?"

He laid his hands over hers and kissed her quickly. In a second, the knot was gone, and he'd unbuttoned the top two buttons of his shirt. He moved his neck as if enjoying the freedom from the tight collar.

"Why are you wearing a suit anyway?"

"I played in a string ensemble at the Country Club earlier this evening."

"Why do you have to take all of these extra gigs? Does the musician-in-residence not pay you at all?" She took hold of his tie and moved it back and forth—swish, swish, swish.

"Yes, it's a stipend, but a modest one. The expectation, though, is that we're available to play and teach." He grasped one end of the tie above her hand and tugged. The other end disappeared through her fingers, and he laid the liberated tie on her other hand. "Plus it's fun. I love to play for anyone who will listen."

Libby looped the tie around her own neck, her fingers rubbing up and down on the textured surface. Byron's attention caught on her movement. His eyebrows arched in interest.

"What?" Libby asked.

Reaching forward, he held the ends of the tie and wrapped it around his hands pulling her to him, laying a long sensuous kiss on her mouth. Sighing, he let go and nudged her off his lap. "This has become my favorite tie because I will always picture you in this moment whenever I wear it."

"I can see why you're a gigolo. You're really good at spouting out pretty lines to whichever woman you're wooing. And who says I'm going to give it back?"

"What are you implying, dear one? I'm completely sincere in every word I utter." He moved to the edge of the bed. "Keep it if you want. I have four others."

"Five ties? That's five more than anyone in my family owns."

"Now, you have one to share." He looked at the television screen, picked up the remote and pointed it. "May I switch the channel?"

"I guess so."

He did. "Oh, lovely. *Animal Cops* is on. May I take off my shoes, recline on your bed, and watch it?"

Libby chuckled. "I like how you ask permission for everything. I'm also enjoying the gradual disrobing."

"This is as far as I'm going. I believe your father would make good on his threat to produce a shotgun and kill me, especially if he comes in here and I'm half dressed."

"The door is locked."

"You should unlock it so our morality won't be in question."

Bouncing on the bed, Libby cast him a sizzling glance.

"Stop tempting me," he chided. "Respect your dad's wishes for us to behave. This is his house, after all."

"So, you'd be willing to jump me if we weren't under my dad's roof? You didn't want to do anything in your dorm room either."

He toed off his shoes and placed them next to the bed. "I told you why that was."

Libby watched him, enjoying his shoes next to her bed. But he did have a point. Somehow making out in her childhood bedroom felt high schoolish. Maybe it was time for her to move out. Was this why people finally decided to leave home, so they could have sleepovers without worrying about parents knocking on their bedroom doors?

Byron sat cross-legged on her bed facing the television. "I haven't seen this episode."

"I bet you never said 'no' to Katrina."

"I said 'no' to her last weekend, but I did it very

humbly, so we stayed friends and she accepted my refusal very graciously."

"So, after her would I be considered your slumming phase?"

He looked at her with furrowed eyebrows. "How can you say that?"

"Because I work in a garage, and I don't have a perfect stupid nose like your sugar mama."

He leaned forward and pulled the tie and her toward him. Placing her on his lap, he kissed the bump on her nose. "I admire you. You came and saved me when I was stranded on the side of the road. And you wept when I played my violin. You're strong and capable and..." His voice dropped to a low murmur. "And you wear very sexy underwear. I've been looking for a tie to match that shade of green panties you wore the other night, but as yet, I have not been successful."

Libby's mouth opened with a soft involuntary moan.

Byron closed his eyes for a moment and cleared his throat. "Now then." He put her next to him on the bed. "Animal Cops."

Chapter Nine

It was Tuesday afternoon, and Libby and Mickey were working on a Ford Ranger truck while Byron stood near the bay entrance and played Bach's violin sonata number two. Libby knew this because he'd told her when she asked.

"The belt isn't on there good," Libby said as they stood at the open hood.

"How can you tell?" Mick said. "I've adjusted it twice. Look at it. Smooth as a baby's bottom."

Libby shook her head. "It looks okay, but it doesn't sound right to me. Shut the motor off, and let's look at it again."

Mick walked to the driver door and killed the engine. Without competition, the music filled the garage.

"Haven't you practiced enough?" Vance called out to Byron. "You took her to lunch. Why do you have to hang around and make the rest of us suffer?" He poured water over a tire on the rotator looking for a leak.

"He's not practicing. He's performing, so shut it so I can hear him before he has to leave in twenty minutes."

"Just because Libby's in love now we all have to act like we like this crap?"

Libby flinched at the love comment. She kept her face under the truck hood.

"You're a terrible actor, little bro," Mickey called out.

Byron paused then launched into 'Row, Row, Row Your Boat'.

Mickey laughed. "Hey, Vance, maybe this is more your speed."

"More my speed is Grateful Dead or Led Zeppelin, not some dead European guy who lived in 1492," Vance groused.

Mickey and Libby exchanged a look. "Vance...."
Mickey shook his head. "I don't know which part of your
dumbass statement to respond to first."

"What?"

Byron began a new tune. It took Libby about half a
minute to identify it.

'Stairway to Heaven.'

With her mouth open in shock, she stood and watched
Byron who shot a glance to Vance apparently to see if he,
too, recognized it. But of course, the idiot never did.

When Byron finished, the customer who had waited on
Vance to fix her tire came up to Byron and asked if he
would be willing to play for her daughter's wedding. After
she went into the office with his business card tucked in her
purse, Libby cleaned her hands and walked over to tell him
goodbye.

"Get a room, why don't you?" Vance yelled from where
he knelt on the pavement replacing the hubcap.

"We're not doing anything but talking," Libby glared at
her brother.

Byron wrapped his arms around her and kissed her
soundly on the lips. "There." He smiled down at her. "Now
he has something to complain about."

Libby was too shocked to respond. Was he crazy? Now
he was going to smell like grease the rest of the day.
Releasing her, Byron began to walk to his car he'd parked
across the street, but pivoted before he reached the road
and strode back to her kissing her one more time. "Would
you call me later?" he asked.

"Umm. Sure."

"Are you free for dinner?"

Libby watched his lips form the question. Her mouth
still tingled from where those lips had touched hers. She
shook her head to clear it. "Okay." He gave her one of his
turn-her-knees-to-jelly smiles and left.

When Libby walked back into the garage, Gene Miller
stood in the doorway leading to the office. He had his arms
crossed over his chest like he did when he was about to

make a pronouncement. His hard stare stopped Libby short.

Uh-oh.

"Mick?" he called.

Mickey appeared from around the corner of the truck. "Yeah, Dad?"

"Why don't you see if Josey can round up some grub for tonight? Tell her we'd like to have a meal with the whole family."

"All right."

"Libby? Call Byron and tell him the dinner bells rings at 6:30."

She shook her head. "I don't think so."

"I do think so."

"He's not family."

"If he's spending time in your bedroom, then he's insinuating himself into the family."

Libby met his gaze boldly. "We haven't done anything." *Hardly.*

The old man arched an eyebrow at her. He wasn't buying it. "Six-thirty tonight."

Byron arrived fifteen minutes before the dinner bell. When Libby opened the door in Josey's borrowed sky blue sweater and knit cotton skirt, he took her hand in his and kissed her knuckles. Libby's eyes widened when she caught sight of his shirt and matching silk tie.

Emerald green with black pencil stripes.

His wicked grin told her the tie was no accident.

Libby stood there struck dumb.

He kept contact and maneuvered their fingers into a handhold.

"You don't know what you're getting into," she finally managed.

"What do you mean?"

"My family. All together. We're horrible."

"Meh. I'm sure it will be fine." He guided them into the house.

"Hi, Byron," Josey greeted him.

He held up a paper shopping bag Libby hadn't noticed. How could she when he'd worn the tie? On purpose.

"I brought a gift."

"Yeah! Presents!" Tony yelled making a beeline for them.

"Not for you, squirt," Mickey told his son.

"I'm not so sure about that," Byron countered. Releasing her hand, he knelt down to Tony and John John who had joined them. Byron reached into the bag and took out two wrapped presents, which he handed to each of them. They ran away leaving a trail of torn paper behind them.

Josey came forward holding Marcus on her hip. Byron stood and held another gift to the baby who took it.

"I also have a bottle of wine here for the adults, and if anyone doesn't drink wine, there's a six pack of beer."

"What kind?" Vance asked from in front of the television. "If you say light, you can just turn right around and—"

"Shut up, Vance. This is my house. He didn't bring the beer for you. You're not supposed to have it anyway until you finish your stint with AA." Mickey came forward and took the bag. "Thanks, Byron. Ahh! Lager. I knew you had good taste."

"I'm only going to AA because of the DUI. I'm not an alcoholic."

"Spoken like a true alcoholic."

"Bite me."

Libby watched the scene critically. All the Miller men wore blue jeans. Byron in his suit stuck out like a sore thumb.

The bickering began even before the meal began. Dad insisted everyone, even the boys, sit at the table. Josey refused his command, and Mick stupidly sided with Gene. Josey and Mickey took the argument into the kitchen, not like it did any good.

"You always do this." Her voice carried through the closed door. "But you and your dad aren't the ones who have to constantly stop what you're doing to take care of the boys."

"They ought to be able to sit at the table for twenty minutes without killing each other," Mick returned. "If you'd actually make them eat at the table, they'd know how to do it by now."

A dish slammed against a surface. Libby was pretty sure that was Josey.

"I tell you what, let's stick John John on one side of you, and Tony on the other side of your dad, with Marcus on the corner between you and see how well you handle them. I will sit on the opposite corner with food on my plate and actually eat during a meal for once in this marriage!"

Mickey laughed, then "Oww! What'd you do that for?"

The door flew open, and Josey, her hostess smile fully in place, came into the room with a glass casserole dish in her oven-mitted hands. "Here we are. Libby, do you mind getting the asparagus casserole from the kitchen?" She set it on a trivet on the middle of the table. "Gene, you sit there." She pointed to each place around the table. "Tony. Vance. Me. Byron. Libby. John John. Mick, and we'll put Marcus there."

"Can I sit in the office chair?" Tony asked referring to one of the two extra chairs they'd had to procure for everyone to have a seat.

"No."

"Oh, come on, Mama. Please?"

Josey bent at the hip and shot daggers at her oldest son. "No. Now sit over there where I told you. Now," she snapped. Straightening, the demon persona fell off as if she'd thrown off a coat. She struck a Martha Stewart pose. "Let's all sit down, shall we?" A brief glimpse of the demon showed again when she tossed out to her husband, "Mick, get the ambrosia."

"The what?"

"The fruit salad in the fridge," she growled.

"Dad." Mickey trudged into the kitchen. "I hope you're

enjoying this family meal. I know *I* am." When he brought back the requested items, he slapped them on the table, and some of the liquid from the fruit slopped on its surface. Sitting down, he took a long swig from his beer bottle.

"I like a family meal," Gene declared with fatherly pride. "Even if Josey can't handle her kids for as long as it takes to feed them."

Josey served herself a helping of chicken casserole. "Last I checked, the kids were only half mine."

"How come they get macaroni and cheese, and we have to eat casserole?" Vance asked.

"Because Josey's coddled them with hotdogs and mac and cheese and chicken nuggets, and now they won't eat anything else."

Josey blinked rapidly. In the process of bringing the fork to her mouth, she stopped. Laying it back down on her plate, she rose and walked out of the room to the stairs.

Libby stood and glared at the Miller men, then cast an apologetic look at Byron. She pushed back her chair and walked to the staircase. She placed her right hand on the banister and looked over her shoulder. "I'm sorry, Byron. Maybe you should just leave now." She jogged up the stairs after her sister-in-law.

Byron stood. "With all due respect, sir. Your concern for my injured feelings is misplaced. Your loyalty and esteem belong to Josey."

He walked toward the front door, but paused at the foot of the stairs. Peering up the stairwell, he hesitated only a moment before he, too, went to the second story of the house.

****

Josey sprayed starch on a flowery sheet and pressed the iron to it. "Is it too much to ask that we could have one dinner, one nice dinner, in which I could be part of the conversation instead of the one wiping snotty noses and jumping up and down a thousand times for more milk, more napkins, or more beer?"

Libby watched the frenetic ironing and debated as to

whether to ask Josey why the heck her sheets needed to be wrinkle-free. "Make Mickey get his own beer."

"What's the point? I'm already up anyway serving everybody else. I might as well serve him too." The ironing board squeaked as she ironed the sheet within an inch of its thread-counted life.

"Make him help you?"

"With the weekend job at the parts store, he's working two jobs. That's no days off. He's tired at the end of the day."

"And you're not? Josey, just because you don't get paid to work doesn't mean it isn't valuable."

She bit her lip.

A knock sounded on the door. Libby went to the door and opened it. She expected to see Mick with Marcus in his arms. She did not expect to see Byron and his green tie.

"Hello. May I come in, or is this a girls-only gathering?"

Libby opened the door all the way, and Byron walked in. "Josey, are you okay?"

"Yeah. Fine." She moved the sheet across the board and pushed the iron over another section.

"Would you like to go out to dinner?"

"What?" both women answered in unison.

"I'd like to take you ladies out for a nice dinner."

"But...." Josey studied Byron. The iron hovered over her forgotten sheet. "The boys."

"Can Mick handle them if we leave?"

Josey stood immobile. "I suppose.... if we're not gone too long. Are you serious?"

"Yes."

Josey cast a hopeful glance to Libby. "What do you think?"

She shrugged. "I guess so." Libby had her doubts Mickey was going to actually allow Josey to leave without another scene.

In twenty minutes, they were on their way. Josey had gone downstairs and told the Miller men she needed to go pick up some feminine items and she'd be back after a while.

Libby thought the ruse was brilliant as no adult still sitting at the table would be caught dead buying tampons. Since Josey was five months pregnant, she didn't have need of anything like that presently. Obviously, that tidbit didn't occur to them.

Once in the car, Byron made a phone call on his cell. "Hello, may I speak to Lane Patterson?... Hi, Lane, this is Byron Venable...Fine, thank you...I'd like to bring two ladies in for a nice dinner, but we don't have a lot of time. Would it be possible for you to prepare three items off the menu for us? One woman is pregnant, so no wine, seafood, or soft cheese." He laughed softly and paused. "My apologies. I'm sure your fish doesn't have high mercury content...About ten minutes...Yes, of course. I'm happy to do that."

He hung up the phone. "We're set, ladies. We're going to the Chimney Nook."

"Wow," Josey said. "I've never been there."

Libby hadn't either, but she did know it was one of the nicest restaurants in town. "Do you have connections with everyone?"

"Only those people who have an affinity for good music."

At the restaurant, they were shown to a table topped with a linen tablecloth and real cotton napkins. A waiter placed crystal goblets of water and long glasses of raspberry spritzer in front of each of them.

"It's alcohol and caffeine free," he said. "And here are some honey biscuits with homemade kiwi and currant jelly on the side. Something to nibble on before the entrées arrive."

By the end of the meal Libby felt like a third wheel. She sat at the table and watched Byron charm the socks off Josey. When he asked Josey to dance, and they danced three songs in a row on the tiny dance floor, jealousy burned in Libby's throat. It rose up in her mouth to settle on her tongue.

It tasted a lot like raspberry spritzer with some black raspberry liqueur added. The liqueur had been the waiter's idea when he'd seen the sour looks Libby directed to her boyfriend and her sister-in-law.

Josey's face was glowing when they came back to the table. "That was so much fun," she said. "I'm going to make Mickey take me out dancing, before I get too big to move."

Libby crossed one leg over the other. Byron held Josey's chair for her as she sat. He was such a damn gentleman. "So, you remember Mickey, huh?"

"Yeah. The man presently texting me asking me why it's taking an hour and a half to buy sanitary napkins. Teeheehee."

Byron stood next to the table. "Is that what you told him? You naughty woman." He executed a little half bow. "If you ladies will excuse me."

Libby assumed he was going to settle the bill. She wondered how many nights he'd be playing here to pay for their meal. She wished she'd ordered a third Black Raspberry Spritzer drink, just for spite.

Later Byron drove them back to the house, and Josey leaned over and kissed him on the cheek while Libby stewed in the backseat. Josey turned and looked over her shoulder at Libby when Byron left the car to open her door for her. "He's a keeper, Libby."

"Which one of us is keeping him, I wonder?"

"Don't be silly. See you later." With her door open, Josey accepted the hand Byron offered and he helped her out of the car. He opened the back door and leaned down to peer at her. "Would you like to get out?"

"Sure." She scooted over the back seat and exited the vehicle from the other side and glared at him over the roof of the car.

"What's wrong?"

"I don't like you hitting on my sister-in-law."

He walked around the car to stand in front of her. "You're kidding, right?"

"No, I'm not. How could you do that? She's married and pregnant and…married. And in front of me."

Byron studied her for a moment. "Are you serious?"

"You danced with her and flirted and—"

"I was not flirting with her, and I asked you to dance first. You said you don't like to dance."

Libby didn't think she liked to dance. She'd never actually done it. And she sure as heck wasn't going to make a fool out of herself learning in public with the gigolo.

"That doesn't mean you should dance with a married woman while I'm sitting there watching you drool all over her."

"*Drool* all over her?"

Doubt niggled at Libby. Maybe there hadn't been anything to what had gone on between Byron and Josey, but until tonight Libby had only witnessed his charm directed at her. Now she'd seen Byron in action. She knew now just how good he was at making any girl feel special. Not just her.

"I guess this is how you got Katrina Bromwell to set you up for …." Byron walked around the car to stand in front of her. Libby took a step back, stumbled, and fell on her butt. "Oww."

Byron reached down, placed his hands under her arms and helped her to her feet. He didn't take his hands away from her waist. "You were saying?"

"Do you have to flirt with every woman?"

His eyebrows furrowed, and Libby lifted her hand to smooth the lines from his forehead.

"Because Josey is married and pregnant…" He took her hand and kissed the palm then held it. "…she needed a night out to feel appreciated."

"That's Mickey's job. Not yours."

"I concur. Perhaps you can make that suggestion."

"Mick and Josey have a great marriage. They love each other very much."

"His behavior tonight didn't demonstrate that. He should defend her when your father is critical, not join in."

Libby extricated herself from his arms. "It's not really your business, Byron."

He began to walk across the lawn to her house. Libby followed and caught up with him before they reached the front porch. Her words echoed in her head with each footstep. Why wasn't he saying anything? Was she wrong?

On the porch, he folded his arms. Libby realized he was waiting for her to go inside. She dug her key out of her pocket.

"Do you want to come inside?"

He shook his head, and unease erupted in Libby like a case of the chicken pox. With her key in hand, she inserted it in the lock and glanced back at him. No movement.

So no goodnight kiss.

Disappointment joined her interior party.

"See you later," she said and slipped inside the house giving him one last regretful look.

Chapter Ten

As mornings went, this one pretty much stank. Libby woke up with a killer headache and a conviction that Byron didn't want to see her again. The drive-through got her breakfast order wrong, and she was at the garage before she realized it. And Mickey was in a worse mood than she was. He chewed her out for parking her car in the wrong spot, and he and Vance nearly had a fistfight when Vance mouthed off to him about a customer complaint. When Dad called her to do a tow for an accident on Highway 23, she thankfully closed up her toolbox, took the clipboard and the truck key, and left.

When she arrived at the scene, cones directed traffic to the other lane on the four-lane highway. A police car with lights flashing was parked on the side of the road. Libby slowed and maneuvered the truck in front of the car and peered along the shoulder for the.... Libby gasped. Byron's car was angled down the embankment, its right front sidled up to a tree. She parked in front of the police car, turned on her hazard lights, and jumped out searching for him.

The policeman met her on the road.

"Where's the driver?"

The policeman shrugged. "The car was abandoned."

"How long has it been here?" Libby climbed down the hill to get a closer look. Maybe it wasn't his. Maybe it just looked like it. Maybe.... Libby's heart skittered to a stop when she saw the Virginia plate and the violin case in the back seat.

"Maybe since last night." The policeman followed her. "Someone spotted it this morning and called it in."

Oh, please. Oh, please, don't let Byron be dead.

"Have you looked for him? Maybe he's hurt and

wandered off in the woods." Her gaze scanned the grass looking for a trail then studied the trees.

"Do you know who this car belongs to?" He was already reaching for his radio.

"Yes." She cupped her hands and shouted through the glass. "Byron?" She tried the driver door and found it locked. She tried the other handles. All locked.

"Byron what?"

"Venable. Byron Venable." She dialed his cell number, but the call went straight to voice mail.

The officer made a call in to check the hospitals for Byron,

Libby contacted her dad and told him what had happened. There was silence on the other end. "Dad?" Libby's voice quivered, and she cleared her throat hoping to hide it.

"Do they know what happened?"

"No. There's only his car. Maybe he swerved to miss a deer or something. Dad." Libby took a shuddering breath. "Maybe he hit his head. If he's wandered off somewhere, I want to help look for him. Something's wrong. Of course, it is. He's not answering his phone."

"Calm down. Can you get the car back here, or do you want me to send Mick?"

Libby ran an unsteady hand through her hair. "I can...I can get the car in unless the police think he might be out here."

"Let me know if I need to send the boys out to help. Try not to worry about Byron. He isn't dead behind the wheel, so wherever he is, he's probably all right."

Libby strode to the car and knelt at the front of the car where it met the tree. Peering underneath the frame, she looked at the axle. It didn't appear to be bent as best she could tell. Standing, she kicked the tire closest to the tree. It stayed firm. No obvious damage. She checked the driver door handle again and peered through the window looking for something. Dark stains on the steering wheel and the edge of the driver's seat stole her breath. Blood.

Please let Byron be all right.

She maneuvered the truck off the road and hooked up his car from the back so she could get it away from the tree with as little damage as possible to the car and the tree. Before she had finished, the sound of a diesel motor pausing on the road filled the air.

The service truck with Gene Miller Garage emblazoned on the side parked on the shoulder, and Vance and Mickey climbed out of the cab. Side by side they traversed the slope to her.

Libby blinked her eyes to hold back the tears forming.

"Hey," Vance said, his eyes on the car. "Did they find him yet?"

Libby shook her head.

Mickey tried the doors. "It's weird that the car is locked. If he were really hurt, he wouldn't have locked the doors. Maybe he wrecked, then walked somewhere to get some help."

"I don't think he'd leave his violin. He takes it everywhere."

The policeman approached them. "He's at the Medical Center."

Libby's gaze flew to Mickey. He nodded and threw her the keys to the service truck. "Go."

****

Libby stood at the reception desk and waited for the woman whose tag identified her as 'Rita' to tell her something. Gazing at a computer screen, Rita sat immobile.

Libby resisted the urge to tap her fingers on the surface of the desk. "He's here, right?"

"The computer is a little slow today."

Hurry up!

"Ah, here we are 4A426. Go down to the A elevator. Do you know where the A elevator is?" The woman wrote down the number on a card.

"I'll find it."

Rita signaled to a man also wearing a blue vest. "Doug? Take her to this patient's room."

"I don't need help. I can...." But already the old guy had stood up from his chair and was walking past her. Sighing, Libby followed him.

Doug took her to the fourth floor and gestured to the nearly-closed door. "Here it is."

Libby's heart raced. How bad was Byron hurt? *Please let him live.* She knocked lightly on the door, and it moved a few inches. Not sure whether she should wait for a summons or not, Libby waited.

"Come in."

Byron's voice. Relief swept over Libby and she pushed the door open. He sat on the edge of the bed, and the sight of him caused Libby to stumble.

Oh, Byron.

His face was a mess. One eye was nearly swollen shut, and his bulging nose was discolored.

The corner of his mouth turned up. "It's not as bad as it looks."

Libby swallowed hoping she wouldn't throw up. She tamped down the panic, which had resurfaced at seeing him. Her feet had frozen when she saw him, but she moved forward again. Standing in front of him, she hesitated then sat next to him on the bed.

"What happened?"

"I believe an appropriate response here is 'You should have seen the other guy.'" He had on the slacks and shoes from the night before but this shirt was gone, and in its place a hospital-issued gown.

"You got in a fight?"

Byron reached up and felt his eyebrow. Libby's gaze followed the movement, and she noticed he had two stitches there. "Well, the term 'fight' might be a bit inaccurate." He closed his other eye as if keeping it open were a strain.

"I thought you had a wreck."

"Oh, there was that, too."

Libby waited for him to say more but he didn't. "Are you okay?"

"Yes. They kept me overnight for observation. Apparently, my heart could hardly stand the excitement." He tugged at the neckline of the hospital gown he wore and revealed several wires attached to round pads sticking to his chest.

"What the heck is that?"

"Heart monitor. I have to wear it for three days." He grimaced. "They've released me though so I can go home."

"Great. I can take you."

He shook his head. "Thank you, but Nic is coming to pick me up."

"And take you to the dorm? No way." Libby pulled out her cell phone. "What's his number? You can tell him to go pick up some clothes for you and bring them to my house." She held her finger over the screen and waited for him to answer her.

"Forgive me, Libby, but I'd rather not have your dad and brothers huffing over me right now."

"I'll lock you in my room."

"I'm not going to be sequestered in your room."

"Just for today. Everyone will be at work anyway except for me. I'll stay with you and be your nurse."

"I don't need a nurse. I just want to go get my violin and—"

"It's in your car which is on its way to the garage. We'll stop by there on the way."

"What?"

"That's how I knew you were here. The police found your car and called for a tow. When I saw it, I freaked out. There's blood all over your steering wheel."

"From my nose. I think it's broken."

"Did you really get in a fight?"

"If you can call it that. I didn't fight back."

"Why not?"

"I make my living with my fingers. I'm not going to break them on someone's face. Besides, I got beat up a lot as a kid. If you hit back, the pummeling lasts longer. It's best just to let them get in their jabs, then limp away…or lay there and groan."

"Are you serious?"

"Not everyone is as tough as you, Liberty Ann Miller. I didn't have two brothers to fight with. I had two sisters who made me play Barbies."

Libby wrinkled her nose. Force play with Barbies. That was worse than getting pounded. "Why would someone do this to you?"

Byron's beautiful lips parted beneath his misshapen nose. "I think I was trespassing on another man's property."

"Why didn't you go straight home last night?"

"I tried, but let us not dwell on the unpleasantness. I may not be as good looking as I was yesterday, but the pain pills have kicked in, and I feel very mellow."

"I will kill whoever did this."

Byron reached over and kissed her gingerly on the cheek. "I believe the correct response to that is two wrongs don't make a right."

A noise from the door caught Libby's attention. Nic walked in, his boots clicking on the tiles. "Oh, dear heavens, Byron. You look terrible."

"Thank you for your tactfulness." Byron stood and picked up a stack of papers on the bed. "Let us go."

A man wearing scrubs walked in pushing a wheelchair. He smiled at them. "I'll wheel you downstairs."

"Can't I walk? I'm certainly capable."

"Have to ride. Sorry." The orderly replied. "If one of you wants to get your car, you can meet us at the south entrance."

Libby stood and met Nic's gaze. "I'd like to take him home."

"Really?" His attention swung to Byron's. "She wants to take you home."

"Her home. It's not convenient. I'm without a car, and I have obligations at the school."

"You can take a few days off," she remarked hoping no one would call her bluff. She really wanted Byron to go home with her. It was stupid. He was okay, but the need to be with him and to know he'd be safe at her house hit her like a tsunami.

'Mine!' her gut claimed. She was the witch attempting to lock her golden-haired Rapunzel in the tower before anything worse happened.

How did that story end again? The witch probably got cooked or something.

Nic grinned as if he'd heard a punch line of a joke. "You can take a few days off," he repeated Libby's words.

"I'm going to get the truck." Libby pulled her keys out of her pocket. "I'll meet you downstairs." She walked out of the room without waiting for Byron to correct her. He *was* going home with her. He could stay in her room and rest and watch Animal Planet. If he absolutely insisted, she'd take him back to Huntington tomorrow.

****

Libby cast a glance at Byron next to her in the truck. Was he okay?

"The light is green, sweetheart."

Libby looked forward and saw that it was. The car behind her honked its horn, and she started to roll her window down to give the jerk her finger.

"Just go. It's all right."

She pressed down on the gas pedal, and the truck jerked forward. "I'm sorry! I didn't mean to jar you."

"Liberty Ann, I'm fine, but let's get to the garage in one piece."

"The garage? I'm taking you to my house."

"For my violin. I'd really like to have it as well as my cell phone. I didn't have it with me at the hospital, so I'm hoping it's still in the car."

Libby huffed. "I'll get your violin and your phone, if it's there."

"No. We go now to the garage," Byron said in a soft but firm voice.

Frustration tore at her. She wanted him at her house away from everyone else—from his wrecked car and the blood and her brothers and dad. She wanted the respite of her room and Byron in it. Safe.

Away. Away from everything else. Away and safe.

"You're going to my house," she snapped. A red light caught them, and she hit the brake a little too hard. It jerked the truck to a stop.

With a click, the door opened and Byron left the cab. His seatbelt hummed as it slid off his body and back into the reservoir.

"Byron! What are you——?"

The door shut, and he walked onto the sidewalk at the park, his hospital gown flapping in the back over his slacks. The garage was close to the hospital—two blocks past the park, but she didn't want him walking it.

And especially not in a hospital gown. People would think he was an escapee.

Rolling down the window, she yelled. "Okay, okay. I'll take you."

He kept walking.

Stubborn idiot.

The light changed to green, and she drove the few yards to where he walked with purposeful steps next to the road. "Byron, get in the truck. I'll take you to the garage."

A horn blasted from the car behind her.

Byron didn't even look her way.

Why was he being so stubborn?

Libby hit the steering wheel in frustration and drove on to the road bisecting the north end of the park. Turning the wheel, she steered the truck next to the curb and jumped out. He was still a long way off. She waited impatiently. Finally, he approached. His swollen and banged up face clenched Libby's gut.

"Byron...please get in. I promise I'll take you to get your violin."

He didn't break his stride. "I'll meet you there."

She let out a howl of frustration. "Why don't you just get in the stupid truck?" No wonder somebody beat him up last night. She was about ready to pound him into submission herself. "Byron!"

He turned around and marched up to her. Grabbing her at the elbows, he pulled her to him, dropped a brief hard kiss on her mouth, and let her go. She stumbled back in shock.

"Drive to the garage, and I will meet you there, darling." He pivoted and continued his trek.

On shaky legs, Libby walked to the driver's door and entered her vehicle. She stared through the windshield and listened to the pounding of her heart. Why was he doing this?

With a sigh of resignation, she turned the key in the ignition and put the truck in gear. She drove forward then turned left onto the other road, which cut through the length of the park. Positioning the truck near the entrance, Libby waited to spot Byron. If he was following the perimeter of the park, she'd see him go by in a few minutes.

She spotted him on the other side of the baseball field and watched him at the corner. The garage was another block over and down four blocks. Would he stay at the park, then cross? He didn't stop at the street, but turn right and stayed on the park sidewalk.

Good. Libby would be able to see him without moving her truck again until he was almost to Central Avenue. Then it was just one block down and one block over, and he'd be at the garage.

He walked on, his movement graceful and steady. The breeze blew the gown away from his pants. Was he cold? Probably, it was in the fifties, and he had no jacket.

He crossed the road where she was parked without acknowledging she was there though the vehicle was only a few feet from the entrance. Was he angry, upset, or just unaware of where she was?

When he was nearly out of her sight, she backed the truck up and exited out of the park. Because of the one-way streets, she'd have to go down an extra block to Carter, but he'd only be out of her field of vision for a moment. He cut through an alley and headed through a bricked parking lot behind a law office. He might even beat her there.

The red light caught her, and she drummed her fingers on the steering wheel and glanced in the rearview mirror. Of course, she couldn't see him. It was dumb to even look.

The no walking sign began to flash on the corner, and the other light turned from green to yellow to red. Two cars were opposite her in the intersection, so she had to wait for them before she could go left. As soon as it was clear, she turned her eyes already looking the block ahead for a sign of him. She parked on the opposite side of the street and jumped out. Byron was just coming to the street, and he didn't pause as he crossed and made a beeline for his car which was parked under the overhang at the far side of the building in front of the storage room. The car's front fender was crushed, the right headlight gone. They didn't do body work at the garage, but Libby had seen enough wrecked cars to assess this one hadn't been totaled. A shudder ran through her. People had been killed in wrecks with less damage than this. She crossed the street and approached him, noticing out of the corner of her eye that Mick had come out of the bay and watched them.

Byron reached into his pocket and pulled out his key ring. He pressed the remote and opened the back door. Bending into the car, he stayed there a moment, and when he backed out, he had his violin and bow in his hands.

"Geez, he looks bad," Vance said. He joined Mick, and the brothers stood next to each other with their arms folded in front of their chests.

Mickey nodded his head in agreement.

A long tone brought Libby's attention back to Byron. He'd tucked the violin under his chin. Holding it reverently, he scraped the length of the bow over the strings, then back again. Closing his eyes, he played a soulful melody that made Libby's throat clog with emotion.

"Great," Vance muttered. "More snooty music." He walked back into the garage.

Mick punched her lightly on her upper arm. "So, I guess he's okay."

Libby couldn't speak so she nodded her head.

"Are *you* okay?"

She glanced at her brother, and the concern on his face brought tears to her eyes. She shrugged her shoulders. "He…." She cleared her throat. "Someone beat him up, and…I don't know…ran him off the road maybe. He won't tell me exactly what happened, but he acts like…it's no b-b-big deal. He could have…could have…." Libby trailed off with a shuddering breath.

Mick put his arm around her shoulders and squeezed her arm then patted her a couple of times comfortingly.

In a moment, she'd calmed down and stepped away from Mickey. "His phone is missing. You didn't find it, did you?" Anytime they worked a wreck site, they cleaned up the debris. Mick and Vance would have found Byron's phone, if it had fallen to the ground next to the car.

"No."

"I tried to call him when I saw the car. I guess I would have heard it if it were there."

"We can look for the phone inside the car since he's unlocked it." Mickey walked past Byron to the vehicle, and Libby followed. Mickey opened the front door and sat in the car. He leaned down and felt on the floorboard under the seats. Libby searched the back.

No luck.

Byron continued to play. The music had morphed into a more energetic and upbeat melody. Libby left him and went into the office to tell her dad she was taking the rest of the day off. By the time she returned, Byron had put his violin in its case and stood next to her car. Silently, they settled inside and she drove to her house. When she looked at Byron, his eyes were closed and he leaned against the headrest. When they arrived at the house, butterflies flitted in Libby's stomach.

She parked behind the house and led Byron inside through the kitchen door.

What now?

"Do you want to lie down?"

"Okay." He cradled his violin case like a baby. His shoulders, stooped, attested to his fatigue. He shuffled to the stairs and ascended without looking back at her.

Libby watched him go, then headed to the laundry room with the bag of his clothes the hospital had sent home. When she pulled his shirt and tie out, a rush of heat overwhelmed her.

She spread them on top of the washing machine. There was so much blood. Obviously, his nose had bled a lot.

Who had beaten him up? And why? He'd said he was trespassing as if it had been a joke. What was he doing at someone else's house after he'd left her? Was Katrina in town, and could his assailant been her husband or boyfriend? Had some jealous lover run him off the road, pulled him out of the car, and hurt him? What if they had killed him?

The dark stains caught her attention again, and panic rose within her.

He could have died.

Libby searched the shelf for the spot cleaner she used to get grease off her coveralls. She poured a generous amount on the shirt and rubbed the cloth against itself, then picked up the tie and examined it.

The material was stiff where the blood had dried contrasting to the normal soft texture. He'd chosen the color for her. He'd worn it for her.

A sob escaped her throat, and she clenched the tie holding it to her face.

What were you doing? You could have died.

The kitchen door opened, and footsteps sounded on the tile. "Libby?" Josey called. "Sweetie, I saw your car. Is everything all right?"

Libby stepped into the kitchen. When Josey caught sight of her, she rushed to her. "What's wrong? What's wrong?"

Libby opened her mouth to speak, but no words came out. Josey's eyes fell to the tie. She slid it from Libby's hand.

"Is this Byron's tie? Is that blood? That's blood!" Her wide eyes searched Libby's face.

"He was…in a wreck or something. I picked him up at the…the hosp-p-pital." Libby burst into tears and covered her face with her hands.

Josey's arms went around her in an embrace. After a moment when Libby had calmed, Josey pulled her toward the backdoor. "I can't stay. The boys are down for a nap, but come over with me to the house. We'll talk."

Libby resisted. "I don't know. He's upstairs. What if he needs me?"

Josey paused. "What's he doing upstairs?"

"Resting."

"He'll be okay for a few minutes." She ushered Libby out the door and next door. When they had settled on the couch in her house, Josey sat back. "Now tell me what happened."

Emotion rose in Libby's chest. "Dad sent me on a wreck tow. When I got there, it was Byron's car crunched up next to the tree. You can't believe what it was like. Seeing the blood and not knowing where he was. I nearly went out of my mind. I think I…I love him."

A smile broke out on Josey's face. "You love him?"

"I want to…to…keep him."

"You want to keep him?" Confusion replaced her pleased expression.

"Yeah. Like…ummm…boyfriend type. Christmas dinner and all that mess."

"Husband type! Children and all that mess."

Libby laughed. "Oh, please. Do I look like the kind of girl Byron would marry? If he ever settles down, it'll be with someone like Katrina Bromwell. He's too refined for someone like me." Libby gestured to the tie still in Josey's hand. "I better put something on this." She stood up.

"It's silk. I don't think you can use the orange cleaner on it."

"No. We can try blotting it with cold saltwater, then I'll hand-wash it with my delicates-detergent." She stood up and went to the kitchen. Libby turned and watched her over the back of the couch. She began to work on the tie. "I wouldn't sell myself short about Byron, if I were you. He had his chance with…what did you call her? A person with clout. Apparently, he'd rather have a real woman who knows how to handle a tool." She laughed and shot Libby a saucy wink. "I didn't mean that exactly like it sounded."

"Of course not." Libby stood up. "I'm going back next door. I don't like leaving him there alone."

Back in the house, Libby put Byron's shirt in the washing machine and started it. She went upstairs and peeked in on him. He lay on her bed on his back on top of the covers. His eyes were close, and she assumed he was asleep. He'd taken off his shoes, and his hand rested on top of his violin case next to him.

She shook her head. *That boy sure loves his violin.*

She tiptoed into the hallway and closed the bedroom door. While he slept, she watched television and folded her clothes and cleaned out the pantry, a job which hadn't been done in years. A little after four that afternoon, footsteps on the stairs alerted Libby that Byron was awake and coming down to join her.

"Hi," she said.

"Hello." His tense expression worried her, and the bruising was more prominent on his face.

"Do you need a pain pill?" They'd stopped at the hospital pharmacy before leaving and filled his prescription.

"Yeah." He set his violin case on the table. "I really could use a shower, though I'm not supposed to get this monitor wet. If I'm careful, I think I can manage it. Do you mind?"

"Not at all." Libby retrieved a glass and filled it with water. She handed it to him along with the pill bottle. "I washed your shirt so it's clean. I can check if Vance has a decent pair of pants and underwear you can wear. You two are about the same size, I bet."

He opened the bottle and shook a pill onto the palm of his hand. "I don't want to impose." Popping the pill into his mouth, he washed it down with a gulp of water.

"You're not going to impose. I bought him a pair of khakis last year for Christmas. They probably still have the tags on them."

"I've got to get back to the college. The orchestra is practicing at six."

A hundred reasons for why he shouldn't go stampeded her brain. The first forty of them were the same: *I don't want you out of my sight.*

"I guess my phone still hasn't shown up, huh?"

Libby shook her head. "My dad would have called if they'd found it." She motioned him to follow her. "You can use this bathroom, if you want." She indicated the full bath next to the kitchen. Reaching into the shallow linen closet, she pulled out a folded towel and bath cloth. "I'll bring you the clothes. Vance wears grippies, so if…." His mouth turned up in a grin, and Libby ignored the embarrassment of discussing his underwear. "Not that I'm really asking, but I'm just telling you what's available."

"It's fine. Thank you."

She retrieved the clothes, knocked on the door, and heard his summons to enter. Her heart raced as she realized he was in the shower as he spoke. She opened the door a few inches and saw the closed shower curtain and the room filling with steam from the hot water.

If she were more bold, she'd get in there with him. It's probably what Katrina Bromwell would do. Libby lay the clothes—neatly stacked—on the edge of the sink and left.

She called Josey. "He's in the shower. I knocked, and he told me to come in."

"Did you go in?"

"Yeah. I brought him some clothes. I went in there while he was naked in the shower."

Josey chortled. "Did you peek?"

"No. He just took a pain pill. I don't think he feels so good."

"I know a great way to make him feel better," she sang.

"You think I should—" Call waiting beeped notifying

Libby she had another call. She looked at the phone screen. The garage. "I better go, Josey. I think Dad's calling in." She switched over. "Hey, what's up?"

"Libby," Gene said. "How's Byron?"

"He's okay. He's in the shower. I'm taking him to the college. He has to practice with the orchestra tonight."

"Huh." He was silent for a moment. "Well, he might want to change his plans. There's a woman here says she's his mother."

"His mother?"

"Uhh…yeah. Apparently, Byron called his sister from the hospital, and they've been trying to call him back. She hasn't been able to get a hold of him. She drove all the way from Virginia. Was beside herself with worry, I bet. Finally called a buddy of his who said all he knew is a woman named Liberty Ann Miller who runs a garage in Ashland took him home. Did you know you ran the garage?"

Libby ignored the question. "Did you tell her he was okay?"

"Yeah. I think…. I think I'll bring them over to the house. You think that'd work?"

"Them?"

"Byron's sister is here, too."

"Wait. Just wait. Let me tell Byron. I'll call you back." She hung up the telephone and knocked on the door. Pushing it open, she stood on the other side of it. "Byron, your mother and sister are here."

"What?"

"Your mom and sister. They're here."

The shower turned off. "My mother and sister are here?" Disbelief filled his voice.

"At the garage. My dad just called. He wants to bring them here to the house."

The rings holding the shower curtain wrenched across the rod with a screech. "Ai yai yai yai yai."

Libby's heart thumped. He was naked. Naked on the other side of the door.

"The hospital called her. She's been trying to get in

touch with you. I'm sure she's very worried."

She heard the towel moving against his body, and goose bumps arose on her skin.

"Should I tell him to bring them over here?"

Cloth moved against skin and a zipper zipped. The door moved, and he appeared shirtless with Vance's pants sitting deliciously low on his hips. A small box attached to several wires hung from a cloth holder around his neck. The wires connected to pads stuck to his chest. "May I use your phone?"

She handed it to him, and he dialed a number. Picking up the shirt, he shrugged into it while he juggled the phone from hand to hand. "Mother?... What are you doing here?... I'm okay. Banged up, but I'm...." He blew out a breath. "Darling, really you shouldn't... Who's with you? Amelia, I suppose... I've got orchestra practice at six. I really can't miss it... He what?... No. I do not believe that's wise... Disaster of epic proportions comes to mind... Well, yes I am, but...." He clicked his tongue in annoyance. He hit the end button and handed the telephone to Libby.

"What is it?"

Byron gave her a pained look. "Guess who's coming to dinner."

Chapter Eleven

In the car, Libby glanced over at Byron trying to read his expression. "What's your mom like? Pushy, I guess?"

"She's very concerned, that's all." He glanced at her. "I'd rather you not mention the heart monitor. I will inform her if there is need after I receive the results." He patted his chest. "I don't know why they felt it necessary. After the events of the night, I think heart palpitations should be expected."

"Byron, what exactly did happen? Did someone run you off the road then beat you up?"

"No. I…." He sighed. "The altercation happened before the wreck. I began to drive home. I was being careless, I suppose, and not paying close attention to the road. Of course, my nose was bleeding profusely, so I have some excuse."

"How did you get to the hospital?"

Byron gave an amused snuffle. "A good Samaritan, or, at the very least, a repentant one."

"What do you mean? Do you know the guy? Was it Katrina Bitchwell's husband, or something?"

"Katrina is a widow, and her last name is Bromwell. This most definitely has nothing to do with her."

"Why don't you want to tell me?"

"Because there's no good reason to. It's over, and I want to move on."

"But what if this lunatic attacks you again? Do you know him?"

"Not really, no." He shifted in his seat. "Listen, since my mother and sister are here, they can take me to Huntington."

"Were you serious about y'all coming back for dinner?"

"I meant it as a metaphor, but your father issued the invitation."

"What do you mean a metaphor?"

"A metaphor is—"

"I know what a metaphor is. I'm not a complete idiot."

"I'm sorry. I didn't mean to imply you were. I've grown so accustomed to the undergraduates and their complete ignorance of anything outside of reality television that it's just easier to explain my clever quips to them rather than watch them stare at me in confusion."

"So, you want to go with your mom and sister over to the college? And you'll come back for dinner?"

"I'm not sure it's a wise idea. Forgive me, but my mother will wipe the floor with the males in your family, if they act the way they did last night. She's quite passionate about respect for a woman in the hearth as well as in the workplace."

Libby digested that bit of information. "Does your mom work outside the home?"

A chuckle rose from Byron's chest and erupted from his mouth.

What was so funny? "What?"

"She works outside the home, yes." He barely contained his laughter enough to answer.

"Is she, like a senator or something?" Libby's stomach roiled in anxiety. She cast a glance Byron's way, and his smile fell.

"She's a woman, Liberty. She's just a person. Don't be nervous. Please."

"*Is* she a senator?"

"No. She…works at a college in Virginia."

"Oh, really? A teacher then?"

"She has her degree in the Classics."

"Like classical music or something?"

"Like ancient languages, culture, and philosophy. The humanities. But don't hold that against her."

Oh no! How would she feel about her son dating a grease monkey? "Does she know that you're…that we're...umm—"

"Apparently. Between Nic telling her you took me home and your father filling her in on the details, well...she's quite anxious to meet you." Byron turned to her, his pinched expression assessing her.

He was dreading this meeting, but why? Because he was ashamed of her?

"I'll try to be...to do the best I can to use my good manners."

"Be yourself. There's nothing wrong with your manners or anything else about you."

His words should have calmed her, but the tension radiating off him contradicted his reassurance. What was wrong? What wasn't he telling her?

In a few minutes, Libby pulled up to the garage and parked. She set the parking brake and turned off the engine. She released her seatbelt and had her hand on the door handle.

"Before we leave the car, would you mind kissing me?"

Libby smiled. "For luck?" She leaned toward him, reaching her finger up and touching his poor swollen flesh at his brow. The darkened skin around both eyes gave him the appearance of a raccoon.

He cupped her cheek. "For posterity," he spoke before fastening his lips onto hers and giving her the sweetest kiss she'd ever received. It felt as if he'd poured all his soul in connecting their mouths, tasting her, drinking her in, memorizing the intimacy of touching each other. Libby wasn't prepared for the intensity of the emotion welling up inside her. When Byron drew back, she took a shuddering breath.

"We who are about to die, salute you," he whispered.

What? Was he really thinking meeting his mom was going to be such a disaster? Had he no confidence in Libby at all?

Reaching forward one more time, he touched her lips once more. He sat back in his seat, his mouth curving up in that beautiful smile, a contrast to the marred appearance of the rest of his face.

Libby's heart ached for his injuries, the discolored skin and swollen flesh.

Why would anyone want to hurt him? He was the best person she knew.

Grasping the door handle, Byron pulled it and with his usual grace, he exited the car. Libby did the same wishing she'd changed clothes and put on something better than blue jeans and a pullover. At least she'd had the good sense to take off her coveralls at the house.

They met at the front of the car, and Byron placed his hand at the small of her back. They walked side by side as a couple. But Libby felt like they were walking toward a funeral. What had Byron said?

We who are about to die salute you.

What did he mean?

Was his mother that bad?

They approached the office, and Byron held the door for her so she stepped inside. Gene Miller wasn't at his usual spot behind the counter. Instead he stood in the small sitting area next to an African American woman dressed in a business suit. Libby nodded to her in greeting before looking around for Byron's mom and sister. Her gaze settled on her dad who watched her. He stepped forward.

"Hey, where's...." Libby realized she didn't even know Byron's mother's name. She turned back to Byron to ask him but saw his attention was on the woman.

"Mother," he said walking to her and embracing her.

The stricken expression on her face as she gazed at his battered continence proved their relationship though shock stopped Libby short.

Was Byron adopted? He wasn't....

The woman smiled, her straight teeth showing through her lips. Byron's smile. But how come he was so light skinned when she was...?

His mother's eyes were closed, relief evident on her face as she returned her son's embrace. "I have been beside myself wondering what happened. Why do you do this to your poor mother?"

"How did you find out?" Byron asked, as he began to step away.

"A missed call from the hospital was on Amelia's cell phone. She called but it was a general number so she asked...." With one hand on his arm and the other on his chest, his mother prevented him from moving further. She studied his face. "What is that?" Her clipped tone demanded an answer.

Byron sighed.

Busted.

"A precaution only."

Her eyes narrowed at him. "What kind of precaution?"

"A monitor, and nothing for you to worry about, darling." He kissed her cheek and took her hand, moving it away from his shirt. "Liberty Ann." He held out his other hand to Libby. "Come here and distract my mother...I mean, meet my mother."

Libby walked the short distance to them.

"Barbara Venable, this is Liberty Ann Miller."

Barbara held her hand out. "Nice to meet you, my dear." She smiled, and her eyes roved over Libby as if assessing her. Libby shook her hand.

"So, did you know Byron was wearing a monitor?"

"I've asked her not to say anything to you about it because it's nothing to concern yourself with." Byron replied, a hint of irritation in his tone.

"You are still my son even if you are an adult. I not only will concern myself with it, but I shall continue to ask until you tell me why you are wearing it."

"It's a heart monitor." Libby said. "His heart rate was elevated when he was at the hospital, so they are checking to be sure there aren't any problems. It does seem to be just a precaution. The hospital here is very thorough. They've rated in the top five nationally for patient care for the last three years." Libby rattled off the information she'd seen on a framed poster in the elevator earlier in the day.

"There. See? The hospital is just being very thorough."

Byron said. "Where's Amelia?"

Barbara moved her hand in a dismissive gesture. "She went to put gas in the car and probably to buy cigarettes. She says she's quit, but every time she vanishes for a few minutes, the aroma of vanilla body spray and smoke accompany her reappearance." She tucked her arm at her waist, her attention on her son. "Tell me what happened."

Byron shifted on his feet. "I was in a car accident."

"Was anyone else injured?"

"No."

She waited for more information but none came forth. She clicked her tongue in frustration and reached forward to kiss him on the cheek. "I worry about you. It's my prerogative to do that, you know."

Libby watched the exchange between mother and son searching for more similarities. Barbara was a beautiful woman, her caramel colored skin was smooth and without blemish. Byron's refinement mirrored hers in speech and posture. But how could Byron's mother be African American, unless Byron's father was a different race?

Did it matter?

No, but it was unexpected. Was this why he had freaked out when he'd found out his mom was here? Did he think Libby would care? Did he think she was a racist? Ire rose in her chest at the possibility. Hadn't she been the one who had called him on his comment about Zeb and Jackie when they'd eaten at their restaurant a couple of weeks....

Aha.

Byron had brought her to Zeb and Jackie's so he could gauge Libby's reaction to a bi-racial couple because he was bi-racial. It had been a test, and she hadn't even known it.

Gene Miller walked over to his usual place behind the counter, and Libby followed him. A customer walked in, and Libby stood there while her dad talked about the repair and the bill. When the customer left, Gene went into his office to file it. Libby stood at the door hoping for his take on Barbara Venable.

"Did you know about his mother?" he asked as he opened a drawer and fingered through several folders.

Libby shook her head.

"I guess it explains a lot. The way he talks and all."

Shock ran through her. "What?" She'd never known her dad to stereotype people because of their skin color.

"I like Byron, but...." He shook his head. "That woman's a good indicator that y'all don't have much in common."

"I can't believe you said that. I never took you for a racist, Dad."

"Racist, hell, I ain't talking about his mama's skin; I'm talking about her education. She's the president of Phipps University in Virginia, and her daughter, Amelia the smoker, is a plastic surgeon. I don't know what Barbara's husband does, but I can tell you this, I bet his name's got a bunch of letters behind it showing how smart he is." Gene pulled out a folder and laid it on the open drawer. "That's what I thought. Buck Tippen told me we hadn't replaced the shocks on his car, but we did back 30,000 miles ago. They shouldn't have gone bad that quick unless he's hitting every pothole in Ashland. Go out there and see if he's left yet, Libby. I want Mick to take another look, if he's willing to leave the car for a little longer."

Libby stepped backward out of the office and pivoted. Across the room, Byron and Barbara had sat down and were talking. Byron reached up and placed his hand over his beat-up eye. Was it bothering him? The pain pill should have kicked in by now.

She resisted the urge to ask if he was okay and went to the door instead looking for the customer, Buck Tippen, but the man had already driven away. Libby stood inside the door uncertainly.

"This isn't about her. This is about you," Barbara said.

"I just find it rather odd that she could get away from the hospital at a moment's notice. She's a resident. They're indentured servants at the hospital."

"Don't be so dramatic, Byron. She knew how

distraught I was and asked if she could have a couple of days off. If you had just picked up your phone when I called you, then I wouldn't have had to come over here worried out of my mind."

"Now who's being dramatic, Mother? I don't know why she even told you. I only called her to ask her if she thought I needed to see someone about my nose." Byron stood up and met Libby's gaze. "I really need to get over to the school. Liberty Ann? Mother and Amelia can take me over to Huntington." He glanced at his watch. "If Amelia ever makes it back," he grumbled.

Barbara stood as well. "Liberty Ann, surely you would like to accompany us. We can converse while Byron is practicing."

"No," Byron said. "I've imposed on her enough. I do thank you for all you've done, Liberty."

Obviously, he didn't want her going with them. Was he ashamed of her? Afraid his family wouldn't think she measured up to their standards? The thoughts cut into Libby's heart.

Movement from outside caught Barbara's attention. "Here she is."

A statuesque woman walked in front of the plate glass window, opened the door, and entered. She favored Byron with her beautifully curly blonde hair and creamy skin. She wore high boots with leggings and a black cashmere sweater. A vanilla-scented cloud accompanied her, and Libby stifled a giggle when she saw Barbara sniff the air and cast a meaningful look to her son.

Byron stepped forward and hugged her. "Hello, Amelia."

She resisted his embrace grabbing his face and peering at him. "This isn't from a car wreck."

He jerked his head from her grasp. "Were you there? I don't recall seeing you."

"Smart ass." She placed her finger on the bridge of his nose and winced. "It's definitely broken. Why don't you come clean about what really happened?"

He stepped around his sister and made eye contact with Libby. "Amelia, this is Liberty Ann Miller. Liberty Ann. Amelia Venable, my sister."

The young woman looked Libby up and down as if she were examining a specimen...on the bottom of her shoe. "You're a mechanic?"

"Yeah."

"You think you could figure out what's wrong with my car? It's been making the put-put-put noise for a couple of weeks now."

"No," Byron stated. "We are going to the University, so let's get in the car."

Amelia arched an eyebrow at Libby. "Liberty and I can ride in the back."

"Liberty Ann is not going with us."

"Why not?" Amelia asked.

"Because she has other things to do, I'm sure," Byron asserted firmly.

Geez, he really didn't want her around.

"This is fine," Barbara replied. "We will have plenty enough time to visit at dinner tonight." She walked over to the counter where Gene had taken is usual spot. "What time should we be back for dinner, Gene?"

"Well, what time can you be back, Barbara?"

Byron shook his head. "No. It will be very late."

"You'll be done by eight tonight, correct?" She turned from Byron to Gene. "We can try to get here by eight-thirty."

"Really, Mother. I believe they eat much earlier than that."

"Eight-thirty is great. Josey can have the boys to bed by then. It will make dinner a lot more enjoyable without the rug rats around."

Barbara set her arm on the counter and settled in for a long talk. "What a shame to miss your grandchildren, Gene. How many do you have?"

"Mother, please. We must go," Byron implored her.

****

Libby had thought a late dinner could save them all. If the holy terrors were in bed, then there'd be less noise and less reason for Dad to pick at Josey for her lack of parenting skills and at Mickey for not having a better handle on Josey or his kids. Libby had even suggested eating at Gene's house and leaving out Mick and Josey altogether, but Dad had insisted. This was for families to meet.

"Ain't you serious about Byron?" he'd asked her.

Libby shrugged then fidgeted like an ant trying to get out of the path of a kid's magnified sunray.

"You aren't fooling me, Libby. He isn't who I would have picked for you, but you could have done worse, I suppose."

"I couldn't have done better," she snapped.

"They run in different circles. Barbara is nice, but...." Gene shook his head. "She's not...the whole family...they're not our kind of people."

"Because she's black?"

"I told you, I don't care if she's blue, purple, pink, or brown. But I've dealt with enough of those high class people who think their education makes them better than the working man. You ain't ever gonna fit in that world, Libby."

"I could have gone to college, if I wanted to." Libby's defensive tone surprised her. "But it wouldn't have made me a better mechanic."

"Exactly."

"I've never pretended to be anything other than who I am to Byron. He likes me."

"But has he pretended to be something else to you?"

The truth of Dad's question bugged her. Byron had never said anything to her about his family—other than having two sisters. But it also hadn't really come up either. Libby had never asked him. She had assumed his family was upper class. Poor uneducated kids didn't grow up to talk, dress, and act like Byron did.

Libby went over to Josey's house around seven to help

with supper.

When Josey saw Libby in jeans, she shook her head. "You're not wearing that, are you?"

"Yes, I am."

"Go upstairs and grab something of mine. I've got a really pretty white pullover that you can wear with some black sparkly leggings. You'll be a knock-out."

"I don't like sparkly. I'm wearing my jeans."

A little boy screamed. John John maybe. Then crying which got louder as he came down the stairs with Tony close behind. "Mom! Tony hit me."

"I did not, Mom!"

"Are you going to get them to bed soon?" Libby asked.

She grabbed each of them by the backs of their shirts. Looking into Tony's face, she said, "Stop hitting your brother."

"I said I didn't do it," Tony yelled.

"Don't do it again, and use your inside voice. I'm right here. You don't need to be so loud." She let go of them.

"I didn't hit him." Tony stepped toward his brother and attempted to kick him, but Josey held him back.

"Don't kick him either. Don't touch him."

"He took my Hero cards."

Josey sighed and looked at Libby. "I still need to get them their baths. These dinners your dad throws on me on short notice aren't easy to pull off."

"Tell him 'no' next time. This isn't fair for him to expect you to feed six extra people in your house with just a few hours to prepare."

"I had to get it from Bob Evans. If I put it on my own platters, though, nobody will know."

"Who cares if they know? Serve it in the to-go boxes. Less clean up that way."

Josey shook her head giving Libby a hard look. "It matters. I want things to be nice. Plastic to-go containers don't say 'welcome'."

"Yeah, they say 'I have a self-centered father-in-law who thinks I run a restaurant.'"

Josey gathered the boys and herded them to the stairs. "I better get them bathed. Do you mind cleaning off the table, Libby? I'll lay that shirt out for you."

Just the table? Libby looked at the living room. It looked like a tornado had hit—toys littered the floor and a turned-over bowl of something sat in front of the television. Something purple covered a portion of the wall next to the dining table. Libby leaned forward and examined it. She touched it with one finger then raised the digit to her nose taking a tentative sniff then touching it to her tongue.

Grape jelly.

Looking down, she saw a piece of purple-smeared bread on the floor. She picked it up. Apparently, someone just wanted the peanut butter portion of the peanut butter and jelly sandwich.

The table itself had Play-Doh and Play-Doh paraphernalia all over it. A plastic bin sat on the floor with a label identifying it as the keeper of the dough. Good. Libby lifted the lid and wrinkled her nose. The peanut butter side of the sandwich was on the bottom.

I'm related to pigs, Libby thought. Byron's mom is going to think his girlfriend, the grease monkey, has pigs for relatives who live in pigsties.

The college president was about to get an education in an alternative context: Hillbilly animal habitats.

Chapter Twelve

Even though the temptation to push the toys in the box was nearly overwhelming, Libby nevertheless reached in the box and removed the food. She walked into the kitchen to wash out the bin and heard heavy footsteps on the stairs. Mickey, his hair still wet from a shower, walked into the room a moment later. He opened the fridge and pulled out a beer can. He popped the tab and turned it up to his mouth taking a long drink. He belched and sighed in satisfaction.

"Go ahead and get all of your gas out now. I don't want you doing that once Byron and his family get here."

"I'll burp in my own house, if I want to."

"I know you can burp in your own house, but please don't."

Mickey walked into the living room and settled on his recliner. The television clicked on. Libby walked back into the dining area, which was really a tiled section of the living room. "Seriously? Look at this house. There are people coming in less than an hour. Get up and do something."

"I'm tired." The volume on the television went up.

"Mickey," Josey yelled from upstairs. "Honey, do you mind raking some of the boys' toys into the den and closing the door?"

"Give me a break, Jose. I just put in ten hours at the garage," he yelled back.

"Come up here then and finish bathing the boys."

With an angry snap, he lowered the footrest on the recliner and stood up. Muttering under his breath, Mickey walked to the back door, opened it, and pulled in a garden rake. He began to drag the toys across the floor.

"You idiot," Libby said. "She didn't mean to literally

rake the toys."

Mickey stopped and looked at his sister with a confused expression. "Yeah, she did."

"With a rake?"

"Yeah. It gives the carpet that just-vacuumed look. Oh, crap." He raked the bowl and found a puddle of Spaghettios underneath. He picked up the bowl and looked at it before setting it on the entertainment center. He looked around, spotted a small rug in front of the couch, retrieved it, and set it over the stain.

Libby noticed a large brown mark he had uncovered by moving the rug—probably from the last time he had raked toys. Shaking her head in amazement, Libby went to the laundry room and found the carpet cleaner. She treated both spots while Mick did his raking and muttering. About the time he had corralled the pile in the den, the back door opened and Gene and Vance walked in the room.

Vance was in the middle of a complaint. "...never had a special dinner for me and my girlfriend. But let Libby just find one fruitcake violin player, and we all got to make nice about it."

"It's an hour of your time and a home-cooked meal. Why are you complaining?" Gene said, strolling to the couch and sitting down.

"I'm still not convinced he's not a fag."

"If you'd a seen the kiss he laid on Libby in the car this afternoon, you wouldn't think so," Mick retorted.

"Libby, did you know he had a black mama?" Vance asked going to the fridge and grabbing a bottle of water. "I don't get it. Is he adopted or something? Do they even let black people adopt white kids or white people adopt black kids? Or Mexicans? Do you have to speak Mexican to adopt one?"

"Or Canadians? Do you have to talk funny to adopt a Canadian kid?" Mick grinned.

Libby's hackles rose in anger. "He's not adopted."

"But he's white," Vance argued. "I expected him to be gay by the way he dresses, but black? I sure didn't see that one coming."

Tension in her right arm caused Libby to look down. She'd balled up her fist ready to punch him. "What's it matter? You're just showing how stupid you are by even asking."

"You know what the King said. He dreamed of people being judged by their character not their skin color," Mick said.

"The King? You mean Elvis?" Vance blinked at his brother.

Mickey laughed. "Martin Luther King, you dumb shit."

"How can his mom be black though? Is he, like, an albino or something? Did you ask him, Libby?"

"No."

"Well, I'm going to."

"If you do, I will kill you," Libby swiped the Play-Doh from the table into the container.

"Vance, don't say anything about it," Gene counseled. "Turn it to the news, Mickey."

Mick aimed the remote.

Vance collapsed on the sofa beside Gene. "We're all thinking it. I'm sure they've been asked before. Amelia is hot, isn't she? Libby, why don't you and Byron and me and her go out on a double date."

Mick ran through the channels before stopping on the news station. "She won't give you the time of day, bro." He laughed. "But dream on."

Libby headed to the kitchen and shut the door behind her before she gave in to the urge to beat Vance to a pulp. She pulled containers out of the paper take-out bags and started to put the food on the platters Josey had set on the counter. In a few minutes, Josey came in with John John in pajamas on her hip. "Oh, thanks. These are oven-safe, so let's stick them in there until Byron and his family arrive." She hurried to the stove and turned a dial. "I don't have enough glasses. You think they mind drinking out of red Solo cups?"

Libby shook her head. "I hate to live up to the

stereotype. Let me run next door and get Mom's crystal. I haven't put it up yet from Thanksgiving."

"Maybe send Vance and Mick to get a few chairs too. Mick said Byron's sister is gorgeous. Do you think so?"

"She looks like a model."

The door opened, and Tony walked in. "Mom, Marcus is crying."

"Did you wake him up, sweetie?"

"No, he woke up by hisself."

Josey turned to Libby. "Do you mind going up and checking on him. And while you're up there, you can change clothes."

"I'm not wearing glittery pants."

"Sweetie, we need all the help we can get tonight. Put them on. They'll give you confidence."

****

Byron had tried to get out of supper. Libby knew it. She could feel it by the way he slunk into the house behind Barbara and Amelia, then stood awkwardly in the corner with his ever-present violin under his arm in its case. If anything, his face looked worse than it had a few hours ago; the skin under his eyes was now black. Libby itched to go to him, place her hand on his face, and soothe away the tension and pain.

"I'm sure everyone is hungry, so let's go ahead and sit down," Josey said. She'd put the boys to bed only about ten minutes ago, and Libby seriously doubted they were asleep.

"Thank you for having us in your home on such short notice." Barbara nodded at Byron who gave Josey a gift bag.

She looked in it and pulled out a bouquet of flowers. "Thank you. They're lovely." Josey disappeared into the kitchen and came out with the flowers tucked into a pitcher with the Kool-Aid man on its side. "I've got a nice vase, but I'm not sure where it is. I'll look for it after supper." She set the flowers in the middle of the table as everyone settled around the table.

"Don't put the flowers there, Josey," Gene said. "All I

can see is flowers. I want to be able to look at who I'm talking to."

They began to pass the food around the table.

"Vance is the only person you can't see. Were you planning on talking to him?" Josey asked. She smiled to soften her comment.

"I'd plan to talk to whoever I felt like talking to. This table's small enough as it is. There's barely enough room for the food, let alone decoration."

Libby leaned forward in her chair to catch a glimpse of Barbara who watched Gene. Looking at Mick who was busy shoveling mashed potatoes on his plate, Libby decided he wasn't going to come to Josey's rescue. Libby opened her mouth to speak, but Josey beat her to it.

"Our table is plenty big for Mick, me, and the boys. This is all we need most of the time. Isn't that true, Mick?"

"Yep." Mickey probably would have agreed with anything since his attention was on the gravy he was pouring all over his plate.

"You keep having kids, you're going to have to get a bigger table," Gene quipped.

"Somebody's got to be responsible for carrying on the family name. Might as well be us. Right, baby?" Mick picked up his water glass and eyed it critically. He stood up. "'Scuse me."

"Where are you going?" Josey asked.

"I'm going to get some…ice for my water. I like my water cold." He walked toward the kitchen. "Icy cold." The door swung shut behind him, and a loud pop of an aluminum can being opened emanated from behind the door. In a moment Mickey returned with water in his glass which looked suspiciously like beer complete with a foam head.

Vance snickered.

"The flowers in the Kool-Aid pitcher look quite charming," Barbara said. "It looks vintage. Is it?"

"I found it at a yard sale. I don't really know." The tension in Josey's voice hinted that she wasn't buying the ice water story either.

"These pork chops taste like they come from Bob Evans. Oww!" Vance glared at Josey. "Who just kicked me?"

"Sorry, Vance." Libby said. "My foot must have slipped."

"That wasn't an accident," Vance grumbled.

"The pork is very tender," Barbara commented as she cut the meat and, placing her fork in her right hand brought the utensil to her mouth. "It's good."

"A little bland, I think," Gene said. "Josey, how about bringing the Tabasco in here."

Josey stood up. Her belly knocked the table overturning Amelia's water glass.

"Oh!"

Both Amelia and Gene jumped out of their chairs to avoid the water rapidly streaming to the edge of the table. Libby also pushed back her chair and ran to the kitchen for a towel.

"It's no problem," Libby said hurrying back into the room and seeing the stricken expression on Josey's face. "Just a little water. No harm. No foul." She threw the towel across the table. Gene caught it and mopped up the mess.

"So, Josey, which of your kids you gonna blame this mess on?" Gene asked.

"The one who knocked the table. When she's born, I'll give her a stern talking to," Josey snapped as she stalked to the kitchen and came back in few seconds later with a massive bottle of Tabasco sauce. She slammed it on the table next to Gene's plate. She shot him a withering glance before turning to Amelia with a pleasant smile on her face. "Can I get you some more water, Amelia?"

"Sure. I'd like my water with ice, too. Perhaps Mickey could get it for me."

Libby couldn't see Amelia's face because of the flowers, but she could hear the playfulness in her tone.

Mick cleared his throat. "Umm. My water is…."

Libby stifled a giggle.

"Icy cold? Yes." Amelia's glass appeared around the flowers. "I like icy cold water."

Gene took the glass from her hand, handed it to Byron who sat next to him, who then handed it to Mickey.

He stood up, still uncertain. "So, you want water with ice?"

Byron's chair scraped against the floor. "Mickey, allow me to help you with the ice." He picked up his own glass. The men walked into the kitchen, and the door swooshed behind them.

"You didn't make any tea, Josey?" Gene asked.

"No, I did not."

"Shame."

"Yeah, real shame, and too bad I'm not allowed any ice water since my unfortunate run-in with the highway patrol," Vance reached for another seconds on the pork and potatoes.

Seeing Josey's nostrils flare in anger and her lips pinch, Libby decided it was time to speak up. "Dad, you didn't give Josey a lot of notice with this dinner." Libby cast an apologetic glance to their guests. "I think she's done a great job considering she had to throw this thing together in just a few hours."

"And really," Barbara added. "You taking care of your children and the house is a fulltime job already. I'm impressed with what you've done."

"Josey don't mind having the family here, do you?" Gene asked.

Barbara reached forward and moved the flowers an inch to the left so that she could have an unobtrusive view of Gene.

"Uh-oh," Amelia said.

"Gene, Josey has been caring for your grandchildren all day. Do you think her day was easier than yours?"

"Probably not. She's not big on discipline so all three of them together are a handful."

"What is discipline to you?" Barbara's eyes glittered but whether from amusement or anger, Libby couldn't tell.

"They need to be spanked every now and then. The Bible says spare the rod spoil the child."

Amelia sighed and shifted in her seat. "Will you all excuse me, please? I'm going outside for a few minutes."

Mick and Byron came back in the room in that moment, and Amelia snagged her beer from Mick without pausing and headed to the front door. The men sat back down at the table.

"Actually, Gene, the verse you're referring to is from Proverbs 13, *Whoever spares the rod hates his son, but he who loves him is diligent to discipline him*. The Hebrew word for rod is *shavet* and usually referred to a scepter, an ornately carved staff of a Monarch to symbolize authority. It's believed that it originated as a staff or a crook that a shepherd used with his sheep."

"Huh."

"Do you believe that a shepherd ever beat the sheep with his staff?" Barbara asked.

Libby looked at Byron. He drank from his glass, emptying about half of the contents. He set it down in front of his plate, and she caught his eye. His eyebrows raised in apology and resignation.

Yeah, I get it. Parents. Whatcha gonna do?

"Well, I wouldn't think so but—"

"Of course not. The staff was used to guide the sheep to where the shepherd wanted them to go. The hook on the end of a crook was to rescue any stray animal that might be in a thicket or crevice. If the staff was ever used as a weapon, it was to beat the wolf or other predator that would harm those in the shepherd's charge. Never the shepherd's own sheep."

"I whipped my own kids when they were little, and they turned out okay. And I don't need a...history lesson or have you telling me my business in this house, Dr. Venable."

Josey's hand slapped the table rattling dishes. "My children are my business, and your name isn't on the mortgage in this house, Gene, even if you are Mickey's boss and his daddy."

"Now, baby—" Mick stood up.

Josey stood up, too, knocking the table once again, her hand rubbing her protruding stomach. "Don't you *now baby* me. This happens every time, and you sit there and let him talk to me like that. Well, I've had enough. I am a good mother, Gene, and if you don't like the way I raise my children, you can leave."

Gene cleared his throat. "Well, I was hoping for dessert first."

Whether Dad was joking or not, Libby couldn't tell. But Josey didn't see any humor in it. She marched into the kitchen and came back out with a perfect coconut cream pie on a raised serving platter. She stood next to Gene and set the platter on top of Gene's plate—food and all.

He studied the pie then cocked his head and raised his eyes to his daughter-in-law who still stood within striking distance. "You got a knife to cut it with?"

"You think it's wise for her to be holding a knife right now, Dad?" Mickey asked.

"Can you guys keep it down? We're trying to sleep." Tony's voice rang out across the room. He and his brother John John stood in pajamas at the foot of the stairs.

****

Instead of the boys' arrival being a good excuse for Josey to make a graceful exit, she settled them on the couch with cups if applesauce. Of course, they didn't stay there. Both wandered over to the table and crowded around Byron.

"What happened to your eyes? You look like a raccoon," Tony said. John John held up his arms, and Byron scooted his chair back and put him in his lap.

Tony backed up to where his dad sat at the end of the table next to Byron. Mick set him on his knee.

"I hurt my nose and my eyes."

John John reached up and touched the dark flesh under Byron's eye. "Owie."

"I'm okay, little one." Byron smiled at the boy.

"Will you play us some songs?" Tony asked.

"Will it help you go back to sleep?" Byron countered.

Both boys chorused, "Uh-huh."

Libby glanced at Barbara and saw she was entranced by the scene, her expression one of yearning. Libby guessed she didn't have any grandchildren yet, but she wanted them.

"All right. Let me get my violin." He patted John John and slid the child onto his chair as he stood up.

Soon he had the youngsters following him up the staircase as he played a lilting piece on his instrument with Josey at the rear.

"Look at the way they're trailing after him. He's the Pied Piper," Gene remarked. He arched an eyebrow at Libby. "He's good with kids."

Yeah. She knew that. She'd seen Byron soothe the savage beasts the night she babysat. With dinner over, people began to move away from the table. Gene and Vance made their excuses and left. Barbara gestured for Libby to sit next to her on the couch.

"Don't you have any grandchildren, Dr. Venable?"

"Please call me Barbara." She settled back against the cushion. "None of my children have married. They've never lived with anyone other than roommates. No grandchildren. Not even a damn cat or dog. My oldest child, Jane, is in China teaching. Amelia is doing her residency at a hospital in Roanoke, and Byron lives to make music."

"You must be very proud."

Barbara's eyes rose to the stairs. "Byron is very good with children. I've never seen him with them. He had applied to teach strings at an elementary school in St. Louis, but this musician-in-residence position fell in his lap." Her gaze fell to Libby. "Have you two known each other long?"

Libby shook her head. She held her breath and waited for Barbara to tell her she wasn't good enough for Byron.

"His father is Irish. He came over here on an education visa at Emory. We met at a hostile where I worked during grad school. I thought my mother was going to have a heart attack when I brought him home the first time. Bi-racial relationships weren't accepted in my mother's generation. Not in Atlanta. Not anywhere in the Deep South. There were some remarks early on." She shrugged. "Mother thought we shouldn't have children. She thought they would suffer because of the prejudice of others."

"Did they?"

"I don't think so. Perhaps there was the occasional slur, but we taught by example." Her brown eyes twinkled. "Education opens many doors that ignorance has held shut."

"I...never went to college."

Barbara crooked her head. "A wise man once told me there are two types of education. There is the kind in a brick and mortar building. We pay tuition, and we sit in a classroom and learn. The other is life. The tuition we pay in that type of setting is much more expensive. Suffering, loss, tears, maybe even blood, but if we learn something of value, then the education was worth the expense. Do you understand me, Liberty Ann?"

Warmth washed over her. "I think you're saying you're not going to hold it against me that I'm a grease monkey."

Barbara's mouth transformed into Byron's smile. "I'll drink to that. Do you think Mickey has any more of his ice cold water?" She stood and walking to the table, she picked up her empty glass. Libby followed.

The front door opened, and Amelia came in laughing. Skinny walked in behind her with a big grin on his face.

"Come, meet my mom," she said pulling him behind her.

"Your mom?" He shook his head and snickered.

Barbara faced them, her expression hardening making it seem that she'd gained about six inches in height. When Skinny caught sight of the woman, his gaze skittered away, but then returned when he saw no other woman in the room but Libby. His eyes widened, and he stumbled to a halt.

"Your mom?"

"Yeah." Amelia watched him, her face full of mirth.

"But she's...black."

"What?" Amelia's face fell. "Mom, you're black?" She gasped and clutched her chest. Barbara rolled her eyes.

"How amusing, Amelia." Barbara held her hand out to Skinny, and he stared at it a moment before grasping it with a shake. "And you are?"

"Umm. Skinny Davis."

Skinny Davis? Is Skinny your given name?"

"My...what?"

"His name's Randolph," Libby supplied unable to stand his discomfort any longer. "Randolph Davis."

Amelia bounced on her heels. "This is my mother, Dr. Barbara Venable, Ph.D. She can speak and read eight languages. Most of them dead, but still impressive, don't you agree?"

Libby watched the other woman. Was Amelia trying to irritate her mother by bringing Skinny in, as if she picked him up off the street, or was she trying to embarrass Skinny by introducing him to her African American Ph.D. mother?

"How do, Mrs...Dr. Venable."

"I do very well, Mr. Davis. How do you do?"

He stuffed his hands in his pants, and the change in his pockets began to rattle. He was wearing his denim jacket, and a dark stain on the shoulder caught Libby's eye. She leaned to the left to get a better look. Whatever it was covered a good portion of his back. What had he been doing, rolling in chocolate syrup?

"I just...well...."

Byron came downstairs with his violin tucked under his arm. Skinny glanced up at him and froze. Byron watched him steadily as he took the last two stairs and walked to stand next to Libby. Byron nodded to Skinny once.

Had they met and Libby didn't remember?

She searched her mind. No. He'd seen Byron in the restaurant with Nic, but he hadn't actually spoken to him. He may have seen him at the garage, but as far as Libby knew, Byron didn't know who Skinny was.

Tension built in the room. What was going on?

Skinny cleared his throat. He reached into his jacket pocket and pulled something out. Reaching his hand forward, he opened his palm. "I found your cell phone."

Byron took the phone from him. "Thank you."

"Do you know my brother?" Amelia asked.

Skinny's eyes narrowed. "Your...?"

Then it clicked.

That wasn't chocolate on Skinny's jacket. It was blood. Byron's blood. Libby's heart raced. She could hear the air being sucked in through her nostrils and back out. She stepped forward, her jaw clenched.

"You," she growled. She lunged at Skinny grabbing his jacket with one hand and punching him in the face with the other. "Wanna know what it feels like? Huh? Do you?" She kneed him then swept his legs with her foot bringing him down on the floor. Noise exploded around her, but she didn't pay much attention to it. Jumping on Skinny, she was about to punch him again when somebody restrained her and pulled her off.

"What is wrong with you?" Mickey asked as he held her arms behind her back and dragged her a safe distance from Skinny.

"He was the one. He beat up Byron last night—sent him to the hospital." She struggled against Mickey. "I'm going to kill you!"

The snake writhed on the floor clutching his crotch and moaning.

Byron stepped in front of her, his dark-ringed eyes focused on her. "Liberty, calm down. He *took* me to the hospital last night. He helped me."

"He hurt you. I know he did."

"Yeah, but afterward...when I wrecked, he was there. He helped me out of the car, put me on the back of his motorcycle, and took me to the emergency room. He stayed with me until they got me in a room."

"It doesn't make it right." She pulled again at her arms. "Let me go, Mick. I'm done. I'm not going after him again."

"Are you sure?"

"Yeah." Libby sighed. "Yeah. I'm sure. Let go."

Mickey released her, and she rolled her shoulders, glaring at Skinny. "Don't you ever touch him again."

Skinny turned on his knees, took a deep breath, and pushed himself to stand.

"I'm not going to, okay? We worked it out, and you didn't need to get involved. It don't have nothing to do with you."

"It had something to do with her," Byron amended.

Skinny and Byron exchanged a look. "Not anymore."

"What do you mean?" Libby asked.

"It's not important. I just came to return the phone and...make sure you were all right." He walked to the door, and with his hand on the knob, he turned back. "Nice to meet you Amelia, Dr...Amelia's mom."

He nodded to them and let himself out.

An uncomfortable silence blanketed the room. Libby was afraid to look at Barbara. Any points she may have scored with the woman were probably nixed now.

"So," Barbara began. "Mickey, I was asking Liberty Ann whether there was any more of the icy cold water left. I certainly could use a glass."

"No," Byron said. "We should go. It's late."

Libby watched him put his violin in its case.

Yeah. Way too late.

Chapter Thirteen

Byron drove the car to Huntington and the hotel where his mother and sister were staying. For half the ride no one spoke.

Then from the backseat, Amelia said, "What kind of people are you involved with, Byron? I feel like I just stepped off the set of a Maury Povitch show. Why did Skinny beat you up?"

"It was a misunderstanding, but as he said, we worked it out."

"I don't know who I'm more embarrassed for. You because Liberty was defending your honor like you're some damsel in distress or Skinny because she beat the crap out of him. How humiliating."

"He could have defended himself, but he didn't. She's a woman. He doesn't hit women. Ever."

"How do you know?"

"He told me."

"Huh. That's good to know, I guess."

"Are you in love with Liberty Ann?" Barbara asked.

Good question. Byron wasn't sure. Had he ever felt this way about a woman before? No, but then again, he'd never met anyone like her. "I don't know."

"What do you and a car-mechanic-tough-girl have in common? Talk about opposites attracting."

"She likes music. The first night I met her, she wept when I played 'Meditation de Thais.' She acts so coarse, but there's this vulnerable place in her that my music touches. I like that about her."

Amelia flicked the back of his head. "Do you love that about her? That's the question."

"I'd rather not discuss matters of the heart with you,

dear sister." Byron reached over to the dashboard and turned on the radio.

"Byron." Barbara shifted in her seat. "A good musician touches the heart of every person who hears him play. I saw the way you looked at Liberty. I even saw you two in the car before you came in the garage this afternoon. Son…" She shook her head as if at a loss for words. "I know what it feels like to love someone from a different background. If she is someone you are serious about, you should think carefully. I don't want to see you give up your career because she wants to live in Ashland, Kentucky, and work in her father's garage."

"Who says she wouldn't be willing to go with me wherever I find work?"

"She's lived in the same house her whole life. You're asking a lot of her."

"I haven't asked anything yet."

"Just be aware. You're talented. You've worked so hard to get where you are thus far. You're on the brink of really making a name for yourself, sweetheart. I don't think you can sustain a professional career here."

Byron sighed. "I know, Mother."

****

Byron walked into the office of Miller Garage shortly before closing time the next day and watched Liberty's dad listen to a woman holding a small dog.

"You know, Gene. I just wonder if there are defects in the tires. I didn't hit anything this time, and it was flat."

"You knew it was flat when you drove over here?" He shook his head. "You don't drive on a flat tire."

"It was only a couple of miles." She lifted her dog to her shoulder and snuggled it. "What did you expect me and Princess Taffy to do?" She turned the dog to look at her face-to-face. "What did he expect, Princess Taffy? That you and me would wait in the cold car? Did he? Did he?"

Gene reared his head back as if the woman had just vomited on the dog. Shaking his head briefly and shutting his eyes as if he hoped to erase the woman/dog image from his mind, Gene then said, "I'll get...errr...Libby to run you home, and we'll bring the car out to you when it's fixed."

His gaze fell on Byron, and relief sparked in the older man's eyes. "Oh, Byron. Good. Can you go out there and tell Libby to run Mrs. Euclid—"

"It's *Miss*. You know I'm not married, Gene, and call me Catherine."

"Right. Byron, would you get Libby? Or better yet, let me go get her." He walked to the door leading to the garage and came back a moment later with Liberty at this heels. Her gaze sought and found his, so Byron knew her dad had told her he was here. "Before Byron speaks to you, I need you to take...ahh...Catherine Euclid home."

"And Princess Taffy."

"Yes," Gene agreed.

Liberty Ann's eyes widened. Apparently, her dad hadn't told her the real reason he'd called her in the office until just now.

"Go on now. It'll just take you a few minutes."

"But...I need my car," the older woman said.

"I'll get Vance to put another tire on it and get it over to you. But if you've messed up the rim by driving on it, then that's something we can't fix until tomorrow at the earliest."

"But what will I do?" she wailed. Tears ran in rivulets down her cheeks. She dipped her face into the dog's fur and dried her face.

Byron recoiled. She was using the dog as a handkerchief. What a sight.

Gene made a shooing gesture with his hand to Liberty.

"Come on, Miss Euclid. Princess Yappy... err... Taffy will be a lot happier at home." Liberty Ann patted the woman's shoulder and propelled her forward. She hovered her hand over the dog's head but quickly hauled it back when Princess Taffy snapped at her.

"I know. I know. It is upsetting, isn't it, Princess Taffy?" Catherine sniffed.

Liberty Ann looked over her shoulder at Byron. "Will

you wait for me?"

Byron nodded, his insides warming at her gaze, which roved over him hopefully. He enjoyed having a beautiful tough girl look at him as if he were a frosty glass of beer. The tension he'd felt from the moment he knew she was going to meet his mother dissipated. Liberty knew his background, and she still seemed to like him. However, they were overdue for an honest heart-to-heart just to be sure he'd read her accurately. The door shut behind them, and he turned back to Gene.

"Oh, my word. That woman, her dog, and her tires." He fished a tissue out of his pocket and wiped his forehead. "How you doing, Byron?"

"Fine, sir."

"I guess you saw Libby beat the crap out of Skinny last night. Was he really the cause of your wreck?"

"Not directly, no."

"Huh." He put away the tissue and leaned his head back to gaze at Byron over his glasses. "What can I do for you?"

"I was wondering what arrangements can be made about my car."

"Well, luckily all your damage was cosmetic." He cocked an eyebrow at Byron's face. "On the car, I mean. We don't do body work as a rule, but Vance has got some skill in that area so I'm going to put him on it."

"I'd rather not you go to any trouble on my behalf."

Gene pursed his lips. "I'm doing it on Libby's behalf. She thinks a lot of you."

"I've seen how you treat Josey, whom I'm sure Mickey thinks a lot of. I mean no disrespect, sir, but I'd rather you not turn your sights on me."

Gene took his glasses off and set them on the counter. "Josey is Mickey's wife. His job is to love, honor, and protect her. Now he does a fair enough job, but what I can't get the boy to understand is that he needs to defend her even against me. Thus far, he hadn't been willing to do that, but he's closer than he was."

Byron blinked at the older man. "Surely you jest."

"Naw."

"You mean you pick on her so that Mickey will stand up for her?"

"Well, I do it so he'll pull his weight mostly. That boy is lazy. She couldn't get him to lift a finger, so I started making comments about the house. Now he picks up and vacuums. With this new baby coming, he's going to have to start doing more as a father. Change a diaper every once in a while and warm up a bottle, take more responsibility with the boys. I fuss at him, but it didn't do no good, until I stumbled on this. I've had some good results."

"Can't you let Josey in on your scheme?"

"Josey can't act. If I tell her, she'll let the cat out of the bag. She says everything that's in her mind and then Mickey will never do anything. When my kids was little, I ran this garage and took care of them without any help. Mickey's spoiled. He thinks just because he brings home the bacon, he ain't got to do anything more than drink beer and watch television and let Josey wait on him hand and foot. But I taught him better than that. A few more dinners, and I think he'll step up to the plate 'cause nothing makes more harmony than uniting against a foe."

Byron laughed. "You son of a gun."

"Now, don't be blabbing my secret to Libby. She and Josey are tight. Them girls stick together, you know." He wiped his glasses on the edge of his shirt and placed them back on his nose. "What are you doing for a car? We got an extra we can loan you."

"I borrowed my friend Nic's car. How long do you think it will take Vance to fix mine?"

"If Skinny's helping him, I figure they can get it done by Saturday, if the parts arrive in time."

Oh. Byron wasn't sure Skinny would be willing to help. Though he'd been civil at the hospital, Byron considered any remorse he had from his actions two nights ago had disappeared about the time Liberty kneed him in the groin.

God help Byron if Liberty ever turned on him similarly.

When she returned ten minutes later, she pulled at his fingers. "Let's go to the house."

"I'll follow you over there."

She stopped and dropped his hand. "Oh. How'd you get here?"

"Nic let me borrow his car."

"We can—"

"No. It's fine. Nic doesn't need his car tonight."

"So, you'll come to the house?"

"Sure."

When he arrived, the front door was open. "Come on in," she yelled from upstairs. "I'll be down in a minute."

Byron assumed she was taking off her coveralls. An image of her taking off said coveralls filled his mind, and his shoe hit the first stair when he stopped himself.

No. They needed to talk.

He pivoted and went to the couch and sat down instead. In a few moments, he heard her footfalls at the stairwell, and he turned. She'd taken her hair out of the ponytail, and it hung loose over her shoulders. A maroon top hugged her breasts and just touched the top of her blue jeans. Without shoes or socks, her slim ankles and bare feet made his hands itch to touch her toes.

Byron watched her perch next to him on the couch. "You're breathtaking."

She gave a Mona Lisa smile. "You're sweet." She tucked her feet underneath her. "I'm sorry for acting like a caveman last night. I'm sure your mom wasn't impressed." She looked away, as if the pattern on the carpet suddenly snagged her attention. "I shouldn't have lost my temper."

"You're forgiven, but I want you to go and work it out with Skinny. You've been friends for a long time. He cares for you."

Liberty turned to him, her full lips open in shock. He wanted to reach forward and kiss her, but he resisted.

"Byron, I don't want to work it out. He attacked you."

"And you attacked him. Are you saying you're no better than he is?"

Her head fell to the side, and she scowled. "I don't want to."

"Of course not. It's hard to admit you're wrong."

"It's not hard to admit it to you."

"I'm not the injured party, my darling."

"Yes, you are."

"Skinny followed me on his motorcycle after he hit me because he was worried. He apologized to me the night he hurt me. He made reparations by assisting me and taking me to the hospital. Now, you should do no less."

"Okay," she said grudgingly.

"Next item of discussion. I value your honesty. Do you believe me?"

She nodded, though her expression became pensive.

"Are you okay with me being bi-racial?"

The scowl returned. "Any racist jokes you want to tell me? Now is the time to do it." Byron said.

"No."

A crease formed between her brows. She was definitely not comfortable with this topic. That was okay with Byron. He'd been down this road before. He'd push her a little bit and see what happened.

"Would you like to hear some? I know a lot of them."

"No. Just because your mother is African American, doesn't make it okay for you to be a...a bigot. I don't care who tells them. They're never funny."

"How about Irish jokes? I'm Irish on my father's side. We drink a lot and eat potatoes all the time when we're not eating fried chicken, watermelon, and listening to rap music."

Liberty jumped up from the couch and paced the room. "Stop it. I don't like this. I don't care if you are Irish and African. It's not funny." She stopped in front of him, her breath coming in gasps. "None of it."

"All of us are a little bit prejudiced, so I want you to know it's okay if you feel a little uneasy. Let me tell you a joke. I know you'll find it amusing."

"No." She hugged herself, her eyes glinting. "You're

sick."

Byron plowed on. He stood up, facing her. "I'd rather know now if this is an issue between us rather than you deny it and then find out later it is. I can deal with it if I know, but if after a while you quit returning my phone calls because you've decided you're not comfortable with who I am, then....Liberty, I'd rather just you tell me now."

"I don't, but I...." She turned away from him. "Your mom is....She's really wonderful. But...."

Byron's heart fell a little bit. Liberty was trying to figure out a way to tell him that his race did matter. He'd thought after what she'd said at Zeb and Jackie's, that she'd be okay when she found out his mother was African American. But sometimes righteous indignation wasn't so easy to feel when it meant becoming involved personally with a black man. And even though his skin color fooled many people, it didn't change his heritage or his history. He was proud of both of his parents.

Maybe he did love Liberty Ann, but if she had a problem with his race, then his feelings didn't matter. Not anymore.

He took a fortifying breath and waited.

Just say it. Just admit that you can't love a man who has African blood in his veins.

"It's all right, Liberty." *I thought you were better than this but....* "I understand."

She turned hopeful eyes to him. "You do?"

He nodded. "Yes." He'd dated a woman in college who'd considered herself open-minded but who'd dropped him like a hot potato when she found out. *In this day and age, one would think we had moved beyond this, but...dammit. Not everyone had apparently.* Byron turned to go.

"I could...you know...take some classes or something. I've been thinking about it."

Byron pivoted. *Take classes?*

"I was never interested before, but I just felt kind of stupid when I was with your friends and your mom. I didn't want to say anything. But it was my issue, so I figured I could learn something new."

"You want to take classes in…?" *What?* Black history? Race relations?

"Music appreciation or world history maybe. You know, so I don't come across like a total hick. So, you…." Her eyes dropped to the carpet. "You wouldn't be embarrassed to be with me."

Oh.

Byron stepped to her. He cradled her face—her beautiful face in his hands. Her eyes widened, then her mouth turned up in the smile that rendered his insides to mush.

Yes. He loved her. He loved Liberty.

"I am going to kiss you," he announced.

Her arms wound around him. "Bring it."

He rested his lips on hers briefly, and he inhaled to catch the scent that was uniquely hers. It reminded him of orange tea sweetened with honey. Her mouth opened, and he tasted her softness. She kissed tentatively as if taking her lead from him. It was a feminine piece of Liberty Ann that allowed him to give and take as a man should kiss a woman. Unexpected considering how forceful he'd seen her in other aspects of her life, which made it that much more intriguing.

Endearing.

He moved to trail kisses to her neck and taste the skin there. He threaded his fingers through the silkiness of her hair. Then he petted her back, enjoying the contrast of the texture of her blouse underneath the nearly liquid softness of her tresses.

"Byron," she whispered.

Snap. Snap. Snap. Snap.

She shrugged out of the shirt revealing breasts clad in a black-lace demi bra. Dropping the blouse to the floor, she shot him a coy gaze through half-closed eyelids, and his heart accelerated to presto tempo.

He laid his lips on top of her shoulder and fingered the strap tracing it down to where the curve of her breast began over the lacy cup. She arched her back as if encouraging him to touch her, learn the curves of her body, explore the exquisite pale skin.

Know her. Love her.

He dipped his head and trailed his tongue over her collarbone. The strap was off her shoulder now, and he touched her through the lace, heard and felt her gasp with pleasure, and he smiled against her skin.

A sound registered in his brain, but he couldn't place it. *The telephone.* Byron raised his head.

"Ignore it. The answering machine will pick up," Liberty said before she sealed her mouth over his again.

Gene's voice spoke from the answering machine speaker. "Libby? This is your daddy. Take it upstairs or somewhere else. I don't want that scene in my living room. Ever again. You got five seconds. Five."

"Shoot!" Libby pushed Byron away and dropped to her knees and picked her blouse off the floor. She wrenched her hands in the sleeves of her clothing.

"Four. Three."

Byron watched her cover herself with a mixture of regret and alarm. If Gene Miller was calling her on the telephone, then he'd likely walked in on them and done the gentlemanly thing and walked back out.

"Two."

Would the man come in and go for his shotgun?

Liberty straightened the collar and closed the snaps. What a beautiful scene that fabric hid.

"One."

The front door opened, and Gene walked in with his phone to his ear. He cast them a withering look and snapped his phone shut.

He slammed the door. "I'd like to think both of you have better sense than to disrespect me by making out in my living room when you know it's quitting time." Headed to the stairs, he began to ascend. "Go away."

Liberty sighed and put her hands on her hips.

The command to leave could have been aimed at them

both or him alone. "Perhaps I should leave."

Her lip jutted out in a cute pout. "Don't leave. Let's go upstairs to my room."

"Liberty." He searched for the right words to say. Something about not wanting to be shot tonight.

"I know. I know. Nothing kills the mood like my dad walking in on us." She leaned forward and put her hands on his shoulders. Reaching up she gave him a quick peck on his mouth. "Let me run upstairs and get a shower. Then we'll go get something to eat."

****

They lingered over their meal. After the plates had been cleared away and cups of untouched coffee sat on the table between them, Byron reached across the table and took Liberty's hand weaving his fingers through hers. He stroked her callused fingers loving the roughened skin against his own string-toughened fingertips.

"Want to go back to my place?" he asked.

"Yes." Her fingers grasped his.

He smiled.

Libby shrugged. "I've never wanted my own place before, but this stinks not having anywhere to go to be alone with you."

He lifted her hand to his lips and kissed her knuckles. "A place to make out isn't a good reason to leave home."

She arched an eyebrow at him. "Really? I think it's as good reason as any other."

"What are you going to do when I leave next year? Find another make-out partner?"

Her gaze clouded. "Where are you going?"

"I'm not sure yet. But my position here ends in July."

She pulled her hand away from his and sat back in the chair. "Bummer. I didn't think about you leaving. Where will you go, do you think?"

"I've applied to several places. Boston, Los Angeles, Melbourne, Munich."

"Australia and Germany?"

"Yes. Those are the pie-in-the-sky ones, as it were."

She watched her finger trace a pattern on the tablecloth. "How pie-in-the-sky? Is it like a snowball's-chance-in-hell kind of pie-in-the-sky?"

Good question. Byron had an audition in Boston on the seventeenth. They wouldn't fly him in if they weren't serious. He hadn't heard any more from Melbourne after his initial application with them, but he'd made the next round to the other two.

Liberty finally looked up from the table. The wary light from her eyes pierced his heart. "How good are you?"

He smiled at her.

"Like Itzhak Perlman good?"

She'd pronounced the famous violinist's name correctly. Interesting. "A fan, are you?"

"He doesn't seem to play as well as you do, but then the acoustics in the garage are pretty good."

Byron laughed. Obviously, she'd been listening to high art music. But had she always liked it, or was it just since she'd met him?

"If you're that good, then what are you doing in Huntington, West Virginia?"

He warmed up to the subject, resting his arms on the table and tenting his hands. "Being a musician-in-residence. It came up when I needed something, and I get to play with the Huntington Orchestra as well as receive invitations as guest violinist in Charleston, Cincinnati, and Louisville. The opportunities for exposure are very good."

"So, do you just live somewhere different every year? Don't you get tired of moving all the time?"

"Not when I get to do what I love."

"Seems like it could be lonely so far from your family," Liberty commented.

Byron couldn't tell if her statement was more curiosity or a reflection of how close-knit her family seemed to be. "It does get lonely at times, yes. That's why it's so nice to have found you."

She'd begun arranging the salt and pepper shakers on the table. "Until July anyway."

He watched her petite hands. Amazing the skill they had considering how dainty they were. "Unless you get tired of me first."

Her hands stilled. "Is that supposed to be a joke?"

He raised his gaze to find her staring at him. "Why? Do you find it amusing?"

"No." She centered the napkin holder. "I find all of this kind of depressing, actually. Because I don't think I'll be tired of you when July gets here."

Ah. Honesty. Byron liked that. "Me neither."

"Really?" She scowled. "Oh, who am I kidding? I bet you say that to all the girls. I bet you said it to Katrina Bitchwell even."

"Bromwell."

"Whatever."

"I haven't had a girl in every port. I certainly have never been involved with someone like you, Liberty Ann."

"Well, I can at least believe the last part." With the table put in order, she rested her chin in her hand. "So, we just go with it until July, then you leave. Right? We part ways, and all of that?"

"Unless we decide that you should go with me."

She laughed. "And do what? Be a roadie? Do they even have roadies for your kind of music?"

"Don't be such a snob. You think only Snoop Dogg has roadies?"

Liberty blinked at him. "Snoop who?"

Byron thought she was teasing him, but her innocent expression was very convincing. He decided to tease back. "And here I was under the mistaken notion that you were culturally literate."

Chapter Fourteen

The bed was too small, and Byron only had one pillow.

In the darkened room, Libby stared at his digital clock with its red glowing numbers. It was midnight, and she wanted to go home to her own bed. She wanted Byron to be with her in her own bed.

Someone walked down the corridor, and a door slammed. In the distance she heard someone singing opera. It sounded okay, she supposed, but it was in the middle of the freakin' night. How in the world did he ever sleep here?

He sighed and shifted as if to lie on his back. Libby held onto the edge of the mattress in case he pushed her off the bed, but when he encountered her, he put his arm around her waist and pulled her closer to him spooning her.

The soft edge of his heart monitor poked her shoulder, and he repositioned it. "You're still here," he murmured, his voice heavy with sleep.

Was that a criticism or compliment? "You brought me here. If you want me gone, you either need to take me or call a taxi."

His hand stroked her hip. "I don't want you gone." He rested his chin on her shoulder, his breath at her ear. His thumb trailed down to her belly button and he circled it, then tapped her stomach with the pads of his fingers.

"Are you playing me?"

"What?" His tone was sharp.

Libby realized he'd misunderstood her question. No. She didn't think he was playing with her emotions. She thought he was playing her body as an instrument. "Your fingers. It feels like you're fretting my stomach."

His hand moved to her breast. "If I were fretting you, I'd fret you up here." Pleasure shot through her. "This is a

C, and this is a B flat." Byron kissed the skin at her neck. He wedged his foot under her leg and lifted her then slid his arm underneath her cozying up closer to her. "Fretting has little effect if the musician doesn't touch the strings."

"I don't have strings, and I'm not an instrument." Libby closed her eyes enjoying Byron's chord changes.

"The shape of a violin was inspired by the body of a woman. A long beautiful neck." His placed an open mouth kiss at her nape. "And an hour-glass shaped body mimicking the breasts and hips." His fingers crept along her thigh and the sensitive skin between leg and trunk. He traced the cord under Libby's skin, leisurely skimming further. "To where—"

"Byron."

"Yes?" His fingers stilled where he'd tucked them. She loved what he was doing, but....

"If you start talking about sawing your bow across my silken parts to make music, honey, I'm going to have to make fun of you because that is really lame."

He burst into laughter, and Libby smiled in response. Chuckling against the curve of her neck, his arms tightened, and he flipped her over his body so that she was now facing the wall.

"Whoa, what are you doing now?"

"I'm not sure how to respond to that since you've said you'll make fun of me if I talk about my bow." His nestled fingers began to move again.

Libby turned on her back and gazed up at Byron. "You keep on, and I'm going to start talking about lubricating the piston so that it slides easily up and down the walls of the cylinder."

Byron shook his head. "If you're trying to demonstrate how absurd my pillow talk is by reverting to your professional jargon, I have to confess it's not working. You're driving me mad."

She snorted. "I'm *driving* you mad?"

"I didn't mean—" He touched a sensitive spot, and lightning zipped through her body. "Hmm, you like that, do you?"

Libby gasped. *Oh, yes*. She liked it very much. She tugged Byron to her and leaned forward to press her lips against his mouth.

His attention to her parts was making her engine purr.

****

Saturday afternoon Libby rang up Fred Smith who paid for a new muffler for his late model Beamer. The clock said it was time to close up, and Stevie's truck pulled up to the far bay.

Libby shook hands with Fred. "See you later, Fred."

"Thank you, Libby. Appreciate you finishing it up today."

"You said you needed it before your trip tomorrow."

"That I did." He waved and headed out the door. Libby followed him and locked up. She went through the other door out to the garage to see what was going on.

Skinny and Vance were unloading parts from the back of the truck and placing them on the concrete next to Byron's car which was parked partway in the bay. Vance had told her he and Skinny had been to a couple of junkyards looking for parts. From the pieces they were assembling on the ground, it looked like they'd been successful.

When Skinny saw her approach, he stopped what he had been doing and stared at her.

"Hi," she said.

He nodded in response. "Libby." His lip had a cut on it from where she'd hit him.

"Y'all need some help?" she asked.

Skinny looked to Vance, and he shrugged his shoulders. "No. We got it." Skinny said finally.

"Can I talk to you for a minute, Skinny?" She looked at Vance. "Alone?"

Vance scratched his head. "Sure. I guess. I'll go grab a cola. You want one?" he asked his friend over his shoulder as he left.

"No. I'm good." Skinny walked to the back of the truck

and opened a toolbox. "What do you want?"

"I wanted to apologize for the other night."

He rested his arms on the side of the truck and studied her.

"Really?"

"Yeah. I shouldn't have done it. It was stupid."

"Here's a first. Libby Miller is apologizing."

"What happened between you and Byron wasn't my business. It was for you two to work out, and Byron said you did. He said you made sure he was okay."

Skinny turned away from her and stared at some point ahead of him.

"I don't like that you hurt him, but I appreciate you helping him later. How come you did that?"

Skinny didn't answer for a while. Then he shook his head. "He wouldn't defend himself. Just stood there and took it. Didn't whimper or nothing. After the second punch, I said 'Ain't you gonna hit me back?' and he said, 'No.' Didn't ask me why. Just waited for the next blow with his hands at his sides. I said, 'Why not?' He said he didn't think it would improve the situation. So, after a minute, he asked if I was done, and I said, 'Yeah,' and he staggered to his car. His nose was bleeding like a stuck pig. It kind of shook me up, so I thought I better follow him and make sure he was all right. I hung back a bit, and was about to go on home, but on Highway 23 his car started weaving pretty bad, and he hit the tree. I thought I'd killed him."

Libby's heart thumped heavily thinking of the possibility.

"He's not a wimp. Took it like a man as if he knew he deserved it."

"He didn't deserve it."

"I know." He cut his eyes to her. "I've never seen a guy who wouldn't even try to defend himself."

By not blocking his face, he was protecting his hands, the tools of his trade.

"Anyway, I waited with him at the ER, and we talked a little. He really is a nice guy. Tough. I know he was in pain, but…." Skinny shrugged. "I told him I was sorry. I am sorry. I saw him and you outside your house that night. The way you looked at him." He sighed. "I thought I had a chance all this time, but when I saw that, I knew. You've never looked at me like that. I've never seen you look at anybody like that. Like…."

"Yeah." The stood in silence for a moment. Libby patted his back. "One day a woman's going to look at you like that, Randolph."

He quirked an eyebrow at her use of his given name. "Amelia might have looked at me like that. She gave me her phone number."

"You know she's a doctor, right?"

"What? You can date her brother, why can't I date her?"

"She lives in Roanoke."

"My motorcycle can get to Roanoke."

Libby sniggered. "How does she like the snake tat?"

"She's got a dragon on her back. The design is sweet. Whoever did it was a master."

****

Libby sat at table for another family gathering with Byron included. After the disaster of last time, she was reticent to have another go, but this request had come from Byron.

"Why would you want to go through that torture again? Is this an excuse to take Josey out dancing?" she'd asked him.

He gave her one of his heart-melting smiles. "If we go out dancing again, we'll invite Mickey the next time, and let your father and Vance stay home with the children."

"Josey won't agree to it. Remember the dog cage incident?"

"Let us just see what happens." He'd had a twinkle in his eye as if he had a secret he wasn't telling.

Now seated next to Byron, Libby braced herself for a repeat performance. Under the table, Byron reached over and took her hand in his, squeezing it.

Jennifer Johnson

Vance glared at them from across the table. "Can you guys tone it down? I don't wanna get sick at the table."

"What are we doing?" Libby asked. "It's not like I'm sitting in his lap or anything."

"You really do want me to puke, don't you?"

"Vance, stop," Gene said.

"Uncle Vance is going to puke, yeah," Tony shouted with glee.

"Tony, eat your macaroni and cheese."

"I am. Get off my back. God." He glowered at his mother.

Gene pursed his lips. "Josey, are you going to let him talk to you like that and blaspheme the Lord God?"

Josey didn't reply. She spooned some peas on Marcus' highchair tray, and he picked them up and threw them. "Marcus, sweetie, don't do that."

He grinned at her and picked up another handful ready to pitch more.

"No."

He screwed up his face and began to cry.

Gene scooted his chair back. "You're not making the other boys eat peas. Why does Marcus have to?"

"Cause we don't like peas, that's why," Tony said.

"Yeah. We don't like peas," John John echoed. "God."

Gene cleared his throat.

Great. He was getting ready to give Josey more parenting advice.

Byron patted her hand and stood. He picked up his glass. "I need more to drink. Excuse me."

Josey looked at him. "I'll get it, Byron."

"Oh, no. No. Please. Mickey can assist me. Right?" He nodded at him.

Mickey who had just taken a bite of food nodded. He stood up as he chewed. "Yeah, sure. Do we still have to call it water since your Ma ain't here?" He led the way into the kitchen. The doors shut behind them.

Whatever Dad was about to say never materialized. The tension dissipated a bit, much to Libby's surprise.

"Would you pass the mac and cheese?" Vance asked.

"You gotta eat your peas," Tony told him.

"You didn't eat yours," Vance returned.

"So? Get off my back, man."

Vance cracked a grin.

In a few minutes Mickey and Byron came out of the kitchen both with cans of beer. As they settled on their chairs, Tony said, "Hey, Dad, can I have some beer?"

"Nope." Mickey tipped his can back and drank.

"Why not? Byron gets one."

Josey spoke. "Because you're not old enough."

"I am too old enough." He yelled and threw his fork. It clanged across the table and fell to the floor.

"Am I the only one who thinks this boy needs correcting?" Gene asked. "Honestly, if my kids had acted like this at the table, they would have gone to bed hungry."

"They're not your kids, Gene," Josey snapped.

Libby shot an *I-told-you-so* look at Byron, but Byron missed it because he and Mickey were passing some silent message to each other. *What?*

"They're my grandkids. I think—"

Mickey stood up. "Dad...look. Josey and I are trying the ignore-the-bad-behavior route with the boys, so either like it and let us be the authority here, or lump it and go home. All right?"

Josey's jaw fell.

Taking a swig of beer, Mickey thumped his chest and belched. "Excuse me."

Gene studied his son. "Seems like you been trying that route most of their lives, Mick."

Mickey lowered himself in the chair. "That's because Josey handles the boys real good most of the time so I don't have to." He flicked a glance at Byron. "But I'm their dad, and I'd never send the boys to bed without supper. I remember when you did it to me, and it wasn't right. My kids won't ever go hungry, if I can help it. Right, Jose?"

Josey blinked at him, her mouth still open.

"Honey?" He waited for her affirmation.

She shook herself out of her stupor. "Of course, Mick."

"Unless all we get is peas, then I'd rather *be* hungry," Tony declared.

Later Libby and Byron reclined on her bed watching television. Byron had his arms around her, and he leaned down to kiss her briefly on the lips.

"Did you have something to do with Mickey saying something to my dad tonight?" she asked.

"Why do you ask?" His hand was under her shirt scratching her back.

"You did. The very fact you didn't deny it immediately tells me you had something to do with it." Libby raised up and studied his expression for any sign of guilt.

"You ever notice how your father only criticizes Josey when Mickey is in the room?"

"No."

"Next time, try to notice."

"Why would he do that?"

"Why indeed."

"You think he's trying to get Mickey to take up for her?"

"I know he is."

"How can you know that?"

"Because he told me. Your father is sneaky." Byron nudged her down next to him. "Listen, I've got to go over the weekend to Cincinnati next month for a concert. Would you like to go?"

"For the weekend?"

"You wouldn't want to come for the whole weekend. I'll be rehearsing most of the time, but you could come over Saturday night for the concert."

"I could find something to do while you're rehearsing."

"You'd really want to go Friday and stay through Sunday? I'd probably only have a few hours Saturday afternoon free."

"Would you want me there? That's really the question."

"Would I want you there?" A smile broke over his face. "Yes."

She began to unbutton his shirt. "Can you stay

tonight?" She kissed the skin above the apex of his undershirt.

"What's Gene going to say when he meets me in the hallway in the morning, hmm?"

"I don't know. Probably move your car so you don't block him in when he leaves at seven." She pushed his shirt off his shoulders and down his arms then carefully laid it on her dresser. She liked him in the undershirt, a casual image she rarely saw.

"You're still his daughter, even if you are an adult."

"Did you get the results of your heart monitor?"

"Yes. They didn't find any problems."

"Would you tell me the truth if there was a problem?"

"The doctor did look at me a little funny. It must have indicated what we were doing the night you stayed in the dorm." He smirked.

"Get out. Really?"

He shrugged and dropped a kiss on her nose.

"You would tell me though, right?"

"Yes, Liberty Ann. I'd tell you. I...don't want to keep secrets from you." He picked up the remote and muted it. "This is why I need you to know that Cincinnati is more than a performance."

"What do you mean?"

"Two people from the Munich Chamber Orchestra will be there to hear me play. If it goes well...really well, I'll get to go to Germany."

"When?"

"As soon as I'm done here. August."

"For how long?"

"Two months, but it could turn into a tenured position."

"In Germany? But...don't you need to know how to speak the language? I mean...." The expression on Byron's face stopped her. "No, you don't."

"Ich spreche Deutsch."

"What? Are you kidding me?"

"No, even though speaking German is not a

requirement. It makes it easier, especially if one is living there."

"How many other languages do you speak?"

"English and German, and just enough Spanish and French to get by, and since I am my mother's son, I can conjugate most Latin verbs in my sleep or translate Koine Greek without too much difficulty."

"So you know six languages? *Six?*"

"I'm only proficient in two."

"Only two, huh?" She shook her head. "That's one more than me, and two more than Vance."

****

Libby hadn't seen Byron in over two weeks. He'd been going to Ohio to practice with the Cincinnati orchestra two nights a week and the other days he'd been too busy to come over to Ashland. On a whim Libby drove over to Huntington to see him one evening and found him in a practice room sawing away on his violin, his body tense, shirt untucked, and hair mussed. He must have missed a note or something because he pulled his instrument away from his body and raised his hands in a gesture of frustration. She knocked on the window. He turned and saw her, and a crease formed between his brows.

He opened the door. "What are you doing here?"

"I missed you. I thought I'd come visit."

He shook his head. "I'm sorry, Liberty Ann. I don't have the time. I can't get this music down for the Munich trial. It's a bear."

"Let me come in and listen."

"There's no chair."

"I'll sit on the floor."

He stood there for a moment, his eyes a storm of emotion. She'd never seen him so unsettled. Finally, he stepped back and opened the door wider. "Suit yourself. It's rather small in here."

He wasn't kidding. The room was not much bigger than a closet, empty except for a metal stand displaying several sheaves of music and his violin case.

Libby came in the room and closed the door. Claiming a corner, she sat down cross legged on the floor. Byron adjusted the stand and craned his face to the paper on it. He positioned his violin and began to play.

After a few minutes Libby decided Byron wasn't playing at all. No. He was working his instrument, and the tones he produced were angry and intense.

Nothing like the beauty of Bach, the sensuousness of Mendelssohn or even the playfulness of Gypsy Airs by...somebody.

Byron stopped. "No, dammit," he muttered. He played it again, and Libby recognized the tune as he repeated it again and again. He turned to the wall and played, but shook his head and looked at the music stand.

He began again, the harsh tones filling the room for several minutes, then ceased suddenly with a loud sigh from Byron. "Come on," he chided himself and launched into it again. After a while he took to pacing as he played and throwing out an occasional curse when he messed up.

After an hour or so, Libby was exhausted. How could he stand this, going over the same section of music constantly? It would be different if the music was beautiful, but it wasn't. Whoever had composed it needed therapy. Big time.

Suddenly, Byron stopped, dropped his arms, and howled. Libby watched him with wide eyes.

He turned to her, his chest heaving.

He stalked to where his open case lay on the floor and placed his violin and bow inside. Closing up the case, he collapsed next to it and closed his eyes, his tortured breathing the only sound in the room.

"Byron?"

For several seconds he didn't move, then with a brief movement of his head toward her, he cracked one eye open.

"Want to go for a strawberry chocolate milkshake? It'll make you feel better."

He turned his face back toward the ceiling, his vacant

stare making Libby wonder if he'd understood her. Then, he sat up. "Okay. Can you drive?"

Chapter Fifteen

By the time the weekend to go to Cincinnati arrived, Libby had become familiar with the tortured music Byron was to play for his try-out. It was written by Claude Allgen, a man who poured his tragic life onto paper in the form of a violin masterpiece. Whether it was the stress of the performance, the pressure of people from Germany flying in, or the ghost of Allgen haunting him, Byron was edgy. Libby offered to drive, and the curvy back road route she'd chosen had him nearly sick.

"I've got something for motion sickness in the glove box." Libby glanced over at the pallor of his face.

"I can't take anything that will make me sleepy. I've got rehearsal as soon as we arrive."

She aimed the vent his way and turned on the air conditioning.

They arrived without further incident and checked into the hotel. She dropped him off at the music hall and finding a mall, Libby wandered around looking for something to wear to the concert the next evening. In a plate glass window, a mannequin caught her attention in a black flowing dress, torn-lace stockings, and black army boots with just a touch of sparkle.

Finally. Something glittery she liked.

Libby walked into the store.

A young woman in ripped jeans and a fur-trimmed purple shirt approached her. "Can I help you find something?"

"I like what that mannequin's wearing, but I don't do stockings."

"Those aren't stockings. They're thigh socks. Very comfortable." She led Libby to a rack of dresses.

Libby found her size and held the hanger and dress up eyeing it critically. "I'm going to a concert tomorrow night with violins and cellos and French horns and oboes. Do you think something like this is dressy enough?"

"I think it's perfect for it. What size shoe do you wear?"

"Eight."

"Be right back."

Goody.

Byron was supposed to call her to pick him up. But when his call came, he said he'd found a ride and would meet her at the hotel. Back in the room, Libby sat on the bed and channel surfed. Was this what it was like to be with Byron? Alone in a hotel room while he spent all evening practicing? He'd told her as much, so her disappointment was self-inflicted. At midnight, Libby left the bathroom light on and cracked the door, then turned off the light and went to sleep. At some point, Byron came in and settled next to her in bed, because when she awoke the next morning he was there.

She slipped out of bed and went to take a shower. And he was still asleep when she came out. Geez, what time had he gone to sleep?

Sitting on the edge of the bed, she leaned down and kissed his curly hair. "Hey, Sleeping Beauty, what time's your rehearsal?"

He scrunched up his eyes. "Nine." His arms wound around her, and he pulled her down next to him snuggling into her. "Mmmm. This is nice. Waking up with a beautiful woman in a towel."

"What time did you get back?"

"About midnight."

She chuckled. "Try again, Cinderella. I gave up on you at midnight."

"There was a one and two in there somewhere." His eyes still closed, his hand unfolded the towel and his fingers moseyed from shoulder to hip to thigh.

"How did rehearsal go?"

"Don't ruin my hotel seduction by asking." He nuzzled

her neck. "Oh, but do you smell nice. Let us stay in bed all weekend."

"Nope. I went to the trouble of buying a dress last night, and you're not taking away my chance to wear it."

"Oh, darn it. I wanted to be the only man whose date was wearing pants."

"Your date may be the only one wearing army boots."

Byron's eyes opened. "Yeah?" he said silkily. "Where are they?"

Libby loved his flirty tone. She nodded toward the closet. Byron turned on his back and propped against the pillow. "Let me see."

"You want me to show you my army boots now?"

"You can model them for me." His hot gaze tickled her insides.

She sat up wrapping the towel around herself. Tucking it in her front, she padded across the room to the closet. Opening the door, she picked up the shoebox from the luggage rest and placed it on the end of the bed. Opening up the box, she picked up a boot and showed him.

"Oh, my, Liberty Ann, aren't they lovely?"

She placed it back in the box.

"Well, come on then. Put them on. Let me see how they look on your feet."

"I have these sock things to wear with them."

"Sock things?" he clasped his hands behind his head and watched her.

"Yeah." Embarrassment poured over her, heating up her skin. Buying the thigh highs seemed kind of ridiculous now. "They…umm…go up....They're like…."

"What, my dear? The suspense is gripping."

"They're thigh-high socks." Libby shrugged. "See?" She held them up briefly from the small plastic hanger.

"Put them on. I'd like to see how they look before tonight."

Liberty studied him to see if he were teasing her. "You know this isn't my thing. Trying on clothes and all." She adjusted the towel.

"Oh, just humor me."

"Okay." She pulled the socks off the hanger and sat on the chair near the bed. Bending over she put the socks on her feet and pulled them up her legs. She raised first one leg then the other to slide them under the towel. Dropping the boots on the floor she nudged her feet into them and stood. "See? Boots and socks." She shrugged as if it were no big deal, as if she didn't feel like an idiot.

"Drop the towel."

****

Byron didn't show up for lunch though rehearsal was only supposed to last until eleven. Libby, who had been waiting in a nearby café, went to look for him and found him in the eaves of the stage playing the tormented notes of Allgen.

"Hey," she said. "Let's go get something to eat."

His bow stilled, but he didn't move the violin. "I can't. I'm not ready for tonight."

"Yes, you are. You've been practicing nonstop. *I* could practically play the piece I've heard it so much."

"Go on without me, Liberty Ann." He dipped the bow and a disharmonious chord played. "I've got to make sure I've got this right."

Byron didn't wear anxiety well. He had that hunted-deer desperation about him, a much different picture than the suave playboy who'd commanded her to drop her towel six hours ago. She shook her head.

"What?" he snapped.

"Put your instrument away, and let's go. You need to trust your hard work, and let the music settle. If you don't, you're going to be like a car that's had its headlights left on. Your battery is going to run low before tonight when you really need your engine strong and your high beams on. You get what I'm saying?"

Byron sighed. "I guess." He lowered his violin and walked over to his case lying on a nearby table.

"I saw a bowling alley on the way over here. Why don't we eat, then bowl a few frames?"

Byron turned to her with a quizzical expression on his face. "Bowling?"

"Yeah. Nothing relieves stress like rolling a heavy ball down a lane and knocking down pins. Have you ever bowled before?"

"Once in elementary school."

"Well, we'll have them set up the bumper guards. Come on."

****

Libby's seat wasn't quite as good as when she'd sat next to Byron on the front row in Huntington, but she was still in the first section on the left side of the stage so she had a pretty good view.

Byron played well as she knew he would though why anyone would choose the demented music of the evening was beyond her. She didn't know a lot about high art music—that's what it was called, as opposed to Classical which Byron had told her only referred to a specific time period.

After the concert, Byron met with the people from the German symphony—whether it was for an audition or an interview or both, Byron hadn't said. When he called her, it was after eleven.

"Are you in bed yet?"

"Nope. Waiting on you. You want me to come pick you up?"

"I'm in the lobby."

"How'd you get here?"

"Someone was kind enough to bring me to the hotel."

"Well, what are you waiting for? Come on up? I kept my boots on just for you."

"Do you mind coming down here, and when you take the elevator, get off on the second floor?"

"What for?"

"Because there is a staircase I'd love to watch you walk down."

Libby knew what staircase he meant—white curved marble with a gilded rail. It crowned the lobby of the antique hotel. She smiled. "Okay. One grease monkey in sparkly army boots on her way down the marble staircase. Look for me."

"I'm breathless with anticipation."

Libby fluffed her skirt and stuffed the card key in her bra then hurried out the door to the elevator. She rode down the five flights then stopped at two where several banquet rooms were located. She approached the glass edged balcony and saw Byron positioned at the bottom of the stairs waiting for her.

In a black tuxedo, he was stunning. His hair shimmered gold under the glittering chandelier. He smiled his GQ grin, the one that had captured her breath the first time she'd met him.

Libby gripped the top of the rail.

Please don't let me stumble, trip, or fall. I want to be graceful and beautiful. I want to be the woman who Byron Venable could fall in love with.

She took a deep breath.

Here we go.

She took a step down, then another. He watched her progress, his eyes drawing her to him, urging her closer.

Desire and, yes, admiration. This is what she saw on his face.

Byron Venable, world-class violinist wanted Libby Miller, a common hillbilly from eastern Kentucky. In his eyes she saw reflected a demure lady in an elegant gown with clean fingernails.

He held his hand out to her, and she placed her hand in his. Touching her fingers, he leaned forward and kissed her knuckles, his eyes never leaving her face.

"Enchanté, Miss Miller. What a pleasure it is to see you."

He tucked her hand into his elbow, and they walked into the lobby. Byron led her to the corner of the lobby with a brocade couch and two champagne glasses sitting on a table.

"We're celebrating," she said. She laughed. "Byron, you

got the job, didn't you? You're going to Germany."

He smiled in response. Picking up the drinks, he held one out to her. "No. I'm not going to Germany, but we're still celebrating." He clicked his glass to hers. "To staying in the good old U.S. of A." He brought the glass to his lips and drank.

Libby examined his expression for disappointment. Of course, he was upset. They'd turned him down. But she saw no sign of sadness or regret. "How could they not want you? You played so well."

"I wasn't the man for the position, I suppose." He shrugged as if were no big deal.

"Those dummies. How could they be such idiots?"

"Drink your champagne. This is a good night for us, Liberty Ann."

****

Libby had an Audi on the lift looking for a leak in the rack and pinion steering system when a bright red Rennen pulled up crossway to the bay. It wasn't an uncommon problem. If the lot was full, a lot of times customers would pull in front of the garage doors, but not too many people blocked both openings, and certainly not in a shiny foreign number like this one.

Libby caught a brief glimpse of a woman who walked from the car to the office.

In a few minutes, her dad appeared next to her. "Can you come in the office for a minute? There's a lady here saying she'd like to speak to you."

"Me? About what?"

"She says you're a friend of a friend."

"She's not selling something is she?"

"I don't think so." Gene quirked his eyebrow. "Quite a looker. I think I've seen her before, but I'm not sure where."

Libby walked to the shelf, squirted some orange cleaner on her hands, and plucked a towel from the box. She followed Gene into the office and saw a woman in a snazzy white suit with incredibly high heels standing in front of the desk. When she saw Libby, she smiled and walked to her with her hand outstretched. Those high heels clicked across the floor.

"Hello, Liberty Miller?"

Libby wiped her hand with the towel and hesitated. "I'm sorry. My hand is…." She gestured with the towel and the woman glanced down and dropped her hand.

"I'm Katrina Bromwell. It is nice to meet you."

Uh-oh. Libby knew what this woman's business was, and it wasn't a car problem. Libby attempted to wipe her hands clean. She pitched the towel in the trashcan.

"May I help you, Ms.…" Libby hesitated to be sure she didn't screw up the name. "Bromwell?"

"I wonder if I could have a few minutes of your time to discuss a mutual friend of ours." She was even more beautiful in person, though her mature age was also apparent. "Perhaps we could go somewhere for coffee after you finish work?"

"Is this mutual friend Byron?"

"Yes."

Whatever this woman wanted to say, Libby didn't want to put it off. "How long will this discussion take, do you think?"

"Oh, not long."

"Half hour?"

She opened and closed her mouth, before she nodded. "Okay."

Libby bet she wasn't used to someone giving her a time limit. "Dad, I'd like to take my lunch now."

"Sure thing, Libby."

"Would you like to meet somewhere? Tim Horton's? It's less than a mile from here on Winchester."

"I can drive us."

"You wouldn't drive me off in the woods somewhere and leave me, would you?"

She blinked. "That is not my intention. No."

She could picture Byron with her. Both of them out somewhere dressed to the nines. Ken and Barbie, or rather,

Ken and Cougar Barbie.

Libby went into the inner office and retrieved her key ring. What did Katrina Bitchwell...err...Bromwell want to talk to her about? Did she want Byron back? Had he told her about Libby?

They walked to her car. It figured that she was the one who had blocked the bays. Typical rich woman behavior is to park wherever she wanted. Libby stumbled on closer inspection of the car. It was nice. Shiny wax job new with leather interior she'd bet.

Libby opened the door.

Yep.

She looked at the woman through the open door. "Are you sure you want me in your car? I'm dirty."

"You're fine." She waved her hand in dismissal as she started up the engine.

Libby quirked her lips. Okay. It seemed like a bad idea, but obviously Katrina really had something to say. Libby climbed in the seat and closed the door. The seat contoured to her body. *Wow.* Nice. Bet it had a butt warmer too.

"So, you want to talk about Byron?" Libby didn't see any reason to wait until they actually got to the restaurant, especially if the woman was going to tell her she wanted him back. What would Libby say to that?

"You were with him in Cincinnati this weekend."

Libby tried to cover her shock. How did Katrina know that? A low whistle began in the car. Libby hit her window button but it didn't move. "Is one of your windows cracked open?"

"No."

The noise continued. "Do you hear that?"

"Hear what?"

Libby looked at the dashboard. The heat was on low. "Do you mind turning off your heater, please."

"Of course." She touched a red-tipped manicured finger to the power button. It didn't change the noise.

"When's the last time you've had your car serviced?"

Katrina gave a delicate snort of disbelief. "I'm not sure.

I take it in every six months for a routine check-up."

"To the dealer, I guess?"

"Yes."

The sound was incessant. How did she stand it?

What else could it be? Libby touched the edge of the windshield testing for tightness. "Do you ever notice any moisture in your car after it rains?"

"Of course not," she said sharply.

Of course not she doesn't notice, or of course not there's no moisture?

"What are you doing?"

"There's a noise—a whistle—really? You don't hear it?"

"I don't know. Liberty, I don't want to talk about my car. I want to talk to you about Byron."

"It's just bugging me. You should take it to the dealer and demand they fix it."

"They didn't find anything to fix," she snapped.

"Really? Did they check—"

Katrina pulled over to the side of the road, put the SUV in park, and faced Libby. "Byron is not going to Germany because of you. Is that what you want for him? To throw away his career and all of his talent so he can live here and...and teach violin lessons to unappreciative children while you fix cars all day?"

Libby stared at the woman because she knew she couldn't have heard Katrina correctly. "What?"

Katrina's eyes glittered angrily. "Do you know how good he is? Can you possibly appreciate that someone like him can't be taught to play as he does? It's a gift that he's just going to give up for what? For this? Can you possibly be so selfish as to rob the world of his talent?"

"He... They offered him the position in Munich?"

"Yes, and he turned it down."

"Idiot," Libby whispered. Why would he do such a stupid thing? Certainly not because.... Libby stared at her hands for a moment. She looked at Katrina. "He didn't turn it down because of me. That's ridiculous."

"Why else would he turn it down?"

Libby laughed. "It can't be because of me. I just…we're just…we're not…" She shook her head. "Well, did you ask him why? Why do you think I had anything to do with it?"

"Because I saw you two walk into the concert hall. I saw how he sought you out once he was on stage. Now, if you love him, great. Do what is best for him, and tell him he must go to Germany without you."

"Without me? Why would I go to Germany with him?"

"Exactly."

It couldn't have anything to do with me.

Could it?

Katrina put the car in gear and began to drive again. The whistling which had stopped when she'd pulled to the side of the road began again.

"Turn around, and take me back to the garage."

Katrina shot her a startled glance. "But coffee—"

"Did you have something else to tell me, or was that it?"

"That, and I wanted to persuade you to convince Byron to take the position."

"Turn around then. I'll talk to Byron and try to change his mind on one condition."

"What?"

"You let me find out why your car is whistling like a tea kettle. Geez, how are you not loopy by now from the noise?"

"With all due respect, you're not touching my car."

"Then I'm not talking to Byron, and he can just stay here and learn how to change a tire. We could use a good tire boy."

Chapter Sixteen

Libby walked across the campus in Huntington feeling self-conscious in her coveralls and work boots. Still. It didn't matter. Not really. She needed to find Byron and...tell him what? *Your sugar mama says you have to go to Germany?*

This doesn't have anything to do with me. He wouldn't not go because of me. That's ridiculous.

Katrina was mistaken.

There was some other reason.

And Libby was going to find out what it was.

He wasn't answering his cell phone which usually meant he was either in class or practicing. It was nearing six now, so she was guessing it was practice.

Finding the music building, she entered and wandered around until she saw several people with instrument cases disappearing into a room. She poked her head in the door and searched for Byron.

String section. String section. Ah, there he was, already seated with his violin across his lap studying paper on a music stand.

Libby took a fortifying breath and went to him. She stopped in front of him, and he did a double take when he spotted her.

"Liberty Ann! Hi." He cradled his violin and bow to his chest and stood. "What are you doing here?"

Libby shifted on her boots. She scanned the people in the room. Several were looking at her. "I have to talk to you. Can we go somewhere?"

"We're about to start. I don't—"

"It's important."

"Very well." He led her across the room to a door and

ushered her inside. It was a tiny office with a bunch of music stands shoved in one corner. Byron shut the door and leaned against it. "Is something wrong? You look so serious."

"Did they offer you the job in Germany?"

Something flickered in his eyes, and there was her answer.

"Why didn't you take it?"

He shook his head. "It didn't feel right."

"It didn't feel right? The position starts right after this one ended. How could that not feel right?"

He watched her, but said nothing.

"Byron, you speak German. It's perfect for you. Why wouldn't you take it? You have to take it."

"No, I don't have to take it."

"What if nothing else works out? What are you going to do then?"

Byron pushed himself from the door and walked the few steps to her. "Something will work out. It always has." He raised a hand and cupped her face.

"Just tell me one thing. This has nothing to do with me, right? You wouldn't stay here just because of us. I can't believe I'm even asking because it's such a stupid question."

His lips parted in a smile. Bending down he touched his mouth to hers. The kiss was so sweet, so tender, emotion prickled Libby's eyes. She pulled away from him and stepped backward.

Her heart beat so hard in her chest, it hurt.

"You're an idiot. Call them and tell them you're going."

"I'm not going."

"Not because of me. If this is because of me, then...then I...I don't want to see you anymore. We're...done." She stepped around him, but he moved to block her. Refusing to look at him in the face, she focused instead on the violin he still held as if it were a baby. "Get out of my way, Byron."

He raised his violin, tucked it under his chin, and began to play. The melody immediately drew her in, tugged at her heartstrings.

"Please move," she said brokenly.

I love you, the violin sang. *I love you. I love you.*

He moved, and she wrenched open the door. Stomping across the large room, she skirted the many people seated in formation with one woman standing in front of them. Most everyone turned toward her.

"Sorry," she muttered.

From behind her, the soulful melody followed her.

I love you. I love you. I love you.

****

She gave him two days to contact her, but he didn't.

She opened the door of the Escort she was working on and sat on the driver's seat. Closing the door for privacy, she dialed Byron's number.

"Hello," he greeted her cheerfully.

"Did you take the job?"

"No, I did not."

"Not because of me though."

"Can you see yourself in Germany?"

"Just admit that it's something else. I know it's not me."

"I'm not willing to plan to be on another continent away from you at this point."

Libby's heart shuddered to a stop for a second. Maybe two. She clutched her chest. "You idiot! Take. The. Job."

"Thank you for your input. However, I am not moving to Germany."

So calm. Didn't he see what a screw-up this was? Didn't he care?

"What if I go with you? Would that make a difference?"

Byron chuckled. "Very amusing. You can't bluff me. I know how much your family means to you. I'd never ask you to leave them or Ashland."

"What are you going to do, wait tables and play in the university orchestra for the rest of your life?"

"Something will come up. An opportunity closer to home. You'll see."

"No, I don't see. Stop being so stupid." She hung up

the phone and hit the steering wheel, causing the horn to blow. Vance showed up at the window.

"What are you doing?" he asked through the glass.

Libby huffed and glared at the phone. "Go away. I'm testing the horn."

"Well, it works."

Libby called Byron back. "I'm sorry I hung up on you."

"It's all right, my darling. But I'm still not taking the job. Would you like to go out Friday night?"

"No, I broke up with you in case you're using me as an excuse to deprive the world of your talent."

"Aha. You've been talking to Katrina. I should have realized that's how you found out."

"She and I agree you should go to Germany."

"I have heard enough of Germany. I'll come pick you up at seven Friday. Would you wear your boots?"

Libby sighed. "I suppose."

"Dress and thigh socks too?"

The way he said *thigh* made her shiver.

"All right."

"Everything will work out splendidly. Do you believe me?"

"Do you define splendidly as you teaching snot-nosed kids music lessons for the rest of your life?"

He laughed again. Why did he think getting stuck here in hillbilly heaven was so funny? Didn't he realize what a big mistake he was making?

Libby ended the call and opened the car door. She stepped onto the pavement and with hunched shoulders, she walked into the office. Her dad was talking to a customer, so she went back out and worked on the car. In a few minutes, he came out to her.

"Did you want something?"

"Dad." She leaned on her elbows on the lip of the car. "What would you say if I told you I was moving to Germany with Byron?"

"Germany? You pulling my leg?"

"He's been offered a job there in August, and he won't

go because of me."

"Really." He tucked in his chin to look at her over his glasses.

"So, I was thinking if I go with him, then he'd go."

"And what are you going to do while he's playing his violin?"

"Find a job, I guess." She picked up a wrench and tightened a bolt on a hose. "Am I crazy for considering this?"

"Yeah, but you're young. You're supposed to do crazy stuff. And it's not like you'd be in Germany alone, if you were with Byron. Is this a permanent job he's taking?"

"It could turn into one."

Gene scratched the thinning hair on top of his head. "Well, try it. If it don't work out, come home."

She shook her head in disbelief. "Just like that? You'd let me go?"

His eyes widened. "Let you go?" He coughed. "You're of legal age. I can't tell you what to do."

"You tell us what to do all the time," Mickey said from his post in the other bay.

"Well, that's work related." He shrugged. "As far as something like this, the best I get to do is advise you."

"So what's your advice?"

"I say go for it. Your mama always wanted to go to Paris, France. I promised her we'd go on our ten-year anniversary, but we never got to do it. She named you Liberty after the Statue of Liberty, you know. She was a gift from France to America. They called her Liberty Enlightening the World." Gene smiled at Libby. "With a namesake like that, well, maybe you ought to do more than fix engines in Eastern Kentucky."

Libby leaned into him affectionately. "Thanks, Dad."

He patted her shoulder. "I don't want to lose you though. You're my best mechanic."

"I heard that," Mickey called.

"Yeah? What of it?" Gene called back.

Later that day, Libby placed another call.

"Hey, Katrina? This is Liberty Miller."

Katrina hesitated before she spoke. "Hello, Liberty."

"Any more problems with the whistling?"

"No. It seems you found the breach in the vent, which was causing the noise. I wish you'd let me pay you for it."

"Do you really want evidence that the garage worked on your car? That will make the warranty void."

She laughed, as if Libby had made a joke.

"Listen, I talked to Byron, and he's not sold on going to Germany. He told me one time your husband used to work for a car company in Europe. So, I was wondering if you had some pull with any German manufacturers or garages. If I had a job and could go over with him, maybe he'd be more willing to go."

The silence stretched so long that Libby thought maybe Katrina had hung up on her.

"Hello?"

"Yes?"

Libby drummed her fingers on the kitchen table. "Umm. So, what do you think?"

"It's an interesting idea."

Libby heard the reluctance in her voice. Guess it was too much to hope that Byron's former girlfriend would be willing to help her. After all, if Byron was alone in Germany, then if Katrina wanted him back, all she'd have to do would be to fly over for a visit.

"Well, anyway, thanks for listening."

They said their goodbyes, and Libby looked online for a German dictionary. She could go over even if she didn't have a job lined up.

And she'd need to get a passport.

Good thing she had until August to get ready.

****

Something was up.

Libby watched Vance run the big squeegee across the garage floor wiping away the bleach water.

Mickey's bay was empty, and his tools were put away. The shelves were orderly and the barrel garbage cans were missing.

They'd been cleaning all week.

"Hurry up with that car, huh? Dad wants everything out so Vance can finish cleaning the floor." Mick said coming back from the storage room.

"Why are we cleaning? It's not April." She shut her cart and pushed it against the wall.

"Because that's what the old man wants."

"I'm not done with this car."

"Well, you'll have to move it out anyway. Aren't you and Byron going out tonight? You better get home and fix your hair or something." Mick gave the shoo-shoo-shoo sign.

Libby stood immobile. Who was this guy? He looked like her brother, but since when did Mick care about her date or her hair?

"Go on. I'll move the car."

Libby finally shrugged and went into the office. Gene wouldn't tell her anything either. He'd denied knowledge of any special occasion. Yet the garage was getting a makeover. Vance had cleaned all the windows two days ago, and the glass was so clear the window was hardly detectable. Was Dad thinking of selling or something? Had her comment about going to Germany worried him?

Surprise birthday party?

Maybe Dad had a date?

"Dad, you didn't finally break down and agree to go out with Catherine Euclid, did you?"

"Give me a break. The moment I agree to get romantically involved with that crazy dog-loving woman will be the day you can put me in the nuthouse."

****

Byron was in his tuxedo again, as handsome as the day she'd met him. His gaze drank her in as if she were a cool glass of sweet tea. "May I come in?"

Libby stepped back from the door and let him enter.

They were alone in the house though why Gene and Vance hadn't gotten home from the garage yet, Libby couldn't fathom.

"Let's sit down, shall we?" Byron led the way to the couch.

"Why are you wearing your tux? Why did you want me to wear this? Where are we going?"

"We're going to a performance later, but for now, let's talk." He took her hand and guided her to sit with him. "You look beautiful. Thank you for dressing up."

"You're welcome."

He kissed her hand then tucked it in his. His gaze reached right through her and warmed her heart. "I love you, Liberty Ann Miller."

"Will you say that in German?"

"No, I will not because I'm not going to Munich, and neither are you."

Libby flinched from the finality of his tone.

"Katrina called me reissuing the proposal to go to Germany, which included a job at a service department in Indolstadt for you." He squeezed her hand. "Apparently, you impressed her with your mechanical prowess. You were able to find and fix a problem in an hour that her husband's company hadn't been able to pinpoint since she's owned her car. Katrina's got it in her mind Germany is my next big thing, but she doesn't really have a say in my life. Not now. She and I are friends, and I appreciate what she's done for me. But I'm not going to Europe any time soon. I don't want to go, and I don't want you to think it is because I'm giving something up to be with you." He settled back on the couch and pulled her close to him. Her dress slid against his trousers making an interesting sound.

She watched their hands entwined on the black fabric of her billowy skirt. "There's not much here in Ashland or in Huntington for someone like you. I think—" Libby decided to push the L-word out of her mouth. Byron had said it without a hint of unease. *I can say it too.* "—loving you means that I'm willing to do whatever is necessary for your best interest. I'm just a mechanic—a dime a dozen. But you have a rare gift with your music, Byron. You shouldn't be stuck here because of me. I think I can get a job most anywhere, if that's what it takes."

He turned, wrapping his arms around her. With his face close to hers, she noted the pleasure radiating from him. "You love me. You love me?"

Libby dropped her eyes in embarrassment. She nodded. "Of course I do. You think I'd sleep in that tiny dorm bed of yours, otherwise?" Finally raising her gaze to his, she continued. "So if you want to…you know…think about me going with you wherever, I'd go if you wanted me to."

His hand caressed her cheek and slid over her chin. Lowering his face, he kissed her, a slow gentle kiss. Desire ignited in Libby. She shifted and tried to pull Byron down to lie down with her. He shook his head.

"Don't distract me from our confession time." He glanced at his watch. "We've only have a few minutes before we must leave."

"Where is this concert?"

He ran his hand under her dress skirt and tapped her thigh at the top of her socks. "It's a surprise. I'm quite excited about it."

"Obviously, you're playing in it."

"Obviously."

"Do I get a good seat?"

"A good seat…hmm…well, you'll have a good view, but it's an outdoor concert. I'm afraid the chairs are the folding kind. Do you own a pashmina?"

"A what?"

"A wrap or a jacket?"

"Oh. No. Maybe Josey has something I can borrow."

"Actually." He slid away from her and stood. "I have a gift for you in the car. One moment, please, and let me fetch it." He left through the front door and came back in a minute later with a flat gift-wrapped box.

"A gift?"

"Hope you like it."

Libby lifted the lid and pushed aside the tissue paper. Black fringed cloth lay inside. She pulled it out. The soft material was warm beneath her fingers.

"Stand up. I'll help you with it. May I?"

Libby stood, and Byron placed the pashmina around her shoulders.

He nodded in approval. "Stunning." He bent down and kissed her. "You are the most beautiful mechanic I've ever kissed."

"I'm the only mechanic you've ever kissed."

"True. Very true. You're also the only mechanic I've ever fallen in love with."

"The only mechanic you've ever slept with? I see a pattern here."

Chapter Seventeen

Libby expected Byron to drive her to Huntington, but he headed to downtown Ashland.

"You're performing at Pendleton?"

"No."

"Not the Paramount?"

"No again."

He turned the corner on Winchester and she glanced up at the marquee of the theater. "The bandstand at the park. Has to be. You said it was outside."

He smiled but didn't say anything.

"The park, right?"

"Liberty Ann, I don't like saying no to you. So try to be patient, okay?" He picked up her hand and kissed her fingers. "We're almost there."

"You like to kiss hands. You're always kissing hands and fingers."

"I do like hands. I especially like your hands and fingers." Placing her hand back on her lap, he patted her.

He flicked on his blinker at the bank and the Presbyterian Church, and Libby glanced down across the plaza to where the garage was.

What the heck?

In front of the garage, someone had strung traffic barricades across the road. Libby saw a whole conglomeration of chairs arranged in a semi-circle with people milling around in eveningwear. She sat up straighter trying to get a better view. "What is going on?"

The traffic light changed to green, and Byron turned onto the road. He parked in the alley behind a church. "This isn't too far to walk, is it? I doubt we'll find anything closer."

"The concert is at our garage?" Libby looked to him for confirmation.

"Surprise."

"Boy howdy. How long has this been in the works?"

"Since Cincinnati."

They exited the car and walked hand in hand down the block. "Your organized this? Why?"

"Because I wanted you to see there's a place for me here. That we could make us work, if we think outside the box." He shrugged. "Play outside the box as it were. And also because the first time you heard me play, you were moved to tears right here in the garage. And I thought on that night you were someone who could capture my heart because my music touched you deeply. Not to mention your hands around the wrench made quite a fetching image which stayed with me." He winked at her eliciting a chuckle.

Gene Miller appeared from the crowd wearing his Sunday suit. He waved to them then made a grand sweeping gesture with his hand.

They walked across the street, and Libby noticed a crowd of about twenty people on chairs facing the orchestra. Josey waved to her. Marcus sat on her lap in a little suit. Mickey who wore slacks and a knit shirt and jacket walked out of the garage bay with Tony on his back and John John under one arm. One of the boys squealed.

"Dad, what the heck?" Libby play punched him on the arm. "Why didn't you give me a clue?"

"You know it's not time for spring cleaning. That was your clue."

"So, I guess this explains why you didn't have too much of a problem with me going to Germany. You knew I wasn't going."

Gene shrugged. "Meh. You might go one day. Just not August of this year."

Libby recognized several people from the day she'd gone to talk to Byron—the day he'd played his love for her on his violin.

A woman in a formal skirt and starched white shirt with a big collar walked over to them.

Byron smiled. "Vera Stolman, this is Liberty Ann Miller."

Vera offered her hand for a shake. Libby accepted her gesture.

"Vera is our conductor tonight. She's a graduate student in conducting and music theory."

Behind them a car stopped. "Hey Gene, what you doing here?"

"We're having a concert. Why don't you park and come listen?"

"We're ready to get started," Vera said. "Are you ready, Byron?"

"Nearly."

He ushered Libby to a chair on the front row next to Josey. Bending down, he kissed her and straightened. "After the concert we're doing karaoke in the garage. I've warned them I'm singing 'The Happiest Girl in the Whole USA' and dedicating it to you."

Libby reached her arms around his neck. "You can't be the happiest girl in the whole USA. Tonight that song belongs to me."

THE END

About Jennifer Johnson

Who am I?

I am a writer.

I write contemporary romantic fiction.

I aspire to be Wonder Woman with the awesome leotard and the criminal-fighting boots on some days.

On other days I am Wonder Woman with my Lasso of Truth and my no-nonsense-pursuit of justice.

I live in the South across the river from the Midwest. I'm married to Super Man with a Tony Stark mind. We have Wonder/Super children and a bionic dog. All in all, it's a comic book kind of life.

Find out more at **www.booksbyjennifer.com**.